MONEY FOR NOTHING

Money for Nothing

P. G. WODEHOUSE

BARRIE & JENKINS

COMMUNICA - EUROPA

First published by
Herbert Jenkins Ltd.
1928
Reprinted in this edition 1976 by
Barrie & Jenkins Ltd.
24 Highbury Crescent,
London N5 1RX

ISBN 0 257 66073 9

*Printed and bound
in Great Britain by*
REDWOOD BURN LIMITED
Trowbridge & Esher

To
IAN HAY BEITH

CONTENTS

CONTENTS

★ 1 ★

Introducing a Young Man in Love

I

THE picturesque village of Rudge-in-the-Vale dozed in the summer sunshine. Along its narrow High Street the only signs of life visible were a cat stropping its backbone against the Jubilee Watering Trough, some flies doing deep-breathing exercises on the hot window-sills, and a little group of serious thinkers who, propped up against the wall of the Carmody Arms, were waiting for that establishment to open. At no time is there ever much doing in Rudge's main thorough-fare, but the hour at which a stranger, entering it, is least likely to suffer the illusion that he has strayed into Broadway, Piccadilly, or the Rue de Rivoli is at two o'clock on a warm afternoon in July.

You will find Rudge-in-the-Vale, if you search carefully, in that pleasant section of rural England where the grey stone of Gloucestershire gives place to Worcestershire's old red brick. Quiet—in fact, almost unconscious—it nestles beside the tiny river Skirme and lets the world go by, somnolently content with its Norman church, its eleven public-houses, its pop.—to quote the Automobile Guide—of 3,541, and its only effort in the direction of modern progress, the emporium of Chas. Bywater, Chemist.

Chas. Bywater is a live wire. He takes no afternoon siesta, but works while others sleep. Rudge as a whole is inclined after luncheon to go into the back room, put a handkerchief over its face and take things easy for a bit. But not Chas. Bywater. At the moment at which this story begins he was all bustle and activity, and had just finished selling to Colonel Meredith Wyvern a bottle of Brophy's Paramount Elixir (said to be good for gnat-bites).

Having concluded his purchase, Colonel Wyvern would

9

have preferred to leave, but Mr. Bywater was a man who liked to sweeten trade with pleasant conversation. Moreover, this was the first time the Colonel had been inside his shop since that sensational affair up at the Hall two weeks ago, and Chas. Bywater, who held the unofficial position of chief gossip-monger to the village, was aching to get to the bottom of that.

With the bare outline of the story he was, of course, familiar. Rudge Hall, seat of the Carmody family for so many generations, contained in its fine old park a number of trees which had been planted somewhere about the reign of Queen Elizabeth. This meant that every now and then one of them would be found to have become a wobbly menace to the passer-by, so that experts had to be sent for to reduce it with a charge of dynamite to a harmless stump. Well, two weeks ago, it seems, they had blown up one of the Hall's Elizabethan oaks and as near as a toucher, Rudge learned, had blown up Colonel Wyvern and Mr. Carmody with it. The two friends had come walking by just as the expert set fire to the train and had had a very narrow escape.

Thus far the story was common property in the village, and had been discussed nightly in the eleven tap-rooms of its eleven public-houses. But Chas. Bywater, with his trained nose for news and that sixth sense which had so often enabled him to ferret out the story behind the story when things happen in the upper world of the nobility and gentry, could not help feeling that there was more in it than this. He decided to give his customer the opportunity of confiding in him.

"Warm day, Colonel," he observed.

"Ur," grunted Colonel Wyvern.

"Glass going up, I see."

"Ur."

"May be in for a spell of fine weather at last."

"Ur."

"Glad to see you looking so well, Colonel, after your little accident," said Chas. Bywater, coming out into the open.

It had been Colonel Wyvern's intention, for he was a man of testy habit, to inquire of Mr. Bywater why the devil he couldn't wrap a bottle of Brophy's Elixir in brown paper and put a bit of string round it without taking the whole afternoon over the task: but at these words he abandoned this project. Turning a bright mauve and allowing his luxuriant eyebrows to meet across the top of his nose, he subjected the other to a fearful glare.

"Little accident?" he said. "Little accident?"

"I was alluding——"

"Little accident!"

"I merely——"

"If by little accident," said Colonel Wyvern in a thick, throaty voice, "you mean my miraculous escape from death when that fat thug up at the Hall did his very best to murder me, I should be obliged if you would choose your expressions more carefully. Little accident! Good God!"

Few things in this world are more painful than the realization that an estrangement has occurred between two old friends who for years have jogged amiably along together through life, sharing each other's joys and sorrows and holding the same views on religion, politics, cigars, wine, and the Decadence of the Younger Generation: and Mr. Bywater's reaction, on hearing Colonel Wyvern describe Mr. Lester Carmody, of Rudge Hall, until two short weeks ago his closest crony, as a fat thug, should have been one of sober sadness. Such, however, was not the case. Rather was he filled with an unholy exultation. All along he had maintained that there was more in that Hall business than had become officially known, and he stood there with his ears flapping, waiting for details.

These followed immediately and in great profusion: and Mr. Bywater, as he drank them in, began to realise that his companion had certain solid grounds for feeling a little annoyed. For when, as Colonel Wyvern very sensibly argued, you have been a man's friend for twenty years and are walking with him in his park and hear warning shouts and look up and realize that a charge of dynamite is shortly about to go off in your immediate neighbourhood, you expect a man who is a man to be a man. You do not expect him to grab you round the waist and thrust you swiftly in between himself and the point of danger, so that, when the explosion takes place, you get the full force of it and he escapes without so much as a singed eyebrow.

"Quite," said Mr. Bywater, hitching up his ears anothe inch.

Colonel Wyvern continued. Whether, if in a condition to give the matter careful thought, he would have selected Chas.

Bywater as a confidant, one cannot say. But he was not in such a condition. The stoppered bottle does not care whose is the hand that removes its cork—all it wants is the chance to fizz: and Colonel Wyvern resembled such a bottle. Owing to the absence from home of his daughter, Patricia, he had had no one handy to act as audience for his grievances, and for two weeks he had been suffering torments. He told Chas. Bywater all.

It was a very vivid picture that he conjured up. Mr. Bywater could see the whole thing as clearly as if he had been present in person—from the blasting gang's first horrified realization that human beings had wandered into the danger zone to the almost tenser moment when, running up to sort out the tangled heap on the ground, they had observed Colonel Wyvern rise from his seat on Mr. Carmody's face and had heard him start to tell that gentleman precisely what he thought of him. Privately, Mr. Bywater considered that Mr. Carmody had acted with extraordinary presence of mind and had given the lie to the theory, held by certain critics, that the landed gentry of England are deficient in intelligence. But his sympathies were, of course, with the injured man. He felt that Colonel Wyvern had been hardly treated and was quite right to be indignant about it. As to whether the other was justified in alluding to his former friend as a jelly-bellied hell-hound, that was a matter for his own conscience to decide.

"I'm suing him," concluded Colonel Wyvern, regarding an advertisement of Pringle's Pink Pills with a smouldering eye.

"Quite."

"The only thing in the world that super-fatted old Blackhander cares for is money, and I'll have his last penny out of him, if I have to take the case to the House of Lords."

"Quite," said Mr. Bywater.

"I might have been killed. It was a miracle I wasn't. Five thousand pounds is the lowest figure any conscientious jury could put the damages at. And, if there were any justice in England, they'd ship the scoundrel off to pick oakum in a prison cell."

Mr. Bywater made non-committal noises. Both parties to this unfortunate affair were steady customers of his, and he did not wish to alienate either by taking sides. He hoped the

Colonel was not going to ask him for his opinion of the rights of the case.

Colonel Wyvern did not. Having relieved himself with some six minutes of continuous speech, he seemed to have become aware that he had bestowed his confidences a little injudiciously. He coughed and changed the subject.

"Where's that Stuff?" he said. "Good God! Isn't it ready yet? Why does it take you fellows three hours to tie a knot in a piece of string?"

"Quite ready, Colonel," said Chas. Bywater hastily. "Here it is. I have put a little loop for the finger, to facilitate carrying."

"Is this Stuff really any good?"

"Said to be excellent, Colonel. Thank you, Colonel. Much obliged, Colonel. Good day, Colonel."

Still fermenting at the recollection of his wrongs, Colonel Wyvern strode to the door: and, pushing it open with extreme violence, left the shop.

The next moment the peace of the drowsy summer afternoon was shattered by a hideous uproar. Much of this consisted of a high, passionate barking, the remainder being contributed by the voice of a retired military man, raised in anger. Chas. Bywater blenched, and, reaching out a hand towards an upper shelf, brought down, in the order named, a bundle of lint, a bottle of arnica, and one of the half-crown (or large) size pots of Sooth-o, the recognized specific for cuts, burns, scratches, nettle-stings and dog-bites. He believed in Preparedness.

II

While Colonel Wyvern had been pouring his troubles into the twitching ear of Chas. Bywater, there had entered the High Street a young man in golf-clothes and an Old Rugbeian tie. This was John Carroll, nephew of Mr. Carmody, of the Hall. He had walked down to the village, accompanied by his dog Emily, to buy tobacco, and his objective, therefore, was the same many-sided establishment which was supplying the Colonel with Brophy's Elixir.

For do not be deceived by that "Chemist" after Mr. Bywater's name. It is mere modesty. Some whim leads this great man to describe himself as a chemist, but in reality he goes much deeper than that. Chas. is the Marshall Field of Rudge, and deals in everything, from crystal sets to mousetraps. There are several places in the village where you can get stuff they call tobacco, but it cannot be considered in the light of pipe-joy for the discriminating smoker. To obtain something that will leave a little skin on the roof of the mouth you must go to Mr. Bywater.

John came up the High Street with slow, meditative strides, a large and muscular young man whose pleasant features betrayed at the moment an inward gloom. What with being hopelessly in love and one thing and another, his soul was in rather a bruised condition these days, and he found himself deriving from the afternoon placidity of Rudge-in-the-Vale a certain balm and consolation. He had sunk into a dreamy trance when he was abruptly aroused by the horrible noise which had so shaken Chas. Bywater.

The causes which had brought about this disturbance were simple and are easily explained. It was the custom of the dog Emily, on the occasions when John brought her to Rudge to help him buy tobacco, to yield to an uncontrollable eagerness and gallop on ahead to Mr. Bywater's shop—where, with her nose edged against the door, she would stand, sniffing emotionally, till somebody came and opened it. She had a morbid passion for cough-drops, and experience had taught her that by sitting and ogling Mr. Bywater with her liquid amber eyes she could generally secure two or three. To-day, hurrying on as usual, she had just reached the door and begun to sniff when it suddenly opened and hit her sharply on the nose. And, as she shot back with a yelp of agony, out came Colonel Wyvern carrying his bottle of Brophy.

There is an etiquette in these matters on which all right-minded dogs insist. When people trod on Emily, she expected them immediately to fuss over her, and the same procedure seemed to her to be in order when they hit her on the nose with doors. Waiting expectantly, therefore, for Colonel Wyvern to do the square thing, she was stunned to find that he apparently had no intention of even apologizing. He was brushing past without a word, and all the woman in Emily rose in revolt against such boorishness.

"Just a minute!" she said dangerously. "Just one minute, if you please. Not so fast, my good man. A word with you, if I may trespass upon your valuable time."

The Colonel, chafing beneath the weight of his wrongs, perceived that they had been added to by a beast of a hairy dog that stood and yapped at him.

"Get out!" he bellowed.

Emily became hysterical.

"Indeed?" she said shrilly. "And who do you think you are, you poor clumsy Robot? You come hitting ladies on the nose as if you were the King of England, and as if that wasn't enough . . ."

"Go away, sir."

"Who the devil are you calling Sir?" Emily had the twentieth century girl's freedom of speech and breadth of vocabulary. "It's people like you that cause all this modern unrest and industrial strife. I know your sort well. Robbers and oppressors. And let me tell you another thing . . ."

At this point the Colonel very injudiciously aimed a kick at Emily.

It was not much of a kick, and it came nowhere near her, but it sufficed. Realizing the futility of words, Emily decided on action. And it was just as she had got a preliminary grip on the Colonel's left trouser-leg that John arrived at the Front.

"Emily! ! !" roared John, shocked to the core of his being.

He had excellent lungs, and he used them to the last ounce of their power. A young man who sees the father of the girl he loves being swallowed alive by a Welsh terrier does not spare his voice. The word came out of him like the note of the Last Trump, and Colonel Wyvern, leaping spasmodically, dropped his bottle of Brophy. It fell on the pavement and exploded, and Emily, who could do her bit in a rough-and-tumble but barred bombs, tucked her tail between her legs and vanished. A faint, sleepy cheering from outside the Carmody Arms announced that she had passed that home from home and was going well.

John continued to be agitated. You would not have supposed, to look at Colonel Wyvern, that he could have had an attractive daughter, but such was the case, and John's manner was as concerned and ingratiating as that of most young men in the presence of the fathers of attractive daughters.

"I'm so sorry, Colonel. I do hope you're not hurt, Colonel."

The injured man, maintaining an icy silence, raked him with an eye before which sergeant-majors had once drooped like withered roses, and walked into the shop. The anxious face of Chas. Bywater loomed up over the counter. John hovered in the background.

"I want another bottle of that Stuff," said the Colonel shortly.

"I'm awfully sorry," said John.

"I dropped the other outside. I was attacked by a savage dog."

"I'm frightfully sorry."

"People ought not to have these pests running loose and not under proper control."

"I'm fearfully sorry."

"A menace to the community and a nuisance to everybody," said Colonel Wyvern.

"Quite," said Mr. Bywater.

Conversation languished. Chas. Bywater, realizing that this was no moment for lingering lovingly over brown paper and toying dreamily with string, lowered the record for wrapping a bottle of Brophy's Paramount Elixir by such a margin that he set up a mark for other chemists to shoot at for all time. Colonel Wyvern snatched it and stalked out, and John, who had opened the door for him and had not been thanked, tottered back to the counter and in a low voice expressed a wish for two ounces of the Special Mixture.

"Quite," said Mr. Bywater. "In one moment, Mr. John."

With the passing of Colonel Wyvern a cloud seemed to have rolled away from the chemist's world. He was his old, charmingly chatty self again. He gave John his tobacco, and, detaining him by the simple means of not handing over his change, surrendered himself to the joys of conversation.

"The Colonel appears a little upset, sir."

"Have you got my change?" said John.

"It seems to me he hasn't been the same man since that unfortunate episode up at the Hall. Not at all the same sunny gentleman."

"Have you got my change?"

"A very unfortunate episode, that," sighed Mr. Bywater.

"My change?"

"I could see, the moment he walked in here, that he was not himself. Shaken. Something in the way he looked at one. I said to myself 'The Colonel's shaken!' "

John, who had had such recent experience of the way Colonel Wyvern looked at one, agreed. He then asked if he might have his change.

"No doubt he misses Miss Wyvern," said Chas. Bywater, ignoring the request with an indulgent smile. "When a man's had a shock like the Colonel's had—when he's shaken, if you understand what I mean—he likes to have his loved ones around him. Stands to reason," said Mr. Bywater.

John had been anxious to leave, but he was so constituted that he could not tear himself away from anyone who had touched on the subject of Patricia Wyvern. He edged a little nearer the counter.

"Well, she'll be home again soon," said Chas. Bywater. "To-morrow, I understand."

A powerful current of electricity seemed to pass itself through John's body. Pat Wyvern had been away so long that he had fallen into a sort of dull apathy in which he wondered sometimes if he would ever see her again.

"What!"

"Yes, sir. She returned from France yesterday. She had a good crossing. She is at the Lincoln Hotel, Curzon Street, London. She thinks of taking the three o'clock train to-morrow. She is in excellent health."

It did not occur to John to question the accuracy of the other's information, nor to be surprised at its minuteness of detail. Mr. Bywater, he was aware, had a daughter in the post office.

"To-morrow!" he gasped.

"Yes, sir. To-morrow."

"Give me my change," said John.

He yearned to be off. He wanted air and space in which he could ponder over this wonderful news.

"No doubt," said Mr. Bywater, "she . . ."

"Give me my change," said John.

Chas. Bywater, happening to catch his eye, did so.

III

To reach Rudge Hall from the door of Chas. Bywater's shop, you go up the High Street, turn sharp to the left down River Lane, cross the stone bridge that spans the slow-flowing Skirme as it potters past on its way to join the Severn, carry on along the road till you come to the gates of Colonel Wyvern's nice little house, and then climb a stile and take to the fields. And presently you are in the park and can see through the trees the tall chimneys and red walls of the ancient home of the Carmodys.

The scene, when they are not touching off dynamite there under the noses of retired military officers, is one of quiet peace. For John it had always held a peculiar magic. In the fourteen years which had passed since the Wyverns had first come to settle in Rudge Pat had contrived, so far as he was concerned, to impress her personality ineffaceably on the landscape. Almost every inch of it was in some way associated with her. Stumps on which she had sat and swung her brown-stockinged legs; trees beneath which she had taken shelter with him from summer storms; gates on which she had climbed, fields across which she had raced, and thorny bushes into which she had urged him to penetrate in search of birds' eggs—they met his eye on every side. The very air seemed to be alive with her laughter. And not even the recollection that that laughter had generally been directed at himself was able to diminish for John the glamour of this mile of Fairyland.

Half way across the park, Emily rejoined him with a defensive, Where-on-earth-did-you-disappear-to manner, and they moved on in company till they rounded the corner of the house and came to the stable-yard. John, who for some years now had looked after the business of the estate for his uncle, had a couple of rooms over the stables, and thither he made his way, leaving Emily to fuss round Bolt, the chauffeur, who was washing the Dex-Mayo.

Arrived in his sitting-room, he sank into a deck-chair, and filled his pipe with Mr. Bywater's Special Mixture. Then, putting his feet up on the table, he stared hard and earnestly at the photograph of Pat which stood on the mantelpiece.

It was a pretty face he was looking at—one whose charm not even a fashionable modern photographer, of the type that prefers to depict his sitters in a grey fog with most of their features hidden from view, could altogether obscure. In the eyes, a little slanting, there was a Puck-like look, and the curving lips hinted demurely at amusing secrets. The nose had that appealing, yet provocative, air which slight tiptiltedness gives. It seemed to challenge, and at the same time to withdraw.

This was the latest of the Pat photographs, and she had given it to him three months ago, just before she left to go and stay with friends at Le Touquet. And now she was coming home. . . .

John Carroll was one of those solid persons who do not waver in their loyalties. He had always been in love with Pat, and he always would be, though he would have had to admit that she gave him very little encouragement. There had been a period when, he being fifteen and she ten, Pat had lavished on him all the worship of a small girl for a big boy who can wiggle his ears and is not afraid of cows. But since then her attitude had changed. Her manner towards him nowadays alternated between that of a nurse towards a child who is not quite right in the head and that of the owner of a clumsy but rather likeable dog.

Nevertheless, he loved her. And she was coming home. . . .

John sat up suddenly. He was a slow thinker, and only now did it occur to him just what the position of affairs would be when she did come home. With this infernal feud going on between his uncle Lester and the old Colonel she would probably look on him as in the enemy's camp and refuse to see or speak to him.

The thought chilled him to the marrow. Something he felt, must be done, and swiftly. And, with a flash of inspiration of a kind that rarely came to him, he saw what that something was. He must go up to London this afternoon, tell her the facts, and throw himself on her clemency. If he could convince her that he was whole-heartedly pro-Colonel and regarded his uncle Lester as the logical successor to Doctor Crippen and the Brides-in-the-Bath murderer, things might straighten themselves.

Once the brain gets working, there is no knowing where it will stop. The very next instant there had come to John Carroll a thought so new and breathtaking that he uttered an audible gasp.

Why shouldn't he ask Pat to marry him?

IV

John sat tingling from head to foot. The scales seemed to have fallen from his eyes, and he saw clearly where he might quite conceivably have been making a grave blunder all these years. Deeply as he had always loved Pat, he had never—now he came to think of it—told her so. And in this sort of situation the spoken word is quite apt to make all the difference.

Perhaps that was why she laughed at him so frequently —because she was entertained by the spectacle of a man, obviously in love with her, refraining year after year from making any verbal comment on the state of his emotions.

Resolution poured over John in a strengthening flood. He looked at his watch. It was nearly three. If he got the two-seater and started at once, he could be in London by seven, in nice time to take her to dinner somewhere. He hurried down the stairs and out into the stable-yard.

"Shove that car out of the way, Bolt," said John, eluding Emily, who, wet to the last hair, was endeavouring to climb up him. "I want to get the two-seater."

"Two-seater, sir?"

"Yes. I'm going to London."

"It's not there, Mr. John," said the chauffeur, with the gloomy satisfaction which he usually reserved for telling his employer that the battery had run down.

"Not there? What do you mean?"

"Mr. Hugo took it, sir, an hour ago. He told me he was going over to see Mr. Carmody at Healthward Ho. Said he had important business and knew you wouldn't object."

The stable-yard reeled before John. Not for the first time in his life, he cursed his light-hearted cousin. "Knew you wouldn't object!" It was just the fat-headed sort of thing Hugo would have said.

★ 2 ★

Healthward Ho

THERE is something about those repellent words, Healthward Ho, that has a familiar ring. You feel that you have heard them before. And then you remember. They have figured in letters to the daily papers from time to time.

"THE STRAIN OF MODERN LIFE.

"To the Editor
The Times.

"Sir,
"In connection with the recent correspondence in your columns on the Strain of Modern Life, I wonder if any of your readers are aware that there exists in the county of Worcestershire an establishment expressly designed to correct this strain. At Healthward Ho (formerly Graveney Court), under the auspices of the well-known American physician and physical culture expert, Doctor Alexander Twist, it is possible for those who have allowed the demands of modern life to tax their physique too greatly to recuperate in ideal surroundings and by means of early hours, wholesome exercise, and Spartan fare to build up once more their debilitated tissues.

"It is the boast of Doctor Twist that he makes New Men for Old.

"I am, sir,

"Yrs. etc.,

"MENS SANA IN CORPORE SANO."

21

"DO WE EAT TOO MUCH?"

"To the Editor
  Daily Mail.

"Sir,
  "The correspondence in your columns on the above subject calls to mind a remark made to me not long ago by Doctor Alexander Twist, the well-known American physician and physical culture expert. 'Over-eating,' said Doctor Twist emphatically, 'is the curse of the Age.'

"At Healthward Ho (formerly Graveney Court), his physical culture establishment in Worcestershire, wholesale exercise and Spartan fare are the order of the day, and Doctor Twist has, I understand, worked miracles with the most apparently hopeless cases.

"It is the boast of Doctor Twist that he makes New Men for Old.

"I am, sir,
    "Yrs. etc.,

"MODERATION IN ALL THINGS."

"SHOULD THE CHAPERONE BE RESTORED?"

"To the Editor
  Daily Express.

"Sir,
  "A far more crying need than that of the Chaperone in these modern days is for a Supervisor of the middle-aged man who has allowed himself to get 'out of shape'.

"At Healthward Ho (formerly Graveney Court), in Worcestershire, where Doctor Alexander Twist, the well-known American physician and physical culture expert, ministers to such cases, wonders have been achieved by means of simple fare and mild, but regular, exercise.

"It is the boast of Doctor Twist that he makes New Men for Old.

"I am, sir,
    "Yrs. etc.,

"VIGILANT."

These letters and many others, though bearing a pleasing variety of signatures, proceeded in fact from a single gifted pen—that of Doctor Twist himself, and among that class of the public which consistently does itself too well when the gong goes and yet is never wholly free from wistful aspirations towards a better liver they had created a scattered but quite satisfactory interest in Healthward Ho. Clients had enrolled themselves on the doctor's books, and now, on this summer afternoon, he was enabled to look down from his study window at a group of no fewer than eleven of them, skipping with skipping-ropes under the eye of his able and conscientious assistant, ex-Sergeant-Major Flannery.

Sherlock Holmes—and even, on one of his bright days, Doctor Watson—could have told at a glance which of those muffled figures was Mr. Flannery. He was the only one who went in instead of out at the waist-line. All the others were well up in the class of man whom Julius Caesar once expressed a desire to have about him. And pre-eminent among them in stoutness, dampness and general misery was Mr. Lester Carmody, of Rudge Hall.

The fact that Mr. Carmody was by several degrees the most unhappy-looking member of this little band of martyrs was due to his distress, unlike that of his fellow-sufferers, being mental as well as physical. He was allowing his mind, for the hundredth time, to dwell on the paralysing cost of these hygienic proceedings.

Thirty guineas a week, thought Mr. Carmody as he bounded up and down. Four pound ten a day. . . . Three shillings and ninepence and hour. . . . Three solid farthings a minute. . . . To meditate on these figures was like turning a sword in his heart. For Lester Carmody loved money as he loved nothing else in this world except a good dinner.

Doctor Twist turned from the window. A maid had appeared bearing a card on a salver.

"Show him in," said Doctor Twist, having examined this. And presently there entered a lissom young man in a grey flannel suit.

"Doctor Twist?"

"Yes, sir."

The newcomer seemed a little surprised. It was as if he had been expecting something rather more impressive, and was

wondering why, if the proprietor of Healthward Ho had the
ability which he claimed, to make New Men for Old, he had
not taken the opportunity of effecting some alterations in himself. For Doctor Twist was a small man, and weedy. He had
a snub nose, features of a markedly simian cast and an expression
of furtive slyness. And he wore a waxed moustache.

However, all this was not the visitor's business. If a man
wishes to wax his moustache, it is a matter between himself and
his God.

"My name's Carmody," he said. "Hugo Carmody."

"Yes. I got your card."

"Could I have a word with my uncle?"

"Sure, if you don't mind waiting a minute. Right now,"
explained Doctor Twist, with a gesture towards the window,
"he's occupied."

Hugo moved to the window, looked out, and started violently.

"Great Scott!" he exclaimed.

He gaped down at the group below. Mr. Carmody and
colleagues had now discarded the skipping-ropes and were
performing some unpleasant-looking bending and stretching
exercises, holding their hands above their heads and swinging
painfully from what one may loosely term their waists. It was
a spectacle well calculated to astonish any nephew.

"How long has he got to go on like that?" asked Hugo,
awed.

Doctor Twist looked at his watch.

"They'll be quitting soon now. Then a cold shower and
rub down, and they'll be through till lunch."

"Cold shower?"

"Yes."

"You mean to say you make my Uncle Lester take cold
shower-baths?"

"That's right."

"Good God!"

A look of respect came into Hugo's face as he gazed upon
this master of men. Anybody who, in addition to making him
tie himself in knots under a blazing sun, could lure Uncle
Lester within ten yards of a cold shower-bath was entitled to
credit.

"I suppose after all this," he said, "they do themselves pretty
well at lunch?"

"They have a lean mutton chop apiece, with green vegetables and dry toast."

"Is that all?"

"That's all."

"And to drink?"

"Just water."

"Followed, of course, by a spot of port?"

"No, sir."

"No port?"

"Certainly not."

"You mean—literally—no port?"

"Not a drop. If your old man had gone easier on the port, he'd not have needed to come to Healthward Ho."

"I say," said Hugo, "did you invent that name?"

"Sure. Why?"

"Oh, I don't know. I just thought I'd ask."

"Say, while I think of it," said Doctor Twist, "have you any cigarettes?"

"Oh, rather." Hugo produced a bulging case. "Turkish this side, Virginian that."

"Not for me. I was only going to say that when you meet your uncle just bear in mind he isn't allowed tobacco."

"Not allowed . . .? You mean to say you tie Uncle Lester into a lover's knot, shoot him under a cold shower, push a lean chop into him accompanied by water, and then don't even let the poor old devil get his lips round a single gasper?"

"That's right."

"Well, all I can say is," said Hugo, "it's no life for a refined Nordic."

Dazed by the information he had received, he began to potter aimlessly about the room. He was not particularly fond of his uncle: Mr. Carmody Senior's practice of giving him no allowance and keeping him imprisoned all the year round at Rudge would alone have been enough to check anything in the nature of tenderness: but he did not think he deserved quite all that seemed to be coming to him at Healthward Ho.

He mused upon his uncle. A complex character. A man with Lester Carmody's loathing for expenditure ought by rights to have been a simple liver, existing off hot milk and triturated sawdust like an American millionaire. That Fate should have given him, together with his prudence in money matters, a recklessness as regarded the pleasures of the table seemed ironic.

"I see they've quit," said Doctor Twist, with a glance out of window. "If you want to have a word with your uncle you could do it now. No bad news, I hope?"

"If there is, I'm the one that's going to get it. Between you and me," said Hugo, who had no secrets from his fellow-men, "I've come to try to touch him for a bit of money."

"Is that so?" said Doctor Twist, interested. Anything to do with money always interested the well-known American physician and physical culture expert.

"Yes," said Hugo. "Five hundred quid, to be exact."

He spoke a little despondently, for, having arrived at the window again, he was in a position now to take a good look at his uncle. And so forbidding had bodily toil and mental disturbance rendered the latter's expression that he found the fresh young hopes with which he had started out on this expedition rapidly ebbing away. If Mr. Carmody were to burst —and he looked as if he might do so at any moment—he, Hugo, being his nearest of kin, would inherit: but, failing that, thère seemed to be no cash in sight whatever.

"Though when I say 'touch'," he went on, "I don't mean quite that. The stuff is really mine. My father left me a few thousand, you see, but most injudiciously made Uncle Lester my trustee, and I'm not allowed to get at the capital without the old blighter's consent. And now a pal of mine in London has written offering me a half share in a new night-club which he's starting if I will put up five hundred pounds."

"I see."

"And what I ask myself," said Hugo, "is will Uncle Lester part? That's what I ask myself."

"From what I have seen of Mr. Carmody, I shouldn't say that parting was the thing he does best."

"He's got absolutely no gift for it whatever," said Hugo gloomily.

"Well, I wish you luck," said Doctor Twist. "But don't you try to bribe him with cigarettes."

"Do what?"

"Bribe him with cigarettes. After they have been taking the treatment for a while, most of these birds would give their soul for a coffin-nail."

Hugo started. He had not thought of this; but, now that it had been called to his attention, he saw that it was most certainly an idea.

"And don't keep him standing around longer than you can help. He ought to get under that shower as soon as possible."

Hugo had an idea.

"I suppose I couldn't tell him that owing to my pleading and persuasion you've consented to let him off a cold shower to-day?"

"No, sir."

"It would help," urged Hugo. "It might just sway the issue, as it were."

"Sorry. He must have his shower. When a man's been exercising and has got himself into a perfect lather of sweat . . ."

"Keep it clean," said Hugo coldly. "There is no need to stress the physical side. Oh, very well, then, I suppose I shall have to trust to tact and charm of manner. But I wish to goodness I hadn't got to spring business matters on him on top of what seems to have been a slightly hectic morning."

He shot his cuffs, pulled down his waistcoat, and walked with a resolute step out of the room. He was about to try to get into the ribs of a man who for a lifetime had been saving up to be a miser and who, even apart from this trait in his character, held the subversive view that the less money young men had the better for them. Hugo was a gay optimist, cheerful of soul and a mighty singer in the bath-tub, but he could not feel very sanguine. However, the Carmodys were a bulldog breed. He decided to have a pop at it.

Theoretically, no doubt, the process of exercising flaccid muscles, opening hermetically sealed pores and stirring up a liver which had long supposed itself off the active list ought to engender in a man a jolly sprightliness. In practice, however, this is not always so. That Lester Carmody was in no radiant mood was shown at once by the expression on his face as he turned in response to Hugo's yodel from the rear. In spite of all that Healthward Ho had been doing to Mr. Carmody this last ten days, it was plain that he had not yet got that Kruschen feeling.

Nor, at the discovery that a nephew whom he had supposed to be twenty miles away was standing at his elbow, did anything in the nature of sudden joy help to fill him with sweetness and light.

"How the devil did you get here?" were his opening words of welcome. His scarlet face vanished for an instant into the folds of a large handkerchief; then reappeared, wearing a look of acute concern. "You didn't," he quavered, "come in the Dex-Mayo?"

A thought to shake the sturdiest man. It was twenty miles from Rudge Hall to Healthward Ho, and twenty miles back again from Healthward Ho to Rudge Hall. The Dex-Mayo, that voracious car, consumed a gallon of petrol for every ten miles it covered. And for a gallon of petrol they extorted from you nowadays the hideous sum of one shilling and sixpence halfpenny. Forty miles, accordingly, meant—not including oil, wear and tear of engines and depreciation of tyres—a loss to his purse of over six shillings—a heavy price to pay for the society of a nephew whom he had disliked since boyhood.

"No, no," said Hugo hastily. "I borrowed John's two-seater."

"Oh," said Mr. Carmody, relieved.

There was a pause, employed by Mr. Carmody in puffing; by Hugo in trying to think of something to say that would be soothing, tactful, ingratiating and calculated to bring home the bacon. He turned over in his mind one or two conversational gambits.

("Well, Uncle, you look very rosy."
?
Not quite right.

"I say, Uncle, what ho the School-Girl Complexion?" Absolutely *no*! The wrong tone altogether.

Ah! That was more like it. "Fit." Yes, that was the word.)

"You look very fit, Uncle," said Hugo.

Mr. Carmody's reply to this was to make a noise like a buffalo pulling its foot out of a swamp. It might have been intended to be genial, or it might not. Hugo could not tell. However, he was a reasonable young man, and he quite understood that it would be foolish to expect the milk of human kindness instantly to come gushing like a geyser out of a two hundred and twenty pound uncle who had just been doing bending and stretching exercises. He must be patient and suave—the Sympathetic Nephew.

"I expect it's been pretty tough going, though," he proceeded.

"I mean to say, all these exercises and cold showers and lean chops and so forth. Terribly trying. Very upsetting. A great ordeal. I think it's wonderful the way you've stuck it out. Simply wonderful. It's character that does it. That's what it is. Character. Many men would have chucked the whole thing up in the first two days."

"So would I," said Mr. Garmody, "only that damned doctor made me give him a cheque in advance for the whole course."

Hugo felt damped. He had had some good things to say about character, and it seemed little use producing them now.

"Well, anyway, you look very fit. Very fit indeed. Frightfully fit. Remarkably fit. Extraordinarily fit." He paused. This was getting him nowhere. He decided to leap straight to the point at issue. To put his fortune to the test, to win or lose it all. "I say, Uncle Lester, what I really came about this afternoon was a matter of business."

"Indeed? I supposed you had come merely to babble. What business?"

"You know a friend of mine named Fish?"

"I do not know a friend of yours named Fish."

"Well, he's a friend of mine. His name's Fish."

"What about him?"

"He's starting a new night-club."

"I don't care," said Mr. Carmody, who did not.

"It's just off Bond Street, in the heart of London's pleasure-seeking area. He's calling it The Hot Spot."

The only comment Mr. Carmody vouchsafed on this piece of information was a noise like another buffalo. His face was beginning to lose its vermilion tinge, and it seemed possible that in a few moments he might come off the boil.

"I had a letter from him this morning. He says he will give me a half share if I put up five hundred quid."

"Then you won't get a half share," predicted Mr. Carmody.

"But I've got five hundred. I mean to say, you're holding a lot more than that in trust for me."

"Holding," said Mr. Carmody, "is the right word."

"But surely you'll let me have this quite trivial sum for a really excellent business venture that simply can't fail? Ronnie Fish knows all about night-clubs. He's practically lived in them since he came down from Cambridge."

"I shall not give you a penny. Have you no conception of

the duties of a trustee? Trust money has to be invested in gilt-edged securities."

"You'll never find a gilter-edged security than a night-club run by Ronnie Fish."

"If you have finished this nonsense I will go and take my shower-bath."

"Well, look here, Uncle, may I invite Ronnie to Rudge, so that you can have a talk with him?"

"You may not. I have no desire to talk with him."

"You'd like Ronnie. He has an aunt in the looney-bin."

"Do you consider that a recommendation?"

"No, I just mentioned it."

"Well, I refuse to have him at Rudge."

"But listen, Uncle. The vicar will be round any day now to get me to perform at the village concert. If Ronnie were on the spot, he and I could do the Quarrel Scene from *Julius Caesar* and really give the customers something for their money. We used to do it at Smokers up at Cambridge and it went big."

Even this added inducement did not soften Mr. Carmody.

"I will not invite your friends to Rudge."

"Right ho," said Hugo, a game loser. He was disappointed, but not surprised. All along he had felt that that Hot Spot business was merely a Utopian dream. There are some men who are temperamentally incapable of parting with five hundred pounds, and his uncle Lester was one of them. But in the matter of a smaller sum it might be that he would prove more pliable, and of this smaller sum Hugo had urgent need. "Well, then, putting that aside," he said, "there's another thing I'd like to chat about for a moment, if you don't mind."

Mr. Carmody said he did.

"There's a big fight on to-night at the Albert Hall. Eustace Rodd and Cyril Warburton are going twenty rounds for the Welter-Weight Championship. Have you ever noticed," said Hugo, touching on a matter to which he had given some thought, "a rather odd thing about boxers these days? A few years ago you never heard of one that wasn't Beefy this or Porky that or Young Cat's-meat or something. But now they're all Claudes and Harolds and Cuthberts. And when you consider that the heavyweight champion of the world is actually named Eugene, it makes you think a bit. However, be that as it may, these two birds are going twenty rounds to-night, and there you are."

"What," inquired Mr. Carmody, "is all this drivel?"

He eyed his young relative balefully. In an association that had lasted many years, he had found Hugo consistently irritating to his nervous system, and he was finding him now rather more trying than usual.

"I only meant to point out that Ronnie Fish has sent me a ticket, and I thought that, if you were to spring a tenner for the necessary incidental expenses—bed, breakfast and so on . . . . well, there I would be, don't you know."

"You mean you wish to go to London to see a boxing contest?"

"That's it."

"Well, you're not going. You know I have expressly forbidden you to visit London. The last time I was weak enough to allow you to go there, what happened? You spent the night in the police station."

"Yes, but that was Boat-Race night."

"And I had to pay five pounds for your fine."

Hugo dismissed the past with a gesture.

"The whole thing," he said, "was an unfortunate misunderstanding, and, if you ask me, the verdict of Posterity will be that the policeman was far more to blame than I was. They're letting a bad type of man into the Force nowadays. I've noticed it on several occasions. Besides, it won't happen again."

"You are right. It will not."

"On second thoughts, then, you will spring that tenner?"

"On first, second, third and fourth thoughts I will do nothing of the kind."

"But, Uncle, do you realise what it would mean if you did?"

"The interpretation I would put upon it is that I was suffering from senile decay."

"What it would mean is that I should feel you trusted me, Uncle Lester, that you had faith in me. There's nothing so dangerous as a want of trust. Ask anybody. It saps a young man's character."

"Let it," said Mr. Carmody callously.

"If I went to London, I could see Ronnie Fish and explain all the circumstances about my not being able to go into that Hot Spot thing with him."

"You can do that by letter."

"It's so hard to put things properly in a letter."

"Then put them improperly," said Mr. Carmody. "Once and for all, you are not going to London."

He had started to turn away as the only means possible of concluding this interview, when he stopped, spell-bound. For Hugo, as was his habit when matters had become difficult and required careful thought, was pulling out of his pocket a cigarette case.

"Goosh!" said Mr. Carmody, or something that sounded like that.

He made an involuntary motion with his hand, as a starving man will make towards bread: and Hugo, with a strong rush of emotion, realized that the happy ending had been achieved and that at the eleventh hour matters could at last be put on a satisfactory business basis.

"Turkish this side, Virginian that," he said. "You can have the lot for ten quid."

"Say, I think you'd best be getting along and taking your shower, Mr. Carmody," said the voice of Doctor Twist, who had come up unobserved and was standing at his elbow.

The proprietor of Healthward Ho had a rather unpleasant voice, but never had it seemed so unpleasant to Mr. Carmody as it did at that moment. Parsimonious though he was, he would have given much for the privilege of heaving a brick at Doctor Twist. For at the very instant of this interruption he had conceived the Machiavellian idea of knocking the cigarette case out of Hugo's hand and grabbing what he could from the debris: and now this scheme must be abandoned.

With a snort which came from the very depths of an overwrought soul Lester Carmody turned and shuffled off towards the house.

"Say, you shouldn't have done that," said Doctor Twist, waggling a reproachful head at Hugo. "No, sir, you shouldn't have done that. Not right to tantalize the poor fellow."

Hugo's mind seldom ran on parallel lines with that of his uncle, but it was animated now by the identical thought which only a short while back Mr. Carmody had so wistfully entertained. He, too, was feeling that what Doctor Twist needed was a brick thrown at him. When he was able to speak, however, he did not mention this, but kept the conversation on a pacific and businesslike note.

"I say," he said, "you couldn't lend me a tenner, could you?"

"I could not," agreed Doctor Twist.

In Hugo's mind the inscrutable problem of why an all-wise Creator should have inflicted a man like this on the world deepened.

"Well, I'll be pushing along, then," he said moodily.

"Going already?"

"Yes, I am."

"I hope," said Doctor Twist, as he escorted his young guest to his car, "you aren't sore at me for calling you down about those students' lamps. You see, maybe your uncle was hoping you would slip him one, and the disappointment will have made him kind of mad. And part of the system here is to have the patients think tranquil thoughts."

"Think what?"

"Tranquil, beautiful thoughts. You see, if your mind's all right, your body's all right. That's the way I look at it."

Hugo settled himself at the wheel.

"Let's get this clear," he said. "You expect my uncle Lester to think beautiful thoughts?"

"All the time."

"Even under a cold shower?"

"Yes, sir."

"God bless you!" said Hugo.

He stepped on the self-starter, and urged the two-seater pensively down the drive. He was glad when the shrubberies hid him from the view of Doctor Twist, for one wanted to forget a fellow like that as soon as possible. A moment later, he was still gladder: for, as he turned the first corner, there popped out suddenly from a rhododendron bush a stout man with a red and streaming face. Lester Carmody had had to hurry, and he was not used to running.

"Woof!" he ejaculated, barring the fairway.

Relief flooded over Hugo. The marts of trade had not been closed after all.

"Give me those cigarettes!" panted Mr. Carmody.

For an instant Hugo toyed with the idea of creating a rising market. But he was no profiteer. Hugo Carmody, the Square Dealer.

"Ten quid," he said, "and they're yours.

Agony twisted Mr. Carmody's glowing features.

"Five," he urged.

"Ten," said Hugo.

"Eight."

"Ten."

Mr. Carmody made the great decision.

"Very well. Give me them. Quick."

"Turkish this side, Virginian that," said Hugo.

The rhododendron bush quivered once more from the passage of a heavy body: birds in the neighbouring trees began to sing again their anthems of joy: and Hugo, in his trousers pocket two crackling five pound notes, was bowling off along the highway.

Even Doctor Twist could have found nothing to cavil at in the beauty of the thoughts he was thinking. He carolled like a linnet in the springtime.

★ 3 ★

Hugo does his Day's Good Deed

"Yes, sir," Hugo Carmody was assuring a listening world as he turned the two-seater in at the entrance of the stable-yard of Rudge Hall some forty minutes later, "That's my baby. No, sir, don't mean maybe. Yes, sir, that's my baby now. And, by the way, by the way . . ."

"Blast you," said his cousin John, appearing from nowhere. "Get out of that car."

"Hullo, John," said Hugo. "So there you are, John. I say, John, I've just been paying a call on the head of the family over at Healthward Ho. Why they don't run excursion-trains of sightseers there is more than I can understand. It's worth seeing, believe me. Large, fat men doing bending and stretching exercises. Tons of humanity leaping about with skipping-ropes. Never a dull moment from start to finish, and all clean, wholesome fun, mark you, without a taint of vulgarity or suggestiveness. Pack some sandwiches and bring the kiddies. And let me tell you the best thing of all, John . . ."

"I can't stop to listen. You've made me late already."

"Late for what?"

"I'm going to London."

"You are?" said Hugo, with a smile at the happy coincidence. "So am I. You can give me a lift."

"I won't."

"I am certainly not going to run behind."

"You're not going to London."

"You bet I'm going to London."

"Well, go by train, then."

"And break into hard-won cash, every penny of which will be needed for the big time in the metropolis? A pretty story!"

"Well, anyway, you aren't coming with me."

"Why not?"

"I don't want you."

35

"John," said Hugo, "there is more in this than meets the eye. You can't deceive me. You are going to London for a purpose. What purpose?"

"If you really want to know, I'm going to see Pat."

"What on earth for? She'll be here to-morrow. I looked in at Chas. Bywater's this morning for some cigarettes—and, gosh, how lucky it was I did!—by the way he's putting them down to you—and he told me she's arriving by the three o'clock train."

"I know. Well. I happen to want to see her very particularly to-night."

Hugo eyed his cousin narrowly. He was marshalling the facts and drawing conclusions.

"John," he said, "this can mean but one thing. You are driving a hundred miles in a shaky car—that left front tyre wants a spot of air, I should look to it before you start, if I were you—to see a girl whom you could see to-morrow in any case by the simple process of meeting the three o'clock train. Your state of mind is such that you prefer—actually prefer—not to have my company. And, as I look at you, I note that you are blushing prettily. I see it all. You've at last decided to propose to Pat. Am I right or wrong?"

John drew a deep breath. He was not one of those men who derive pleasure from parading their inmost feelings and discussing with others the secrets of their hearts. Hugo, in a similar situation, would have advertised his love like the hero of a musical comedy; he would have made the round of his friends, confiding in them; and, when the supply of friends had given out, would have buttonholed the gardener. But John was different. To hear his aspirations put into bald words like this made him feel as if he were being divested of most of his more important garments in a crowded thoroughfare.

"Well, that settles it," said Hugo briskly. "Such being the case, of course you must take me along. I will put in a good word for you. Pave the way."

"Listen," said John, finding speech. "If you dare to come within twenty miles of us . . ."

"It would be wiser. You know what you're like. Heart of gold but no conversation. Try to tackle this on your own and you'll bungle it."

"You keep out of this," said John, speaking in a low, husky

voice that suggested the urgent need of one of those throat-lozenges purveyed by Chas. Bywater and so esteemed by the dog Emily. "You keep right out of this."

Hugo shrugged his shoulders.

"Just as you please. Hugo Carmody is the last man," he said, a little stiffly, "to thrust his assistance on those who do not require same. But a word from me would make all the difference, and you know it. Rightly or wrongly Pat has always looked up to me, regarded me as a wise elder brother, and, putting it in a nutshell, hung upon my lips. I could start you off right. However, since you're so blasted independent, carry on, only bear this in mind—when it's all over and you are shedding scalding tears of remorse and thinking of what might have been, don't come yowling to me for sympathy, because there won't be any."

John went upstairs and packed his bag. He packed well and thoroughly. This done he charged down the stairs, and perceived with annoyance that Hugo was still inflicting the stable-yard with his beastly presence.

But Hugo was not there to make jarring conversation. He was present now, it appeared, solely in the capacity of Good Angel.

"I've fixed up that tyre," said Hugo, "and filled the tank and put in a drop of oil and passed an eye over the machinery in general. She ought to run nicely now."

John melted. His mood had softened, and he was in a fitter frame of mind to remember that he had always been fond of his cousin.

"Thanks. Very good of you. Well, good-bye."

"Good-bye," said Hugo. "And heaven speed your wooing, boy."

Freed from the restrictions placed upon a light two-seater by the ruts and hillocks of country lanes, John celebrated his arrival on the broad main road that led to London by placing a large foot on the accelerator and keeping it there. He was behind time, and he intended to test a belief, which he had long held, that a Widgeon Seven can, if pressed, do fifty. To the scenery, singularly beautiful in this part of England, he paid no attention. Automatically avoiding wagons by an inch and dreamily putting thoughts of the hereafter into the startled minds of dogs and chickens, he was out of Worcestershire and into Gloucestershire almost before he had really settled in his seat. It was only when the long wall that fringes Blenheim Park came into view that it was borne in upon him that he would be reaching Oxford in a few minutes and could stop for a well-earned cup of tea. He noted with satisfaction that he was nicely ahead of the clock.

He drifted past the Martyrs' Memorial, and, picking his way through the traffic, drew up at the door of the Clarendon. He alighted stiffly, and stretched himself. And as he did so, something caught his attention out of the corner of his eye. It was his cousin Hugo, climbing down from the dickey.

"A very nice run," said Hugo with satisfaction. "I should say we made pretty good time."

He radiated kindliness and satisfaction with all created things. That John was looking at him in rather a peculiar way, and apparently trying to say something, he did not seem to notice.

"A little refreshment would be delightful," he observed. "Dusty work, sitting in dickeys. By the way, I got on to Pat on the 'phone before we left, and there's no need to hurry. She's dining out and going to a theatre to-night."

"What!" cried John, in agony.

"It's all right. Don't get the wind up. She's meeting us at eleven-fifteen at the Mustard Spoon. I'll come on there from the fight and we'll have a nice home evening. I'm still a member, so I'll sign you in. And, what's more, if all goes well at the Albert Hall and Cyril Warburton is half the man I think he is and I can get some sporting stranger to bet the other way at reasonable odds, I'll pay the bill."

"You're very kind!"

"I try to be, John," said Hugo modestly. "I try to be. I don't think we ought to leave it all to the Boy Scouts."

★ 4 ★

Disturbing Occurrences at a Night-Club

I

A MAN whose uncle jerks him away from London as if he were picking a winkle out of its shell with a pin and keeps him for months and months immured in the heart of Worcestershire must inevitably lose touch with the swiftly-changing kaleidoscope of metropolitan night-life. Nothing in a big city fluctuates more rapidly than the status of its supper-dancing clubs; and Hugo, had he still been a lad-about-town in good standing, would have been aware that recently the Mustard Spoon had gone down a good deal in the social scale. Society had migrated to other, newer institutions, leaving it to become the haunt of the lesser ornaments of the stage and the Portuguese, the Argentines and the Greeks.

To John Carroll, however, as he stood waiting in the lobby, the place seemed sufficiently gay and glittering. Nearly a year had passed since his last visit to London: and the Mustard Spoon rather impressed him. An unseen orchestra was playing with extraordinary vigour, and from time to time ornate persons of both sexes drifted past him into the brightly lighted supper-room. Where an established connoisseur of night-clubs would have pursed his lips and shaken his head, John was conscious only of feeling decidedly uplifted and exhilarated.

But then he was going to see Pat again, and that was enough to stimulate any man.

She arrived unexpectedly, at a moment when he had taken his eye off the door to direct it in mild astonishment at a lady in an orange dress who, doubtless with the best motives, had dyed her hair crimson and was wearing a black-rimmed monocle. So absorbed was he with this spectacle that he did not see her enter, and was only made aware of her presence when there spoke from behind him a clear little voice which, even when it was laughing at you, always seemed to have in it something of the song of larks on summer mornings and winds whispering across the fields in Spring.

"Hullo, Johnnie."

The hair, scarlet though it was, lost its power to attract. The appeal of the monocle waned. John spun round.

"Pat!"

She was looking lovelier than ever. That was the thing that first presented itself to John's notice. If anybody had told him that Pat could possibly be prettier than the image of her which he had been carrying about with him all these months, he would not have believed him. But so it was. Some sort of a female with plucked eyebrows and a painted face had just come in, and she might have been put there expressly for purposes of comparison. She made Pat seem so healthy, so wholesome, such a thing of the open air and the clean sunshine, so pre-eminently fit. She looked as if she had spent her time at Le Touquet playing thirty-six holes of golf a day.

"Pat!" cried John, and something seemed to catch at his throat. There was a mist in front of his eyes. His heart was thumping madly.

She extended her hand composedly.

"Well, Johnnie. How nice to see you again. You're looking very brown and rural. Where's Hugo?"

It takes two to hoist a conversation to an emotional peak. John choked, and became calmer.

"He'll be here soon, I expect," he said.

Pat laughed indulgently.

"Hugo'll be late for his own funeral—if he ever gets to it. He said eleven-fifteen and it's twenty-five to twelve. Have you got a table?"

"Not yet."

"Why not?"

"I'm not a member," said John, and saw in her eyes the scorn which women reserve for male friends and relations who show themselves wanting in enterprise. "You have to be a member," he said, chafing under the look.

"I don't," said Pat with decision. "If you think I'm going to wait all night for old Hugo in a small lobby with six draughts whizzing through it, correct that impression. Go and find the head waiter and get a table while I leave my cloak. Back in a minute."

John's emotions as he approached the head waiter rather resembled those with which years ago he had once walked up to a bull in a field, Pat having requested him to do so because she wanted to know if bulls in fields really are fierce or if the artists who depict them in comic papers are simply trying to be funny. He felt embarrassed and diffident. The head waiter was a large, stout, smooth-faced man who would have been better for a couple of weeks at Healthward Ho, and he gave the impression of having disliked John from the start.

John said it was a nice evening. The head waiter did not seem to believe him.

"Has—er—has Mr. Carmody booked a table?" asked John.

"No, monsieur."

"I'm meeting him here to-night."

The head waiter appeared uninterested. He began to talk to an underling in rapid French. John, feeling more than ever an intruder, took advantage of a lull in the conversation to make another attempt.

"I wonder . . . Perhaps . . . Can you give me a table?"

Most of the head waiter's eyes were concealed by the upper strata of his cheeks, but there was enough of them left visible to allow him to look at John as if he was something unpleasant that had come to light in a portion of salad.

"Monsieur is a member?"

"Er—no."

"If you will please wait in the lobby, thank you."

"But I was wondering . . ."

"If you will wait in the lobby, please," said the head waiter, and, dismissing John from the scheme of things, became gruesomely obsequious to an elderly man with diamond studs, no hair, an authoritative manner and a lady in pink. He waddled before them into the supper room, and Pat reappeared.

"Got that table?"

"I'm afraid not. He says . . ."

"Oh, Johnnie, you are helpless."

Women are unjust in these matters. When a man comes into a night-club of which he is not a member and asks for a table he feels that he is butting in, and naturally is not at his best. This is not helplessness, it is fineness of soul. But women won't see that.

"I'm awfully sorry."

The head waiter had returned, and was either doing sums or drawing caricatures on a large pad chained to a desk. He seemed so much the artist absorbed in his work that John would not have dreamed of venturing to interrupt him. Pat had no such delicacy.

"I want a table, please," said Pat.

"Madame is a member?"

"A table, please. A nice, large one. I like plenty of room. And when Mr. Carmody arrives tell him that Miss Wyvern and Mr. Carroll are inside."

"Very good, Madame. Certainly, Madame. This way, Madame."

Just as simple as that! John, making a physically impressive but spiritually negligible tail to the procession, wondered, as he crossed the polished floor, how Pat did these things. It was not as if she were one of those massive imperious women whom you would naturally expect to quell head waiters with a glance. She was no Cleopatra, no Catherine of Russia— just a slim, slight girl with a tip-tilted nose. And yet she had taken this formidable magnifico in her stride, kicked him lightly in the face and passed on. He sat down, thrilled with a wor- shipping admiration.

Pat, as always happened after one of her little spurts of irritability, was apologetic.

"Sorry I bit your head off, Johnnie," she said. "It was a shame, after you had come all this way, just to see an old friend. But it makes me so angry when you're meek and sheep-y and let people trample on you. Still I suppose it's not your fault." She smiled across at him. "You always were a slow, good- natured old thing, weren't you, like one of those big dogs that come and bump their head on your lap and snuffle. Poor old Johnnie!"

John felt depressed. The picture she had conjured up was not a flattering one; and, as for this "Poor old Johnnie!" stuff, it struck just the note he most wanted to avoid. If one thing is certain in the relations of the sexes, it is that the Poor Old Johnnies of this world get nowhere. But before he could put any of these feelings into words Pat had changed the subject.

"Johnnie," she said, "what's all this trouble between your uncle and father? I had a letter from father a couple of weeks ago, and as far as I could make out Mr. Carmody seems to have been trying to murder him. What's it all about?"

Not so eloquently, nor with such a wealth of imagery as Colonel Wyvern had employed in sketching out the details of the affair of the dynamite outrage for the benefit of Chas. Bywater, Chemist, John answered the question.

"Good heavens!" said Pat.

"I—I hope . . . " said John.

"What do you hope?"

"Well, I—I hope it's not going to make any difference?"

"Difference? How do you mean?"

"Between us. Between you and me, Pat."

"What sort of difference?"

John had his cue.

"Pat, darling, in all these years we've known one another haven't you ever guessed that I've been falling more and more in love with you every minute? I can't remember a time when I didn't love you. I loved you as a kid in short skirts and a blue jersey. I loved you when you came back from that school of yours, looking like a princess. And I love you now more than I have ever loved you. I worship you, Pat darling. You're the whole world to me, just the one thing that matters the least little bit. And don't you try to start laughing at me again now, because I've made up my mind that, whatever else you laugh at, you've got to take me seriously. I may have been Poor Old Johnnie in the past, but the time has come when you've got to forget all that. I mean business. You're going to marry me, and the sooner you make up your mind to it, the better."

That was what John had intended to say. What he actually did say was something briefer and altogether less effective.

"Oh, I don't know," said John.

"Do you mean you're afraid I'm going to stop being friends with you just because my father and your uncle have had a quarrel?"

"Yes," said John. It was not quite all he had meant, but it gave the general idea.

"What a weird notion! After all these years? Good heavens, no. I'm much too fond of you, Johnnie."

Once more John had his cue. And this time he was determined that he would not neglect it. He stiffened his courage. He cleared his throat. He clutched the tablecloth.

"Pat . . ."

"Oh, there's Hugo at last," she said, looking past him. "And about time. I'm starving. Hullo! Who are the people he's got with him? Do you know them?"

John heaved a silent sigh. Yes, he could have counted on Hugo arriving at just this moment. He turned, and perceived that unnecessary young man crossing the floor. With him were a middle-aged man and a younger and extremely dashing-looking girl. They were complete strangers to John.

II

Hugo pranced buoyantly up to the table, looking like the Laughing Cavalier, clean-shaved.

He was wearing the unmistakable air of a man who has been to a welter-weight boxing contest at the Albert Hall and backed the winner.

"Hullo, Pat," he said jovially. "Hullo, John. Sorry I'm late. Mitt—if that is the word I want—my dear old friend . . . I've forgotten your name," he added, turning to his companion.

"Molloy, brother. Thomas G. Molloy."

Hugo's dear old friend spoke in a deep, rich voice, well in keeping with his appearance. He was a fine, handsome, open-faced person in the early forties, with grizzled hair that swept in a wave off a massive forehead. His nationality was plainly American, and his aspect vaguely senatorial.

"Molloy," said Hugo, "Thomas G. and daughter. This is Miss Wyvern. And this is my cousin, Mr. Carroll. And now," said Hugo, relieved at having finished with the introductions, "let's try to get a bit of supper."

The service at the Mustard Spoon is not what it was; but by the simple process of clutching at the coat tails of a passing waiter and holding him till he consented to talk business Hugo contrived to get fairly rapid action. Then, after an interval of the rather difficult conversation which usually marks the first stages of this sort of party, the orchestra burst into a sudden torrent of what it evidently mistook for music, and Thomas G. Molloy rose and led Miss Molloy out on to the floor. He danced a little stiffly, but he knew how to give the elbow and he appeared, as the crowd engulfed him, to be holding his own.

"Who are your friends, Hugo?" asked Pat.

"Thos. G. . . ."

"Yes, I know. But who are they?"

"Well, there," said Hugo, "you rather have me. I sat next to Thos. at the fight, and I rather took to the fellow. He seemed to me a man full of noble qualities, including a loony idea that Eustace Rodd was some good as a boxer. He actually offered to give me three to one, and I cleaned up substantially at the end of the seventh round. After that, I naturally couldn't very well get out of giving the man supper. And as he had promised to take his daughter out to-night, I said bring her along. You don't mind?"

"Of course not. Though it would have been cosier, just we three."

"Quite true. But never forget that, if it had not been for this Thos., you would not be getting the jolly good supper which I have now ample funds to supply. You may look on Thos. as practically the Founder of the Feast." He cast a wary eye at his cousin, who was leaning back in his chair with the abstracted look of one in deep thought. "Has old John said anything to you yet?"

"John? What do you mean? What about?"

"Oh, things in general. Come and dance this. I want to have a very earnest word with you, young Pat. Big things are in the wind."

"You're very mysterious."

"Ah!" said Hugo.

Left alone at the table with nothing to entertain him but his thoughts, John came almost immediately to the conclusion that his first verdict on the Mustard Spoon had been an erroneous one. Looking at it superficially, he had mistaken it for rather an attractive place: but now, with maturer judgment, he saw it for what it was—a blot on a great city. It was places like the Mustard Spoon that made a man despair of progress. He disliked the clientèle. He disliked the head waiter. He disliked the orchestra. The clientèle was flashy and offensive and, as regarded the male element of it, far too given to the use of hair oil. The head waiter was a fat parasite who needed kicking. And, as for Ben Baermann's Collegiate Buddies, he resented the fact that they were being paid for making the sort of noises which he, when a small boy, had produced—for fun and with no thought of sordid gain—on a comb with a bit of tissue paper over it.

He was brooding on the scene in much the same spirit of captious criticism as that in which Lot had once regarded the Cities of the Plain, when the Collegiate Buddies suddenly suspended their cacophony, and he saw Pat and Hugo coming back to the table.

But the Buddies had only been crouching, the better to spring. A moment later they were at it again, and Pat, pausing, looked expectantly at Hugo.

Hugo shook his head.

"I've just seen Ronnie Fish up in the balcony," he said. "I positively must go and confer with him. I have urgent matters to discuss with the old leper. Sit down and talk to John. You've got lots to talk about. See you anon. And, if there's anything you want, order it, paying no attention whatever to the prices in the right-hand column. Thanks to Thos., I'm made of money to-night."

Hugo melted away: Pat sat down: and John, with another abrupt change of mood, decided that he had misjudged the Mustard Spoon. A very jolly little place, when you looked at it in the proper spirit. Nice people, a distinctly lovable head waiter, and as attractive a lot of musicians as he remembered ever to have seen. He turned to Pat, to seek her confirmation of these views, and, meeting her gaze, experienced a rather severe shock. Her eyes seemed to have frozen over. They were cold and hard. Taken in conjunction with the fact that her nose turned up a little at the end, they gave her face a scornful and contemptuous look.

"Hullo!" he said, alarmed. "What's the matter?"

"Nothing."

"Why are you looking like that?"

"Like what?"

"Well . . ."

John had little ability as a word-painter. He could not on the spur of the moment give anything in the nature of detailed description of the way Pat was looking. He only knew he did not like it.

"I suppose you expected me to look at you 'with eyes overrunning with laughter'?"

"Eh?"

" 'Archly the maiden smiled, and with eyes overrunning with laughter said in a tremulous voice "Why don't you speak for yourself, John"? ' "

"I don't know what you're talking about."

"Don't you know *The Courtship of Miles Standish*? I thought that must have been where you got the idea. I had to learn chunks of it at school, and even at that tender age I always thought Miles Standish a perfect goop. 'If the great captain of Plymouth is so very eager to wed me, why does he not come himself and take the trouble to woo me? If I am not worth the wooing, I surely am not worth the winning'. And yards more of it. I knew it by heart once. Well, what I want to know is, do you expect my answer direct, or would you prefer that I communicated with your agent?"

"I don't understand."

"Don't you? No? Really?"

"Pat, what's the matter?"

"Oh, nothing much. When we were dancing just now, Hugo proposed to me."

A cold hand clutched at John's heart. He had not a high opinion of his cousin's fascinations, but the thought of anybody but himself proposing to Pat was a revolting one.

"Oh, did he?"

"Yes, he did. For you."

"For me? How do you mean, for me?"

"I'm telling you. He asked me to marry you. And very eloquent he was, too. All the people who heard him—and there must have been dozens who did—were much impressed."

She stopped: and, as far as such a thing is possible at the Mustard Spoon when Ben Baermann's Collegiate Buddies are giving an encore of "My Sweetie Is A Wow", there was silence. Emotion of one sort or another had deprived Pat of words: and, as for John, he was feeling as if he could never speak again.

He had flushed a dusky red, and his collar had suddenly become so tight that he had all the sensations of a man who is being garrotted. And so powerfully had the shock of this fearful revelation affected his mind that his only coherent thought was a desire to follow Hugo up to the balcony, tear him limb from limb, and scatter the fragments on to the tables below.

Pat was the first to find speech. She spoke quickly, stormily.

"I can't understand you, Johnnie. You never used to be such a jellyfish. You did have a mind of your own once. But now . . . I believe it's living at Rudge all the time that has done it. You've got lazy and flabby. It's turned you into a vegetable. You just loaf about and go on and on, year after year, having your three fat meals a day and your comfortable rooms and your hot-water bottle at night . . ."

"I don't!" cried John, stung by this monstrous charge from the coma which was gripping him.

"Well, bed-socks, then," amended Pat. "You've just let yourself be cosseted and pampered till the You that used to be there has withered away and you've gone blah. My dear, good Johnnie," said Pat vehemently, riding over his attempt at speech and glaring at him above a small, perky nose whose tip had begun to quiver even as it had always done when she lost her temper as a child. "My poor, idiotic, fat-headed Johnnie, do you seriously expect a girl to want to marry a man who hasn't the common, elementary pluck to propose to her for himself and has to get someone else to do it for him?"

"I didn't!"

"You did."

"I tell you I did not."

"You mean you never asked Hugo to sound me out?"

"Of course not. Hugo is a meddling, officious idiot, and if I'd got him here now, I'd wring his neck."

He scowled up at the balcony. Hugo, who happened to be looking down at the moment, beamed encouragingly and waved a friendly hand as if to assure his cousin that he was with him in spirit. Silence, tempered by the low wailing of the Buddy in charge of the saxophone and the unpleasant howling of his college friends, who had just begun to sing the chorus, fell once more.

"This opens up a new line of thought," said Pat at length. "Our Miss Wyvern appears to have got the wires crossed." She looked at him meditatively. "It's funny. Hugo seemed so convinced about the way you felt."

John's collar tightened up another half-inch, but he managed to get his vocal chords working.

"He was quite right about the way I felt."

"You mean . . . Really?"

"Yes."

"You mean you're . . . fond of me?"

"Yes."

"But, Johnnie!"

"Damn it, are you blind?" cried John, savage from shame and the agony of harrowed feelings, not to mention a collar which appeared to have been made for a man half his size. "Can't you see? Don't you know I've always loved you? Yes, even when you were a kid."

"But, Johnnie, Johnnie, Johnnie!" Distress was making Pat's silver voice almost squeaky. "You can't have done. I was a horrible kid. I did nothing but bully you from morning till night."

"I liked it."

"But how can you want me to marry you? We know each other too well. I've always looked on you as a sort of brother."

There are words in the language which are like a knell. Keats considered "forlorn" one of them. John Carroll was of opinion that "brother" was a second.

"Oh, I know. I was a fool. I knew you would simply laugh at me."

Pat's eyes were misty. The tip of her nose no longer quivered, but now it was her mouth that did so. She reached out across the table and her hand rested on his for a brief instant.

"I'm not laughing at you, Johnnie, you—you chump. What would I want to laugh at you for? I'm much nearer crying. I'd do anything in the world rather than hurt you. You must know that. You're the dearest old thing that ever lived. There's no one on earth I'm fonder of." She paused. "But this . . . it —it simply isn't on the board."

She was looking at him, furtively, taking advantage of the fact that his face was turned away and his eyes fixed on the broad, swallow-tailed back of Mr. Ben Baermann. It was odd, she felt, all very odd. If she had been asked to describe the sort of man whom one of these days she hoped to marry, the description, curiously enough, would not have been at all unlike dear old Johnnie. He had the right clean, fit look— she knew she could never give a thought to anything but an outdoor man—and the straightness and honesty and kind-liness which she had come, after moving for some years in a world where they were rare, to look upon as the highest of masculine qualities. Nobody could have been farther than

John from the little, black-moustached dancing-man type which was her particular aversion, and yet . . . well, the idea of becoming his wife was just simply too absurd and that was all there was to it.

But why? What, then, was wrong with Johnnie? Simply, she felt, the fact that he was Johnnie. Marriage, as she had always envisaged it, was an adventure. Poor cosy, solid old Johnnie would have to display quite another side of himself, if such a side existed, before she could regard it as an adventure to marry him.

"That man," said John, indicating Mr. Baermann, "looks like a Jewish black beetle."

Pat was relieved. If by this remark he was indicating that he wished the recent episode to be taken as concluded, she was very willing to oblige him.

"Doesn't he?" she said. "I don't know where they can have dug him up from. The last time I was here, a year ago, they had another band, a much better one. I think this place has gone down. I don't like the look of some of these people. What do you think of Hugo's friends?"

"They seem all right." John cast a moody eye at Miss Molloy, a prismatic vision seen fitfully through the crowd. She was laughing, and showing in the process teeth of a flashing whiteness. "The girl's the prettiest girl I've seen for a long time."

Pat gave an imperceptible start. She was suddenly aware of a feeling which was remarkably like uneasiness. It lurked at the back of her consciousness like a small formless cloud.

"Oh!" she said.

Yes, the feeling was uneasiness. Any other man who at such a moment had said those words she would have suspected of a desire to pique her, to stir her interest by a rather obviously assumed admiration of another. But not John. He was much too honest. If Johnnie said a thing, he meant it.

A quick flicker of concern passed through Pat. She was always candid with herself, and she knew quite well that, though she did not want to marry him, she regarded John as essentially a piece of personal property. If he had fallen in love with her, that was, of course, a pity: but it would, she realised, be considerably more of a pity if he ever fell in love with someone else. A Johnnie gone out of her life and assimilated into that of another girl would leave a frightful gap. The Mustard Spoon was one of those stuffy, overheated places, but, as she meditated upon this possibility, Pat shivered.

"Oh!" she said.

The music stopped. The floor emptied. Mr. Molloy and his daughter returned to the table. Hugo remained up in the gallery, in earnest conversation with his old friend, Mr. Fish.

III

Ronald Overbury Fish was a pink-faced young man of small stature and extraordinary solemnity. He had been at school with Hugo and also at the University. Eton was entitled to point with pride at both of them, and only had itself to blame if it failed to do so. The same remark applies to Trinity College, Cambridge. From earliest days Hugo had always entertained for R. O. Fish an intense and lively admiration, and the thought of being compelled to let his old friend down in this matter of the Hot Spot was doing much to mar an otherwise jovial evening.

"I'm most frightfully sorry, Ronnie, old thing," he said immediately the first greetings were over. "I sounded the aged relative this afternoon about that business and there's nothing doing."

"No hope?"

"None."

Ronnie Fish surveyed the dancers below with a grave eye. He removed the stub of his cigarette from its eleven-inch holder, and recharged that impressive instrument.

"Did you reason with the old pest?"

"You can't reason with my Uncle Lester."

"I could," said Mr. Fish.

Hugo did not doubt this. Ronnie, in his opinion, was capable of any feat.

"Yes, but the only trouble is," he explained, "you would have to do it at long range. I asked if I might invite you down to Rudge and he would have none of it."

Ronnie Fish relapsed into silence. It seemed to Hugo, watching him, that that great brain was busy, but upon what train of thought he could not conjecture.

"Who are those people you're with?" he asked at length.

"The big chap with the fair hair is my cousin John. The girl in green is Pat Wyvern. She lives near us."

"And the others? Who's the stately-looking bird with the brushed-back hair who has every appearance of being just about to address a gathering of constituents on some important point of policy?"

"That's a fellow named Molloy. Thos. G. I met him at the fight. He's an American."

"He looks prosperous."

"He isn't so prosperous as he was before the fight started. I took thirty quid off him."

"Your uncle, from what you have told me, is pretty keen on rich men, isn't he?"

"All over them."

"Then the thing's simple," said Ronnie Fish. "Invite this Mulcahy or whatever his name is to Rudge, and invite me at the same time. You'll find that in the ecstasy of getting a millionaire on the premises your uncle will forget to make a fuss about my coming. And once I am in I can talk this business over with him. I'll guarantee that if I can get an uninterrupted half-hour with the old boy I can easily make him see the light."

A rush of admiration for his friend's outstanding brain held Hugo silent for a moment. The bold simplicity of the move thrilled him.

"What it amounts to," continued Ronnie Fish, "is that your uncle is endeavouring to do you out of a vast fortune. I tell you, the Hot Spot is going to be a gold mine. To all practical intents and purposes he is just as good as trying to take thousands of pounds out of your pocket. I shall point this out to him, and I shall be surprised if I can't put the thing through. When would you like me to come down?"

"Ronnie," said Hugo, "this is absolute genius." He hesitated. He had no wish to discourage his friend, but he desired to be fair and above-board. "There's just one thing. Would you have any objection to performing at the village concert?"

"I should enjoy it."

"They're sure to rope you in. I thought you and I might do the Quarrel scene from *Julius Caesar* again."

"Excellent."

"And this time," said Hugo generously, "you can be Brutus."

"No, no," said Ronnie, moved.

"Yes, yes."

"Very well. Then fix things up with this American bloke, and leave the rest to me. Shall I like your uncle?"

"No."

"Ah, well," said Mr. Fish equably, "I don't for a moment suppose he'll like me."

IV

The respite afforded to their patrons' ear-drums by the sudden cessation of activity on the part of the Buddies proved of brief duration. Men like these ex-Collegians, who have really got the saxophone virus into their systems, seldom have long lucid intervals between the attacks. Very soon they were at it again, and Mr. Molloy, rising, led Pat gallantly out on to the floor. His daughter, following them with a bright eye as she busied herself with her lip-stick, laughed amusedly.

"She little knows!"

John, like Pat a short while before, had fallen into a train of thought. From this he now woke with a start to the realization that he was alone with this girl and presumably expected by her to make some effort at being entertaining.

"I beg your pardon?" he said.

Even had he been less preoccupied, he would have found small pleasure in this tete-à-tète. Miss Molloy—her father addressed her as Dolly—belonged to the type of girl in whose society a diffident man is seldom completely at ease. There hung about her like an aura a sort of hard glitter. Her challenging eyes were of a bright hazel—beautiful but intimidating. She looked supremely sure of herself. She reminded him of a leopardess, an animal of which he had never been fond.

"I was saying," she explained, "that your Girl Friend little knows what she has taken on, going out to step with Soapy."

"Soapy?"

It seemed to John that his companion had momentarily the appearance of being a little confused.

"My father, I mean," she said quickly. "I call him Soapy."

"Oh?" said John.

"Soapy," said Miss Molloy, developing her theme, "is full

of Sex-Appeal, but he has two left feet." She emitted another little gurgle of laughter. "There! Would you just look at him now!"

John was sorry to appear dull, but, eyeing Mr. Molloy as requested, he could not see that he was doing anything wrong. On the contrary, for one past his first youth, the man seemed to him enviably efficient.

"I'm afraid I don't know anything about dancing," he said apologetically.

"At that, you're ahead of Soapy. He doesn't even suspect anything. Whenever I get out on the floor with him and come back alive I reckon I've broke even. It isn't so much his dancing on my feet that I mind—it's the way he jumps on and off that slays me. Don't you ever hoof?"

"Oh, yes. Sometimes. A little."

"Well, come and do your stuff, then. I can't sit still while they're playing that thing."

John rose reluctantly. Their brief conversation had made it clear to him that in the matter of dancing this was a girl of high ideals, and he feared he was about to disappoint her. If she regarded with derision a quite adequate performer like Mr. Molloy, she was obviously no partner for himself. But there was no means of avoiding the ordeal. He backed her out into mid-stream, hoping for the best.

Providence was in a kindly mood. By now the floor had become so congested that skill was at a discount. Even the sallow youths with the marcelled hair and the india-rubber legs were finding little scope to do anything but shuffle. This suited John's individual style. He, too, shuffled: and, playing for safety, found that he was getting along better than he could have expected. His tension relaxed, and he became conversational.

"Do you often come to this place?" he asked, resting his partner against the slim back of one of the marcelled hair brigade who, like himself, had been held up in the traffic block.

"I've never been here before. And it'll be a long time before I come again. A more gosh-awful aggregation of yells for help than this gang of whippets," said Miss Molloy, surveying the company with a critical eye, "I've never seen. Look at that dame with the eyeglass."

"Rather weird," agreed John.

"A cry for succour," said Miss Molloy severely. "And why,

when you can buy insecticide at any drug-store, people let these boys with the shiny hair go around loose beats me."

John began to warm to this girl. At first, he had feared that he and she could have little in common. But this remark told told him that on certain subjects, at any rate, they saw eye to eye. He, too, had felt an idle wonder that somebody did not do something about these youths.

The Buddies had stopped playing: and John, glowing with the strange, new spirit of confidence which had come to him, clapped loudly for an encore.

But the Buddies were not responsive. Hitherto, a mere tapping of the palms had been enough to urge them to renewed epileptic spasms; but now an odd lethargy seemed to be upon them, as if they had been taking some kind of treatment for their complaint. They were sitting, instruments in hand, gazing in a spell-bound manner at a square-jawed person in ill-fitting dress clothes who had appeared at the side of Mr. Baermann. And the next moment, there shattered the stillness a sudden voice that breathed Vine Street in every syllable.

"Ladies and gentlemen," boomed the voice, proceeding, as nearly as John could ascertain, from close to the main entrance, "will you kindly take your seats."

"Pinched!" breathed Miss Molloy in his ear. "Couldn't you have betted on it!"

Her diagnosis was plainly correct. In response to the request, most of those on the floor had returned to their tables, moving with the dull resignation of people to whom this sort of thing has happe..ed before: and, enjoying now a wider range of vision, John was able to see that the room had become magically filled with replicas of the sturdy figure standing beside Mr. Baermann. They were moving about among the tables, examining with an offensive interest the bottles that stood thereon and jotting down epigrams on the subject in little note-books. Time flies on swift wings in a haunt of pleasure like the Mustard Spoon, and it was evident that the management, having forgotten to look at its watch, had committed the amiable error of serving alcoholic refreshment after hours.

"I might have known," said Miss Molloy querulously, "that something of the sort was bound to break loose in a dump like this."

John, like all dwellers in the country as opposed to the wicked inhabitants of cities, was a law-abiding man. Left to himself, he would have followed the crowd and made for his table, there to give his name and address in the sheepish undertone customary on these occasions. But he was not left to himself. A moment later, it had become plain that the dashing exterior of Miss Molloy was a true index to the soul within. She grasped his arm and pulled him commandingly.

"Snap into it!" said Miss Mollo~

The "it" into which she desired him to snap was apparently a small door that led to the club's service quarters. It was the one strategic point not yet guarded by a stocky figure with large feet and an eye like a gimlet. To it his companion went like a homing rabbit, dragging him with her. They passed through; and John, with a resourcefulness of which he was surprised to find himself capable, turned the key in the lock.

"Smooth!" said Miss Molloy approvingly. "Nice work! That'll hold them for awhile."

It did. From the other side of the door there proceeded a confused shouting, and somebody twisted the handle with a good deal of petulance, but the Law had apparently forgotten to bring its axe with it to-night, and nothing further occurred. They made their way down a stuffy passage, came presently to a second door: and passing through this, found themselves in a back-yard, fragrant with the scent of old cabbage stalks and dish-water.

Miss Molloy listened. John listened. They could hear nothing but a distant squealing and tooting of horns, which, though it sounded like something out of the repertoire of the Collegiate Buddies, was in reality the noise of the traffic in Regent Street.

"All quiet along the Potomac," said Miss Molloy with satisfaction. "Now," she added briskly, "if you'll just fetch one of those ash-cans and put it alongside that wall and give me a leg-up and help me round that chimney and across that roof and down into the next yard and over another wall or two, I think everything will be more or less jake."

V

John sat in the lobby of the Lincoln Hotel in Curzon Street. A lifetime of activity and dizzy hustle had passed, but it had all been crammed into just under twenty minutes: and, after seeing his fair companion off in a taxi cab, he had made his way to the Lincoln, to ascertain from a sleepy night-porter that Miss Wyvern had not yet returned. He was now awaiting her coming.

She came some little while later, escorted by Hugo. It was a fair summer night, warm and still, but with her arrival a keen east wind seemed to pervade the lobby. Pat was looking pale and proud, and Hugo's usually effervescent demeanour had become toned down to a sort of mellow sadness. He had the appearance of a man who has recently been properly ticked off by a woman for Taking Me to Places Like That.

"Oh, hullo, John," he murmured in a low, bedside voice. He brightened a little, as a man will who, after a bad quarter of an hour with an emotional girl, sees somebody who may possibly furnish an alternative target for her wrath. "Where did you get to? Left early to avoid the rush?"

"It was this way . . ." began John. But Pat had turned to the desk, and was asking the porter for her key. If a female martyr in the rougher days of the Roman Empire had had occasion to ask for a key, she would have done it in just the voice which Pat employed. It was not a loud voice, nor an angry one—just the crushed, tortured voice of a girl who has lost her faith in the essential goodness of humanity.

"You see . . ." said John.

"Are there any letters for me?" asked Pat.

"No, no letters," said the night-porter: and the unhappy girl gave a little sigh, as if that was just what might be expected in a world where men who had known you all your life took you to Places which they ought to have Seen from the start were just Drinking-Hells, while other men, who also had known you all your life, and, what was more, professed to love you, skipped through doors in the company of flashy women and left you to be treated by the police as if you were a common criminal.

"What happened," said John, "was this . . ."

"Good night," said Pat.

She followed the porter to the lift, and Hugo, producing a handkerchief, dabbed it lightly over his forehead.

"Dirty weather, shipmate!" said Hugo. "A very deep depression off the coast of Iceland, laddie."

He placed a restraining hand on John's arm, as the latter made a movement to follow the Snow Queen.

"No good, John," he said gravely. "No good, old man, not the slightest. Don't waste your time trying to explain to-night. Hell hath no fury like a woman scorned, and not many like a girl who's just had to give her name and address in a raided night-club to a plain-clothes cop who asked her to repeat it twice and then didn't seem to believe her."

"But I want to tell her why . . ."

"Never tell them why. It's no use. Let us talk of pleasanter things. John, I have brought off the coup of a lifetime. Not that it was my idea. It was Ronnie Fish who suggested it. There's a fellow with a brain, John. There's a lad who busts the seams of any hat that isn't a number eight."

"What are you talking about?"

"I'm talking about this amazingly intelligent idea of old Ronnie's. It's absolutely necessary that by some means Uncle Lester shall be persuaded to cough up five hundred quid of my capital to enable me to go into a venture second in solidity only to the Mint. The one person who can talk him into it is Ronnie. So Ronnie's coming to Rudge."

"Oh?" said John, uninterested.

"And to prevent Uncle Lester making a fuss about this, I've invited old man Molloy and daughter to come and visit us as well. That was Ronnie's big idea. Thos. is rolling in money, and once Uncle Lester learns that he won't kick about Ronnie being there. He loves having rich men around. He likes to nuzzle them."

"Do you mean," cried John, "that that girl is coming to stay at Rudge?"

He was appalled. Limpidly clear though his conscience was, he was able to see that his rather spectacular association with Miss Dolly Molloy had displeased Pat, and the last thing he wished for was to be placed in a position which was virtually tantamount to hobnobbing with the girl. If she came to stay at Rudge, Pat might think . . . What might not Pat think?

He became aware that Hugo was speaking to him in a quiet, brotherly voice.

"How did all that come out, John?"

"All what?"

"About Pat. Did she tell you that I paved the way?"

"She did! And look here . . ."

"All right, old man," said Hugo, raising a deprecatory hand. "That's absolutely all right. I don't want any thanks. You'd have done the same for me. Well, what has happened? Everything pretty satisfactory?"

"Satisfactory!"

"Don't tell me she turned you down?"

"If you really want to know, yes, she did."

Hugo sighed.

"I feared as much. There was something about her manner when I was paving the way that I didn't quite like. Cold. Not responsive. A bit glassy-eyed. What an amazing thing it is," said Hugo tapping a philosophical vein, "that in spite of all the ways there are of saying Yes, a girl on an occasion like this nearly always says No. An American statistician has estimated that, omitting substitutes like 'All right', 'You bet', 'O.K.' and nasal expressions like 'Uh-huh', the English language provides nearly fifty different methods of replying in the affirm-ative, including Yeah, Yeth, Yum, Yo, Yaw, Chess, Chass, Chuss, Yip, Yep, Yop, Yup, Yurp . . ."

"Stop it!" cried John forcefully.

Hugo patted him affectionately on the shoulder.

"All right, John. All right, old man. I quite understand. You're upset. A little on edge, yes? Of course you are. But listen, John, I want to talk to you very seriously for a moment, in a broad-minded spirit of cousinly good will. If I were you, laddie, I would take myself firmly in hand at this juncture. You must see for yourself by now that you're simply wasting your time fooling about after dear old Pat. A sweet girl, I grant you—one of the best: but if she won't have you she won't, and that's that. Isn't it or is it? Take my tip and wash the whole thing out and start looking round for someone else. Now, there's this Miss Molloy, for instance. Pretty. Pots of money. If I were you, while she's at Rudge, I'd have a decided pop at her. You see, you're one of those fellows that Nature intended for a married man right from the start. You're a con-firmed settler-down, the sort of chap that likes to roll the garden lawn and then put on his slippers and light a pipe and sit side by side with the little woman, sharing a twin set of head phones. Pull up your socks, John, and have a dash at this Molloy girl. You'd be on velvet with a rich wife."

At several points during this harangue John had endeavoured to speak, and he was just about to do so now, when there occurred that which rendered speech impossible. From immediately behind them, as they stood facing the door, a voice spoke.

"I want my bag, Hugo."

It was Pat. She was standing within a yard of them. Her face was still that of a martyr, but now she seemed to suggest by her expression a martyr whose tormentors have suddenly thought up something new.

"You've got my bag," she said.

"Oh, ah," said Hugo.

He handed over the beaded trifle, and she took it with a cold aloofness. There was a pause.

"Well, good night," said Hugo.

"Good night," said Pat.

"Good night," said John.

"Good night," said Pat.

She turned away, and the lift bore her aloft. Its machinery badly needed a drop of oil, and it emitted, as it went, a low wailing sound that seemed to John like a commentary on the whole situation.

VI

Some half a mile from Curzon Street, on the fringe of the Soho district, there stands a smaller and humbler hotel named the Belvidere. In a bedroom on the second floor of this, at about the moment when Pat and Hugo had entered the lobby of the Lincoln, Dolly Molloy sat before a mirror, cold-creaming her attractive face. She was interrupted in this task by the arrival of the senatorial Thomas G.

"Hello, sweetie-pie," said Miss Molloy. "There you are."

"Yes," replied Mr. Molloy. "Here I am."

Although his demeanour lacked the high tragedy which had made strong men quail in the presence of Pat Wyvern, this man was plainly ruffled. His fine features were overcast and his frank grey eyes looked sombre.

"Gee! If there's one thing in this world I hate," he said, "it's having to talk to policemen."

"What happened?"

"Oh, I gave my name and address. A name and address, that is to say. But I haven't got over yet the jar it gave me seeing so many cops all gathered together in a small room. And that's not all," went on Mr. Molloy, ventilating another grievance. "Why did you make me tell those folks you were my daughter?"

"Well, sweetie, it sort of cramps my style, having people know we're married."

"What do you mean, cramps your style?"

"Oh, just cramps my style."

"But, darn it," complained Mr. Molloy going to the heart of the matter, "it makes me out so old, folks thinking I'm your father." The rather pronounced gap in years between himself and his young bride was a subject on which Soapy Molloy was always inclined to be sensitive. "I'm only forty-two."

"And you don't seem that, not till you look at you close," said Dolly with womanly tact. "The whole thing is, sweetie, being so dignified, you can call yourself anybody's father and get away with it."

Mr. Molloy, somewhat soothed, examined himself not without approval, in the mirror.

"I do look dignified," he admitted.

"Like a Professor or something."

"That isn't a bald spot coming there, is it?"

"Sure it's not. It's just the way the light falls."

Mr. Molloy resumed his examination with growing content.

"Yes," he said complacently, "that's a face which for business purposes is a face. Just a Real Good Face. I may not be the World's Sweetheart, but nobody can say I haven't got a map that inspires confidence. I suppose I've sold more dud oil-stock to suckers with it than anyone in the profession. And that reminds me, honey, what do you think?"

"What?" asked Mrs. Molloy, removing cream with a towel.

"We're sitting in the biggest kind of luck. You know how I've been wanting all this time to get hold of a really good prospect—some guy with money to spend who might be interested in a little oil deal? Well, that Carmody fellow we met to-night has invited us to go and visit at his country home."

"You don't say!"

"Yes, ma'am!"

"Well, isn't that great. Is he rich?"

"He's got an uncle that must be, or he couldn't be living

in a place like he was telling me. It's one of those stately homes of England you read about."

Mrs. Molloy mused. The soft smile on her face showed that her day dreams were pleasant ones.

"I'll have to get me some new frocks . . . and hats . . . and shoes . . . and stockings . . . and . . ."

"Now, now, now!" said her husband, with that anxious alarm which husbands exhibit on these occasions. "Be yourself, baby! You aren't going to stay at Buckingham Palace."

"But a country-house party with a lot of swell people . . ."

"It isn't a country-house party. There's only the uncle besides those two boys we met to-night. But I'll tell you what. If I can plant a good block of those Silver River shares on the old man, you can go shopping all you want."

"Oh, Soapy! Do you think you can?"

"Do I think I can?" echoed Mr. Molloy scornfully. "I don't say I've ever sold Central Park or Brooklyn Bridge to anybody, but if I can't get rid of a parcel of home-made oil stock to a guy that lives in the country I'm losing my grip and ought to retire. Sure I'll sell him those Silver Rivers, honey. These fellows that own these big estates in England are only glorified farmers when you come right down to it, and a farmer will buy anything you offer him, just so long as it's nicely engraved and shines when you slant the light on it."

"But, Soapy . . ."

'Now what?"

"I've been thinking. Listen, Soapy. A home like this one where we're going is sure to have all sorts of things in it, isn't it? Pictures, I mean, and silver and antiques and all like that. Well, why can't we, once we're in the place, get away with them and make a nice clean-up?"

Mr. Molloy, though conceding that this was the right spirit, was obliged to discourage his wife's pretty enthusiasm.

"Where could you sell that sort of stuff?"

"Anywhere, once you got it over to the other side. New York's full of rich millionaires who'll buy anything and ask no questions, just so long as it's antiques."

Mr. Molloy shook his head.

"Too dangerous, baby. If all that stuff left the house same time as we did, we'd have the bulls after us in ten minutes. Besides it's not in my line. I've got my line, and I like to stick to it. Nobody ever got anywhere in the long run by going out-side of his line."

"Maybe you're right."

"Sure I'm right. A nice conservative business, that's what I aim at."

"But suppose when we get to this joint it looks dead easy?"

"Ah! Well then, I'm not saying. All I'm against is risks. If something's handed to you on a plate, naturally no one wouldn't ever want to let it get past them."

And with this eminently sound commercial maxim Mr. Molloy reached for his pyjamas and prepared for bed. Something attempted, something done, had earned, he felt, a night's repose.

★ 5 ★

Money for Nothing

I

SOME years before the date of the events narrated in this story, at the time when there was all that trouble between the aristocratic householders of Riverside Row and the humbler dwellers in Budd Street (arising, if you remember, from the practice of the latter of washing their more intimate articles of underclothing and hanging them to dry in back-gardens into which their exclusive neighbours were compelled to gaze every time they looked out of the window), the vicar of the parish, the Rev. Alistair Pond-Pond, always a happy phrase-maker, wound up his address at the annual village sports of Rudge with an impressive appeal to the good feeling of those concerned.

"We must not," said the Rev. Alistair, "consider ourselves as belonging to this section of Rudge-in-the-Vale or to that section of Rudge-in-the-Vale. Let us get together. Let us recollect that we are all fellow-members of one united community. Rudge must be looked on as a whole. And what a whole it is!"

With the concluding words of this peroration Pat Wyvern, by the time she had been home a little under a week, found herself in hearty agreement. Walking with her father along High Street on the sixth morning she had to confess herself disappointed with Rudge. Her home-coming, she had now definitely decided, was not a success.

Elderly men with a grievance are seldom entertaining companions for the young, and five days of the undiluted society of Colonel Wyvern had left Pat with the feeling that, much as she loved her father, she wished he would sometimes change the subject of his conversation. Had she been present in person she could not have had a fuller grasp of the facts of that dynamite outrage than she now possessed.

But this was not all. After Mr. Carmody's thug-like behaviour on that fatal day, she was given to understand, the Hall and its grounds were as much forbidden territory to her as the piazza of the townhouse of the Capulets would have been to a young Montague.

Accordingly she had not been within half a mile of the Hall since her arrival, and, having been accustomed for fourteen years to treat the place and its grounds as her private property, found Rudge, with a deadline drawn across the boundaries of Mr. Carmody's park, a poor sort of place. Unlovable character though Mr. Carmody was in many respects, she had always been fond of him, and she missed seeing him. She also missed seeing Hugo. And, as for John, not seeing him was the heaviest blow of all.

From the days of childhood, John had always been her stand-by. Men might come and men might go, but John went on for ever. He had never been too old, like Mr. Carmody, or too lazy, like Hugo, to give her all the time and attention she required, and she did think that, even though there was this absurd feud going on, he might have had the enterprise to make an opportunity of meeting her. As day followed day her resentment grew, until now she had reached the stage when she was telling herself that this was simply what from a knowledge of his character she might have expected. John—she had to face it—was a jellyfish. And if a man is a jellyfish, he will behave like a jellyfish, and it is at times of crisis that his jellyfishiness will be most noticeable.

It was conscience that had brought Pat to the High Street this morning. Her father had welcomed her with such a pathetic eagerness, and had been so plainly pleased to see her back, that she was ashamed of herself for not feeling happier And it was in a spirit of remorse that now, though she would have preferred to stay in the garden with a book, she had come with him to watch him buy another bottle of Brophy's Paramount Elixir from Chas. Bywater, Chemist.

Brophy, it should be mentioned, had proved a sensational success. His Elixir was making the local gnats feel perfect fools. They would bite Colonel Wyvern on the face and stand back, all ready to laugh, and he would just smear Brophy on himself and be as good as new. It was simply sickening, if you were a gnat; but fine, of course, if you were Colonel Wyvern, and that just man, always ready to give praise where praise was due, said as much to Chas. Bywater.

"That Stuff," said Colonel Wyvern, "is good. I wish I'd heard of it before. Give me another bottle."

Mr. Bywater was delighted—not merely at this rush of trade, but because, good kindly soul, he enjoyed ameliorating the lot of others

"I thought you would find it capital, Colonel. I get a great many requests for it. I sold a bottle yesterday to Mr. Carmody, senior."

Colonel Wyvern's sunniness vanished as if someone had turned it off with a tap.

"Don't talk to me about Mr. Carmody," he said gruffly.

"Quite," said Chas. Bywater.

Pat bridged a painful silence.

"Is Mr. Carmody back, then?" she asked. "I heard he was at some sort of health place."

"Healthward Ho, Miss, just outside Lowick."

"He ought to be in prison," said Colonel Wyvern.

Mr. Bywater stopped himself in the nick of time from saying "Quite," which would have been a deviation from his firm policy of never taking sides between customers.

"He returned the day before yesterday, Miss, and was immediately bitten on the nose by a mosquito."

"Thank God!" said Colonel Wyvern.

"But I sold him one of the three-and-sixpenny size of the Elixir," said Chas. Bywater, with quiet pride, "and a single application completely eased the pain."

Colonel Wyvern said he was sorry to hear it, and there is no doubt that conversation would once more have become difficult had there not at this moment made itself heard from the other side of the door a loud and penetrating sniff.

A fatherly smile lit up Chas. Bywater's face.

"That's Mr. John's dog," he said, reaching for the cough-drops.

Pat opened the door and the statement was proved correct. With a short wooffle, partly of annoyance at having been kept waiting and partly of happy anticipation, Emily entered, and, seating herself by the counter, gazed expectantly at the chemist.

"Hullo, Emily," said Pat.

Emily gave her a brief look in which there was no pleased recognition, but only the annoyance of a dog interrupted during an important conference. She then returned her gaze to Mr. Bywater.

"What do you say, doggie?" said Mr. Bywater, more paternal than ever, poising a cough-drop.

"Oh, Hell! Snap into it!" replied Emily curtly, impatient at this foolery.

"Hear her speak for it?" said Mr. Bywater. "Almost human, that dog is."

Colonel Wyvern, whom he had addressed, did not seem to share his lively satisfaction. He muttered to himself. He regarded Emily sourly, and his right foot twitched a little.

"Just like a human being, isn't she, Miss?" said Chas. Bywater, damped but persevering.

"Quite," said Pat absently.

Mr. Bywater, startled by this infringement of copyright, dropped the cough-lozenge and Emily snapped it up.

Pat, still distrait, was watching the door. She was surprised to find that her breath was coming rather quickly and that her heart had begun to beat with more than its usual rapidity. She was amazed at herself. Just because John Carroll would shortly appear in that doorway must she stand fluttering, for all the world as though poor old Johnnie, an admitted jellyfish, were something that really mattered? It was too silly, and she tried to bully herself into composure. She failed. Her heart, she was compelled to realize, was now simply racing.

A step sounded outside, a shadow fell on the sunlit pavement, and Dolly Molloy walked into the shop.

II

It is curious, when one reflects, to think how many different impressions a single individual can make simultaneously on a number of his or her fellow-creatures. At the present moment it was almost as though four separate and distinct Dolly Molloys had entered the establishment of Chas. Bywater.

The Dolly whom Colonel Wyvern beheld was a beautiful woman with just that hint of diablerie in her bearing which makes elderly widowers feel that there is life in the old dog yet. Drawing himself up, he automatically twirled his moustache. To Colonel Wyvern Dolly represented Beauty.

To Chas. Bywater, with his more practical and worldly outlook, she represented Wealth. Although Soapy had contrived with subtle reasoning to head her off from the extensive purchases which she had contemplated making in preparation for her visit to Rudge, Dolly undoubtedly took the eye, and in Chas. Bywater's mind she awoke roseate visions of large orders for face-creams, imported scents and expensive bath-salts.

Emily, it was evident, regarded Mrs. Molloy as Perfection. A dog who, as a rule, kept herself to herself and looked on the world with a cool and rather sardonic eye, she had conceived for Dolly the moment they met one of those capricious adorations which come occasionally to the most hard-boiled Welsh terriers. Hastily swallowing her cough-drop, she bounded up and fawned on her.

So far, the reactions caused by the newcomer's entrance have been unmixedly favourable. It is only when we come to Pat that we find Disapproval rearing its ugly head. Piercing with woman's intuitive eye through an outer crust which to vapid and irreflective males might possibly seem attractive, Pat saw Dolly as a vampire and a menace.

For beyond a question, felt Pat, this girl must have come to Rudge in brazen pursuit of poor old Johnnie. The fact that she took her walks abroad accompanied by Emily showed that she was staying at the Hall; and what reason could she have had for getting herself invited to the Hall if not that she wished to continue the acquaintance begun at the Mustard Spoon ? This, then, was the explanation of John's failure to come and pass the time of day with an old friend. What she had assumed to be Jelly-fishiness was in reality base treachery. Like Emily, whom, slavering over Mrs. Molloy's shoes, she could gladly have kicked, he had been hypnotized by this woman's specious glamour and had forsaken old allegiances.

Pat, eyeing Dolly coldly, was filled with a sisterly desire to save John from one who could never make him happy.

Dolly was all friendliness.

"Why, hello," she said, removing a shapely foot from Emily's mouth, "I was wondering when I was going to run into you. I heared you lived in these parts."

"Yes ?" said Pat frigidly.

"I'm staying at the Hall."

"Yes ?"

"What a wonderful old place it is."

"Yes."

"All those pictures and tapestries and things."

"Yes."

"Is this your father?"

"Yes. This is Miss Molloy, father. We met in London."

"Pleased to meet you," said Dolly.

"Charmed," said Colonel Wyvern.

He gave another twirl of his moustache. Chas. Bywater hovered beamingly. Emily, still ecstatic, continued to gnaw one of Dolly's shoes. The whole spectacle was so utterly revolting that Pat turned to the door.

"I'll be going along, father," she said. "I want to buy some stamps."

"I can sell you stamps, Miss," said Chas. Bywater affably.

"Thank you, I will go to the post office," said Pat. Her manner suggested that you got a superior brand of stamp there. She walked out. Rudge, as she looked upon it, seemed a more depressing place than ever. Sunshine flooded the High Street. Sunshine fell on the Carmody Arms, the Village Hall, the Plough and Chickens, the Bunch of Grapes, the Waggoner's Rest and the Jubilee Watering Trough. But there was no sunshine in the heart of Pat Wyvern.

III

And, curiously enough, at this very moment up at the Hall the same experience was happening to Mr. Lester Carmody. Staring out of his study window, he gazed upon a world bathed in a golden glow: but his heart was cold and heavy. He had just had a visit from the Rev. Alistair Pond-Pond, and the Rev. Alistair had touched him for five shillings.

Many men in Mr. Carmody's place would have considered that they had got off lightly. The vicar had come seeking subscriptions to the Church Organ Fund, the Mothers' Pleasant Sunday Evenings, the Distressed Cottagers Aid Society, the Stipend of the Additional Curate and the Rudge Lads' Annual Summer Outing, and there had been moments of mad optimism when he had hoped for as much as a ten pound note. The actual bag, as he totted it up while riding pensively away on his motor-bicycle, was the above-mentioned five shillings and a promise that the Squire's nephew Hugo and his friend Mr. Fish should perform at the village concert next week.

And even so, Mr. Carmody was looking on him as a robber. Five shillings gone—just like that!

Nor was this all that was poisoning a perfect summer day for Mr. Carmody. There was in addition the soul-searing behaviour of Doctor Alexander Twist, of Healthward Ho.

When Doctor Twist had undertaken the contract of making a new Lester Carmody out of the old Lester Carmody, he had cannily stipulated for cash down in advance—this to cover a course of three weeks. But at the end of the second week Mr. Carmody, learning from his nephew Hugo that an American millionaire was arriving at the Hall, had naturally felt compelled to forgo the final stages of the treatment and return home. Equally naturally, he had invited Doctor Twist to refund one third of the fee. This the eminent physician and physical culture expert had resolutely declined to do, and Mr. Carmody, re-reading the man's letter, thought he had never set eyes upon a baser document.

The lot of the English landed proprietor, felt Mr. Carmody, is not what it used to be in the good old times. When the first Carmody settled in Rudge he had found little to view with alarm. Those were the days when churls were churls, and a scurvy knave was quite content to work twelve hours a day, Saturdays included, in return for a little black bread and an occasional nod of approval from his overlord. But in this twentieth century England's peasantry has degenerated. Modern sons of the soil expect coddling. Their roofs leak, and you have to mend them, their walls fall down and you have to build them up; their lanes develop holes and you have to restore the surface, and all this runs into money. The way things were shaping, felt Mr. Carmody, in a few years a landlord would be expected to pay for the repairs of his tenants' wireless sets.

He stood at the window and looked out on the sunlit garden. And as he did so there came into his range of vision the sturdy figure of his guest, Mr. Molloy, and for the first time that morning Lester Carmody seemed to hear, beating faintly in the distance, the wings of the blue bird. In a world containing anybody as rich-looking as Thomas G. Molloy there was surely still hope.

Ronald Fish's prediction that Hugo's uncle would appreciate a visit from so solid a citizen of the United States as Mr. Molloy had been fulfilled to the letter. Mr. Carmody had welcomed his guest with open arms. The more rich men he could gather about him, the better he was pleased, for he was a man of vision, and had quite a number of schemes in his mind for which he was anxious to obtain financial support.

He decided to go and have a chat with Mr. Molloy. On a morning like this, with all Nature smiling, an American millionaire might well feel just in the mood to put up a few hundred thousand dollars for something. For July had come in on golden wings, and the weather now was the kind of weather to make a poet sing, a lover love, and a Scotch business man subscribe largely to companies formed for the purpose of manufacturing diamonds out of coal-tar. On such a morning, felt Mr. Carmody, anybody ought to be willing to put up any sum for anything.

IV

Nature continued to smile for about another three and a quarter minutes, and then, as far as Mr. Carmody was concerned, the sun went out. With a genial heartiness which gashed him like a knife, the plutocratic Mr. Molloy declined to invest even a portion of his millions in a new golf-course, a cinema de luxe to be established in Rudge High Street, or any of the four other schemes which his host presented to his notice.

"No, sir," said Mr. Molloy, "I'm mighty sorry I can't meet you in any way, but the fact is I'm all fixed up in Oil. Oil's my dish. I began in Oil and I'll end in Oil. I wouldn't be happy outside of Oil."

"Oh?" said Mr. Carmody, regarding this Human Sardine with as little open hostility and dislike as he could manage on the spur of the moment.

"Yes, sir," proceeded Mr. Molloy, still in lyrical vein, "I put my first thousand into Oil and I'll put my last thousand into Oil. Oil's been a good friend to me. There's money in Oil."

"There is money," urged Mr. Carmody, "in a cinema in Rudge High Street."

"Not the money there is in Oil."

"You are a stranger in England," went on Mr. Carmody patiently, "so you have no doubt got a mistaken idea of the potentialities of a place like Rudge. Rudge, you must remember is a centre. Small though it is, never forget that it lies just off the main road in the heart of a prosperous county. Worcester is only seven miles away, Birmingham only eighteen. People would come in their motors . . ."

"I'm not stopping them," said Mr. Molloy generously. "All I'm saying is that my money stays in little old Oil."

"Or take Golf," said Mr. Carmody, side-stepping and attacking from another angle. "The only good golf-course in Worcestershire at present is at Stourbridge. Worcestershire needs more golf-courses. You know how popular Golf is nowadays."

"Not so popular as Oil. Oil," said Mr. Molloy, with the air of one making an epigram, "is Oil."

Mr. Carmody stopped himself just in time from saying what he thought of Oil. To relieve his feelings he ground his heel into the soft gravel of the path, and had but one regret, that Mr. Molloy's most sensitive toe was not under it. Half-turning in the process of making this bitter gesture, he perceived that Providence, since the days of Job always curious to know just how much a good man can bear, had sent Ronald Overbury Fish to add to his troubles. Young Mr. Fish was sauntering up behind his customary eleven inches of cigarette-holder, his pink face wearing that expression of good-natured superiority which, ever since their first meeting, had afflicted Mr. Carmody sorely.

From the list of Mr. Carmody's troubles, recently tabulated, Ronnie Fish was inadvertently omitted. Although to Lady Julia Fish, his mother, this young gentleman, no doubt, was all the world, Lester Carmody had found him nothing but a pain in the neck. Apart from the hideous expense of entertaining a man who took twice of nearly everything and helped himself unblushingly to more port, he chafed beneath his guest's curiously patronising manner. He objected to being treated as a junior—and, what was more, as a half-witted junior—by solemn young men with pink faces.

"What's the argument?" asked Ronnie Fish, anchoring self and cigarette-holder at Mr. Carmody's side.

Mr. Molloy smiled genially.

"No argument, brother," he replied with that bluff heartiness which Lester Carmody had come to dislike so much. "I was merely telling our good friend and host here that the best investment under the broad blue canopy of God's sky is Oil."

"Quite right," said Ronnie Fish. "He's perfectly correct, my dear Carmody."

"Our good host was trying to interest me in golf-courses."

"Don't touch 'em," said Mr. Fish.

"I won't," said Mr. Molloy. "Give me Oil. Oil's oil. First in war, first in peace, first in the hearts of its countrymen, that's what Oil is. The Universal Fuel of the Future."

"Absolutely," said Ronnie Fish. "What did Gladstone say in '88? You can fuel some of the people all the time, and you can fuel all the people some of the time, but you can't fuel all the people all the time. He was forgetting about Oil. Probably he meant coal."

"Coal?" Mr. Molloy laughed satirically. You could see he despised the stuff. "Don't talk to me about Coal."

This was another disappointment for Mr. Carmody. Cinemas *de luxe* and golf-courses having failed, Coal was just what he had been intending to talk about. He suspected its presence beneath the turf of the park, and would have been glad to verify his suspicions with the aid of someone else's capital.

"You listen to this bird, Carmody," said Mr. Fish, patting his host on the back. "He's talking sense. Oil's the stuff. Dig some of the savings out of the old sock, my dear Carmody, and wade in. You'll never regret it."

And, having delivered himself of this advice with a fatherly kindliness which sent his host's temperature up several degrees, Ronnie Fish strolled on.

Mr. Molloy watched him disappear with benevolent approval. He said to Mr. Carmody that that young man had his head screwed on the right way, and seemed not to notice a certain lack of responsive enthusiasm on the other's part. Ronnie Fish's head was not one of Mr. Carmody's favourite subjects at the moment.

"Yes, sir," said Mr. Molloy, resuming. "Any man that goes into Oil is going into a good thing. Oil's all right. You don't see John D. Rockefeller running round asking for hand-outs from his friends, do you? No, sir! John's got his modest little competence, same as me, and he got it, like I did, out of Oil. Say, listen, Mr. Carmody, it isn't often I give up any of my holdings, but you've been mighty nice to me, inviting me to your home and all, and I'd like to do something for you in return. What do you say to a good, solid block of Silver River stock at just the price it cost me? And let me tell you I'm offering you something that half the big men on our side would give their eye-teeth for. Only a couple of days before I sailed I was in Charley Schwab's office, and he said to me 'Tom,' said Charley, 'right up till now I've stuck to Steel and I've done well. Understand,' he said, 'I'm not knocking Steel. But Oil's the stuff, and if you want to part with any of that Silver River of yours, Tom,' he said, 'pass it across this desk and write your own ticket.' That'll show you."

There is no anguish like the anguish of the man who is trying to extract cash from a fellow human being and suddenly finds the fellow human being trying to extract it from him. Mr. Carmody laughed a bitter laugh.

"Do you imagine," he said, "that I have money to spare for speculative investments?"

"Speculative?" Mr. Molloy seemed to suspect his ears of playing tricks. "Silver River spec. . . . ?"

"By the time I've finished paying the bills for the expenses of this infernal estate I consider myself lucky if I've got a few hundred that I can call my own."

There was a pause.

"Is that so?" said Mr. Molloy in a thin voice.

Strictly speaking, it was not. Before succeeding to his present position of head of the family and squire of Rudge Hall, Lester Carmody had contrived to put away in gilt-edged securities a very nice sum indeed, the fruit of his labours in the world of business. But it was his whim to regard himself as a struggling pauper.

"But all this . . ." Mr. Molloy indicated with a wave of his hand the smiling gardens, the rolling park and the opulent-looking trees reflected in the waters of the moat. "Surely this means a barrel of money?"

"Everything that comes in goes out again in expenses. There's no end to my expenses. Farmers in England to-day sit up at night trying to think of new claims they can make against a landlord."

There was another pause.

"That's bad," said Mr. Molloy thoughtfully. "Yes, sir, that's bad."

His commiseration was not all for Mr. Carmody. In fact, very little of it was. Most of it was reserved for himself. It began to look, he realised, as though in coming to this stately home of England he had been simply wasting valuable time. It was not as if he enjoyed staying at country-houses in a purely aesthetic spirit. On the contrary, a place like Rudge Hall afflicted his town-bred nerves. Being in it seemed to him like living in the first act set of an old-fashioned comic opera. He always felt that at any moment a band of villagers and retainers might dance out and start a drinking-chorus.

"Yes, sir," said Mr. Molloy, "that must grind you a good deal."

"What must?"

It was not Mr. Carmody who had spoken, but his guest's attractive young wife, who, having returned from the village, had come up from the direction of the rose-garden. From afar she had observed her husband spreading his hands in broad, per-suasive gestures, and from her knowledge of him had gathered that he had embarked on one of those high-pressure sales-talks of his which did so much to keep the wolf from the door. Then she had seen a shadow fall athwart his fine face: and, scenting a hitch in the negotiations, had hurried up to lend wifely assistance.

"What must grind him?" she asked.

Mr. Molloy kept nothing from his bride.

"I was offering our host here a block of those Silver River shares. . . ."

"Oh, you aren't going to sell Silver Rivers!" cried Mrs. Molloy in pretty concern. "Why, you've always told me they're the biggest thing you've got."

"So they are. But. . . ."

"Oh, well," said Dolly with a charming smile, "seing it's Mr. Carmody. I wouldn't mind Mr. Carmody having them."

"Nor would I," said Mr. Molloy sincerely. "But he can't afford to buy."

"What!"

"You tell her," said Mr. Molloy.

Mr. Carmody told her. He was never averse from speaking of the unfortunate position in which the modern owner of English land found himself.

"Well, I don't get it," said Dolly, shaking her head. "You call yourself a poor man. How can you be poor, when that gallery place you showed us round yesterday is jam-full of pictures worth a fortune an inch and tapestries and all those gold coins?"

"Heirlooms."

"How's that?"

"They're heirlooms," said Mr. Carmody bitterly.

He always felt bitter when he thought of the Rudge Hall heirlooms. He looked upon them as a mean joke played on him by a gang of sardonic ancestors.

To a man who, lacking both reverence for family traditions and appreciation of the beautiful in Art, comes into possession of an ancient house and its contents there must always be something painfully ironical about heirlooms. To such a man they are simply so much potential wealth which is being allowed to lie idle, doing no good to anybody. Mr. Carmody had always had that feeling very strongly.

Unlike the majority of heirs, he had not been trained from boyhood to revere the home of his ancestors and to look forward to its possession as a sacred trust. He had been the second son of a second son, and his chance of ever succeeding to the property was at the outset so remote that he had seldom given it a thought. He had gone into business at an early age; and when, in middle life, a series of accidents made him squire of Rudge Hall, he had brought with him to the place a practical eye and the commercial outlook. The result was that when he walked in the picture-gallery and thought how much solid cash he could get for its contents if only he were given a free hand, the iron entered into Lester Carmody's soul. They was one Elizabethan salt-cellar, valued at about three thousand pounds, at which he could scarcely bear to look.

"They're heirlooms," he said. "I can't sell them."

"How come? They're yours, aren't they?"

"No," said Mr. Carmody, "they belong to the estate."

On Mr. Molloy, as he listened to his host's lengthy exposition of the laws governing heirlooms, there descended a deepening cloud of gloom. You couldn't, it appeared, dispose of the darned things without the consent of trustees; while even if the trustees gave their consent they collared the money and invested it on behalf of the estate. And Mr. Molloy, though ordinarily a man of sanguine temperament, could not bring himself to believe that a bunch of trustees, most of them probably lawyers with tight lips and suspicious minds, would ever have the sporting spirit to take a flutter in Silver River Ordinaries.

"Hell!" said Mr. Molloy with a good deal of feeling.

Dolly linked her arm in his with a pretty gesture of affectionate solicitude.

"Poor old Pop!" she said. "He's all broken up about this."

Mr. Carmody regarded his guest sourly.

"What's he got to worry about?" he asked with a certain resentment.

"Why, Pop was sort of hoping he'd be able to buy all this stuff," said Dolly. "He was telling me only this morning that, if you felt like selling, he would write you out his cheque for whatever you wanted without thinking twice."

V

Moodily scanning his wife's face during Mr. Carmody's lecture on Heirloom Law, Mr. Molloy had observed it suddenly light up in a manner which suggested that some pleasing thought was passing through her always agile brain: but, presented now in words, this thought left him decidedly cold. He could not see any sense in it.

"For the love of Pete . . .!"

His bride had promised to love, honour and obey Mr. Molloy, but she had never said anything about taking any notice of him when he tried to butt in on her moments of inspiration. She ignored the interruption.

"You see," she said, "Pop collects old junk—I mean antiques and all like that. Over in America he's got a great big museum place full of stuff. He's going to present it to the nation when he hands in his dinner-pail. Aren't you, Pop ?"

It became apparent to Mr. Molloy that at the back of his wife's mind there floated some idea at which, handicapped by his masculine slowness of wit, he could not guess. It was plain to him, however, that she expected him to do his bit, so he did it.

"You betcher," he said.

"How much would you say all that stuff in your museum was worth, Pop ?"

Mr. Molloy was still groping in outer darkness, but he persevered.

"Oo," he said, "Worth ? Call it a million. . . . Two millions. . . . Three, maybe."

"You see," explained Dolly, "the place is so full up, he doesn't really know what he's got. But Pierpont Morgan offered you a million for the pictures alone, didn't he ?"

Now that figures had crept into the conversation, Mr. Molloy was feeling more at his ease. He liked figures.

"You're thinking of Jake Shubert, honey," he said. "It was the tapestries that Pierp. wanted. And it wasn't a million, it was

seven hundred thousand. I laughed in his face. I asked him if he
thought he was trying to buy cheese-sandwiches at the de-
licatessen store or something. Pierp. was sore." Mr. Molloy
shook his head regretfully, and you could see he was thinking
that it was too bad that his little joke should have caused a coolness between himself and an old friend. "But, great guns!" he
said, in defence of his attitude. "Seven hundred thousand! Did
he think I wanted car-fare?"

Mr. Carmody's always rather protuberant eyes had been
bulging farther and farther out of their sockets all through this
exchange of remarks, and now they reached the farthest point
possible and stayed there. His breath was coming in little gasps,
and his fingers twitched convulsively. He was suffering the
extreme of agony.

It was all very well for a man like Mr. Molloy to speak sneer-
ingly of seven hundred thousand dollars. To most people—and
Mr. Carmody was one of them—seven hundred thousand dollars
is quite a nice little sum. Mr. Molloy, if he saw seven hundred
thousand dollars lying in the gutter, might not think it worth his
while to stoop and pick it up, but Mr. Carmody could not
imitate that proud detachment. The thought that he had as his
guest at Rudge a man who combined with a bottomless purse a
taste for antiquities and that only the imbecile laws relating to
Heirlooms prevented them consummating a deal racked him
from head to foot.

"How much would you have given Mr. Carmody for all those
pictures and things he showed us yesterday?" asked Dolly,
twisting the knife in the wound.

Mr. Molloy spread his hands carelessly.

"Two hundred thousand . . . Three . . . we wouldn't have
quarrelled about the price. But what's the use of talking? He
can't sell 'em."

"Why can't he?"

"Well, how can he?"

"I'll tell you how. Fake a burglary."

"What!"

"Sure. Have the things stolen and slipped over to you without
anybody knowing, and then you hand him your cheque for two
hundred thousand or whatever it is, and you're happy and he's
happy and everybody's happy. And, what's more, I guess all this
stuff is insured, isn't it? Well then, Mr. Carmody can stick to

the insurance money, and he's that much up besides whatever he gets from you."

There was a silence. Dolly had said her say, and Mr. Molloy felt for the moment incapable of speech. That he had not been mistaken in supposing that his wife had a scheme at the back of her head was now plain, but, as outlined, it took his breath away. Considered purely as a scheme, he had not a word to say against it. It was commercially sound and did credit to the ingenuity of one whom he had always regarded as the slickest thinker of her sex. But it was not the sort of scheme, he considered, which ought to have emanated from the presumably innocent and unspotted daughter of a substantial Oil millionaire. It was calculated, he felt, to create in their host's mind doubts and misgivings as to the sort of people he was entertaining.

He need have had no such apprehension. It was not righteous disapproval that was holding Mr. Carmody dumb.

It has been laid down by an acute thinker that there is a subtle connection between felony and fat. Almost all embezzlers, for instance, says this authority, are fat men. Whether this is or is not true, the fact remains that the sensational criminality of the suggestion just made to him awoke no horror in Mr. Carmody's ample bosom. He was startled, as any man might be who had this sort of idea sprung suddenly on him in his own garden, but he was not shocked. A youth and middle age spent on the London Stock Exchange had left Lester Carmody singularly broad-minded. He had to a remarkable degree that spacious charity which allows a man to look indulgently on any financial project, however fishy, provided he can see a bit in it for himself.

"It's money for nothing," urged Dolly, misinterpreting his silence. "The stuff isn't doing any good, just lying around the way it is now. And it isn't as if it didn't really belong to you. All what you were saying awhile back about the law is simply mashed potatoes. The things belong to the house, and the house belongs to you, so where's the harm in your selling them? Who's supposed to get them after you?"

Mr. Carmody withdrew his gaze from the middle distance. "Eh? Oh. My nephew Hugo."

"Well, you aren't worrying about him?"

Mr. Carmody was not. What he was worrying about was the practicability of the thing. Could it, he was asking himself, be put safely through without the risk, so distasteful to a man of sen-

sibility, of landing him for a lengthy term of years in a prison cell?
It was on this aspect of the matter that he now touched.

"It wouldn't be safe," he said, and few men since the world
began have ever spoken more wistfully. "We would be found out."

"Not a chance. Who would find out? Who's going to say
anything? You're not. I'm not. Pop's not."

"You bet your life Pop's not," assented Mr. Molloy.

Mr. Carmody gazed out over the waters of the moat. His
brain, quickened by the stimulating prospect of money for
nothing, detected another doubtful point.

"Who would take the things?"

"You mean get them out of the house?"

"Exactly. Somebody would have to take them. It would be
necessary to create the appearance of an actual burglary."

"Well, there'll be an actual burglary."

"But whom could we trust in such a vital matter?"

"That's all right. Pop's got a friend who would put this thing
through just for the fun of it, to oblige Pop. You could trust him."

"Who?" asked Mr. Molloy, plainly surprised that any friend
of his could be trusted.

"Chimp," said Dolly briefly.

"Oh, Chimp," said Mr. Molloy, his face clearing. "Yes,
Chimp would do it."

"Who," asked Mr. Carmody, "is Chimp?"

"A good friend of mine. You wouldn't know him."

Mr. Carmody scratched at the gravel with his toe, and for a
long minute there was silence in the garden. Mr. Molloy looked
at Mrs. Molloy. Mrs. Molloy looked at Mr. Molloy. Mr. Molloy
closed his left eye for a fractional instant, and in response Mrs.
Molloy permitted her right eyelid to quiver. But, perceiving that
this was one of the occasions on which a strong man wishes to be
left alone to commune with his soul, they forbore to break in
upon his reverie with jarring speech.

"Well, I'll think it over," said Mr. Carmody.

"Atta-boy!" said Mr. Molloy.

"Sure. You take a nice walk around the block all by yourself,"
advised Mrs. Molloy, "and then come back and issue a bulletin."

Mr. Carmody moved away, pondering deeply, and Mr. Molloy
turned to his wife.

"What made you think of Chimp?" he asked doubtfully.

"Well, he's the only guy on this side that we really know. We can't pick and choose, same as if we were in New York."

Mr. Molloy eyed the moat with a thoughtful frown.

"Well, I'll tell you, honey. I'm not so darned sure that I sort of kind of like bringing Chimp into a thing like this. You know what he is—as slippery as an eel that's been rubbed all over with axle-grease. He might double-cross us."

"Not if we double-cross him first."

"But could we?"

"Sure we could. And, anyway, it's Chimp or no one. This isn't the sort of affair you can just go out into the street and pick up the first man you run into. It's a job where you've got to have somebody you've worked with before."

"All right, baby. If you say so. You always were the brains of the firm. If you think it's kayo, then it's all right by me and no more to be said. Cheese it! Here's his nibs back again."

Mr. Carmody was coming up the gravel path, his air that of a man who has made up his mind. He had evidently been following a train of thought, for he began abruptly at the point to which it had led him.

"There's only one thing," he said. "I don't like the idea of bringing in this friend of yours. He may be all right or he may not. You say you can trust him, but it seems to me the fewer people who know about this business, the better."

These were Mr. Molloy's sentiments, also. He would vastly have preferred to keep it a nice, cosy affair among the three of them. But it was no part of his policy to ignore obvious difficulties.

"I'd like that, too," he said. "I don't want to call in Chimp any more than you do. But there's this thing of getting the stuff out of the house."

"What you were saying just now," Mrs. Molloy reminded Mr. Carmody. "It's got to look like an outside job, what I mean."

"As it's called," said Mr. Molloy hastily. "She's always reading these detective stories," he explained. "That's where she picks up these expressions. Outside job, ha, ha! But she's dead right, at that. You said yourself it would be necessary to create the appearance of an actual burglary. If we don't get Chimp, who is going to take the stuff?"

"I am."

"Eh?"

"I am," repeated Mr. Carmody stoutly. "I have been thinking the whole matter out, and it will be perfectly simple. I shall get up very early to-morrow morning and enter the picture-gallery through the window by means of a ladder. This will deceive the police into supposing the theft to have been the work of a professional burglar."

Mr. Molloy was regarding him with affectionate admiration.

"I never knew you were such a hot sketch!" said Mr. Molloy. "You certainly are one smooth citizen. Looks to me as if you'd done this sort of thing before."

"Wear gloves," advised Mrs. Molloy.

"What she means," said Mr. Molloy, again speaking with a certain nervous haste, "is that the first thing the bulls—as the expression is—they always call the police bulls in these detective stories—the first thing the police look for is finger-prints. The fellows in the books always wear gloves."

"A very sensible precaution," said Mr. Carmody, now thoroughly in the spirit of the thing. "I am glad you mentioned it. I shall make a point of doing so."

★ 6 ★

Mr. Carmody Among the Birds

I

THE picture-gallery of Rudge Hall, the receptacle of what Mrs. Soapy Molloy had called the antiques and all like that, was situated on the second floor of that historic edifice. To Mr. Carmody, at five-thirty on the following morning, as he propped against the broad sill of the window facing the moat a ladder which he had discovered in one of the barns, it looked much higher. He felt, as he gazed upward, like an inexpert Jack about to mount the longest bean-stalk on record.

Even as a boy, Lester Carmody had never been a great climber. While his young companions, reckless of risk to life and limb, had swarmed to the top of apple-trees, Mr. Carmody had preferred to roam about on solid ground, hunting in the grass for windfalls. He had always hated heights, and this morning found him more prejudiced against them than ever. It says much for Crime as a wholesome influence in a man's life that the lure of the nefarious job which he had undertaken should have induced him eventually after much hesitation to set foot on the ladder's lowest rung. Nothing but a single-minded desire to do down an innocent insurance company could have lent him the necessary courage.

Mind having triumphed over matter to this extent, Mr. Carmody found the going easier. Carefully refraining from looking down, he went doggedly upward. Only the sound of his somewhat stertorous breathing broke the hushed stillness of the summer morning. As far as the weather was concerned, it was the start of a perfect day. But Mr. Carmody paid no attention to the sunbeams creeping over the dewy grass, nor, when the quiet was broken by the first piping of birds, did he pause to listen. He had not, he considered, time for that sort of thing. He was to have ample leisure later, but of this he was not aware.

He continued to climb, using the extreme of caution—a method which, while it helped to ease his mind, necessarily rendered progress slow. Before long, he was suffering from a feeling that he had been climbing this ladder all his life. The thing seemed to have no end. He was now, he felt, at such a distance from the earth that he wondered the air was not more rarefied, and it appeared incredible to him that he should not long since have reached the window-sill.

Looking up at this point, a thing he had not dared to do before, he found that steady perseverance had brought about its usual result. The sill was only a few inches above his head, and with the realization of this fact there came to him something that was almost a careless jauntiness. He quickened his pace, and treading heavily on an upper rung snapped it in two as if it had been matchwood.

When this accident occurred, he had been on a level with the sill and just about to step warily on to it. The effect of the breaking of the rung was to make him execute this movement at about fifteen times the speed which he had contemplated. There was a moment in which the whole universe seemed to dissolve, and then he was on the sill, his fingers clinging with a passionate grip to a small piece of lead piping that protruded from the wall and his legs swinging dizzily over the abyss. The ladder, urged outwards by his last frenzied kick, tottered for an instant, then fell to the ground.

The events just described, though it seemed longer to the principal actor in them, had occupied perhaps six seconds. They left Mr. Carmody in a world that jumped and swam before his eyes, feeling as though somebody had extracted his heart and replaced it with some kind of lively firework. This substitute appeared to be fizzing and leaping inside his chest, and its gyrations interfered with his breathing. For some minutes his only conscious thought was that he felt extremely ill. Then becoming by slow degrees more composed, he was enabled to examine the situation.

It was not a pleasant one. At first, it had been agreeable enough simply to allow his mind to dwell on the fact that he was alive and in one piece. But now, probing beneath this mere surface aspect of the matter, he perceived that, taking the most conservative estimate, he must acknowledge himself to be in a peculiarly awkward position.

The hour was about a quarter to six. He was thirty feet or so above the ground. And, though reason told him that the window-sill on which he sat was thoroughly solid and quite capable of bearing a much heavier weight, he could not rid himself of the feeling that at any moment it might give way and precipitate him into the depths.

Of course, looked at in the proper spirit, his predicament had all sorts of compensations. The medical profession is agreed that there is nothing better for the health than the fresh air of the early morning: and this he was in a position to drink into his lungs in unlimited quantities. Furthermore, nobody could have been more admirably situated than he to compile notes for one of those Country Life articles which are so popular with the readers of daily papers.

"As I sit on my second-floor window-sill and gaze about me," Mr. Carmody ought to have been saying to himself, "I see Dame Nature busy about her morning tasks. Everything in my peaceful garden is growing and blowing. Here I note that most gem-like of all annuals, the African nemesia with its brilliant ruby and turquoise tints; there the lovely tangle of blue, purple and red formed by the blending shades of delphiniums, Canterbury bells, and the popular geum. Birds, too, are chanting everywhere their morning anthems. I see the Jay (*Garrulus Glandarius Rufitergum*), the *Corvus Monedula Spermologus* or Jackdaw, the Sparrow (better known, perhaps, to some of my readers as *Prunella Modularis Occidentails*) and many others . . ."

But Mr. Carmody's reflections did not run on these lines. It was with a gloomy and hostile eye that he regarded the grass, the trees, the flowers, the birds and the dew that lay like snow upon the turf: and of all these, it was possibly the birds that he disliked most. They were an appalling crowd—noisy, fussy and bustling about with a sort of overdone heartiness that seemed to Mr. Carmody affected and offensive. They got on his nerves and stayed there: and outstanding among the rest in general lack of charm was a certain Dartford Warbler (*Melizophilus Undatus Dartfordiensis*) which, instead of staying in Dartford, where it belonged, had come all the way up to Worcestershire simply, it appeared, for the purpose of adding to his discomfort.

This creature, flaunting a red waistcoat which might have been all right for a frosty day in winter but on a summer morning seemed intolerably loud and struck the jarring note of a Fair

Isle sweater in the Royal Enclosure at Ascot, arrived at five minutes past six and, sitting down on the edge of Mr. Carmody's window-sill, looked long and earnestly at that unfortunate man with its head cocked on one side.

"This can't be real," said the Dartford Warbler in a low voice.

It then flew away and did some rough work among the insects under a bush. At six-ten it returned.

"It is real," it soliloquized. "But, if real, what is it?"

Pondering this problem, it returned to its meal, and Mr. Carmody was left for some considerable time to his meditations. It may have been about twenty-five minutes to seven when a voice at his elbow aroused him once more. The Dartmouth Warbler was back again, its eye now a little glazed and wearing the replete look of the bird that has done itself well at the breakfast-table.

"And why?" mused the Dartmouth Warbler, resuming at the point where he had left off.

To Mr. Carmody, conscious now of a devouring hunger, the spectacle of this bloated bird was the last straw. He struck out at it in a spasm of irritation and nearly overbalanced. The Warbler uttered a shrill exclamation of terror and disappeared, looking like an absconding bookmaker. Mr. Carmody huddled back against the window, palpitating. And more time passed.

It was at half-past seven, when he was beginning to feel that he had not tasted food since boyhood, that there sounded from somewhere below on his right a shrill whistling.

II

He looked cautiously down. It gave him acute vertigo to do so, but he braved this in his desire to see. Since his vigil began, he had heard much whistling. In addition to the *Garrulus Glandarius Rufitergum* and the *Corvus Monedula Spermologus*, he had been privileged for the last hour or so to listen to a never ceasing concert featuring such artists as the *Dryobates Major Anglicus*, the *Sturnus Vulgaris*, the *Emberiza Curlus*, and the *Muscicapa Striata*, or Spotted Fly-catcher: and, a moment before, he would have said that in the matter of whistling he had had all he wanted. But this latest outburst sounded human. It stirred in his bosom something approaching hope.

So Mr. Carmody, craning his neck, waited: and presently round the corner of the house, a towel about his shoulders, suggesting that he was on his way to take an early morning dip in the moat, came his nephew Hugo.

Mr. Carmody, as this chronicle has shown, had never entertained for Hugo quite that warmth of affection which one likes to see in an uncle towards his nearest of kin, but at the present moment he could not have appreciated him more if he had been a millionaire anxious to put up capital for a new golf-course in the park.

"Hoy!" he cried, much as the beleaguered garrison of Lucknow must have done to the advance guard of the relieving Highlanders. "Hoy!"

Hugo stopped. He looked to his right, then to his left, then in front of him, and then, turning, behind him. It was a spectacle that chilled in an instant the new sensation of kindliness which his uncle had been feeling towards him.

"Hoy!" cried Mr. Carmody. "Hugo! Confound the boy! Hugo!"

For the first time the other looked up. Perceiving Mr. Carmody in his eyrie, he stood rigid, gazing with opened mouth. He might have been posing for a statue of Young Man Startled By Snake In Path While About to Bathe.

"Great Scott!" said Hugo, looking to his uncle's prejudiced eye exactly like the Dartford Warbler. "What on earth are you doing up there?"

Mr. Carmody would have writhed in irritation, had not prudence reminded him that he was thirty feet too high in the air to do that sort of thing.

"Never mind what I'm doing up here! Help me down."

"How did you get there?"

"Never mind how I got here!"

"But what," persisted Hugo insatiably, "is the big idea?"

Withheld from the relief of writhing, Mr. Carmody gritted his teeth.

"Put that ladder up," he said in a strained voice.

"Ladder?"

"Yes, ladder."

"What ladder?"

"There is a ladder on the ground."

"Where?"

"There. No, not there. There. There. Not there, I tell you. There. There."

Hugo, following these directions, concluded a successful search.

"Right," he said. "Ladder, long, wooden, one. Correct as per memo. Now what?"

"Put it up."

"Right."

"And hold it very carefully."

"Esteemed order booked," said Hugo. "Carry on."

"Are you sure you are holding it carefully?"

"I'm giving my popular imitation of a vice."

"Well, don't let go."

Mr. Carmody, dying a considerable number of deaths in the process, descended. He found his nephew's curiosity at close range even more acute than it had been from a distance.

"What on earth were you doing up there?" said Hugo starting again at the beginning.

"Never mind."

"But what were you?"

"If you wish to know, a rung broke and the ladder slipped."

"But what were you doing on a ladder?"

"Never mind!" cried Mr. Carmody, regretting more bitterly than ever before in his life that his late brother Eustace had not lived and died a bachelor. "Don't keep saying What—What—What!"

"Well, why?" said Hugo, conceding the point. "Why were you climbing ladders?"

Mr. Carmody hesitated. His native intelligence returning, he perceived now that this was just what the great public would want to know. It was little use urging a human talking-machine like his nephew to keep quiet and say nothing about this incident. In a couple of hours it would be all over Rudge. He thought swiftly.

"I fancied I saw a swallow's nest under the eaves."

"Swallow's nest?"

"Swallow's nest."

"Did you think swallows nested in July?"

"Why shouldn't they?"

"Well, they don't."

"I never said they did. I merely said . . ."

"No swallow has ever nested in July."

"I never . . ."

"April," said our usually well-informed correspondent.

"What?"

"April. Swallows nest in April."

"Damn all swallows!" said Mr. Carmody. And there was silence for a moment, while Hugo directed his keen young mind at other aspects of this strange affair.

"How long have you been up there?"

"I don't know. Hours. Since half-past five."

"Half-past five? You mean you got up at half-past five to look for swallows' nests in July?"

"I did not get up to look for swallows' nests."

"But you said you were looking for swallows' nests."

"I did not say I was looking for swallows' nests. I merely said I fancied I saw a swallow's nest . . ."

"You couldn't have done. Swallows don't nest in July . . . April."

The sun was peeping over the elms. Mr. Carmody raised his clenched fists to it.

"I did not say I saw a swallow's nest. I said I thought I saw a swallow's nest."

"And got a ladder out and climbed up for it?"

"Yes."

"Having risen from couch at five-thirty ante meridian?"

"Will you kindly stop asking me all these questions."

Hugo regarded him thoughtfully.

"Just as you like, uncle. Well, anything further this morning? If not, I'll be getting along and taking my dip."

III

"I say, Ronnie," said Hugo, some two hours later, meeting his friend en route for the breakfast table. "You know my uncle?"

"What about him?"

"He's loopy."

"What?"

"Gone clean off his castors. I found him at seven o'clock this morning sitting on a second-floor window-sill. He said he'd got up at five-thirty to look for swallow's nests."

"Bad," said Mr. Fish, shaking his head with even more than his usual solemnity. "Second-floor window-sill, did you say?"

"Second-floor window-sill."

"Exactly how my aunt started," said Ronnie Fish. "They found her sitting on the roof of the stables, playing the ukelele in a blue dressing-gown. She said she was Boadicea. And she wasn't. That's the point, old boy," said Mr. Fish earnestly. "She wasn't. We must get you out of this as quickly as possible, or before you know where you are you'll find yourself being murdered in your bed. It's this living in the country that does it. Six consecutive months in the country is enough to sap the intellect of anyone. Looking for swallows' nests, was he?"

"So he said. And swallows don't nest in July. They nest in April."

Mr. Fish nodded.

"That's how I always heard the story," he agreed. "The whole thing looks very black to me, and the sooner you're safe out of this and in London, the better."

<h2 style="text-align:center">IV</h2>

At about the same moment, Mr. Carmody was in earnest conference with Mr. Molloy.

"That man you were telling me about," said Mr. Carmody. "That friend of yours who you said would help us."

"Chimp?"

"I believe you referred to him as Chimp. How soon could you get in touch with him?"

"Right away, brother."

Mr. Carmody objected to being called brother, but this was no time for being finicky.

"Send for him at once."

"Why, have you given up the idea of getting that stuff out of the house yourself?"

"Entirely," said Mr. Carmody. He shuddered slightly. "I have been thinking the matter over very carefully, and I feel that this is an affair where we require the services of some third party. Where is this friend of yours? In London?"

"No. He's right around the corner. His name's Twist. He runs a sort of health-farm place only a few miles from here."

"God bless my soul! Healthward Ho?"

"That's the spot. Do you know it?"

"Why, I have only just returned from there."

Mr. Molloy was conscious of a feeling of almost incredulous awe. It was the sort of feeling which would come to a man who saw miracles happening all round him. He could hardly believe that things could possibly run as smoothly as they appeared to be doing. He had anticipated a certain amount of difficulty in selling Chimp Twist to Mr. Carmody, as he phrased it to himself, and had looked forward with not a little apprehension to a searching inquisition into Chimp Twist's *bona fides*. And now, it seemed, Mr. Carmody knew Chimp personally and was, no doubt, prepared to receive him without a question. Could luck like this hold? That was the only thought that disturbed Mr. Molloy.

"Well, isn't that interesting!" he said slowly. "So you know my old friend Twist, do you?"

"Yes," said Mr. Carmody, speaking, however, as if the acquaintanceship were not one to which he looked back with any pleasure. "I know him very well."

"Fine!" said Mr. Molloy. "You see, if I thought we were getting in somebody you knew nothing about and felt you couldn't trust, it would sort of worry me."

Mr. Carmody made no comment on this evidence of his guest's nice feeling. He was meditating and did not hear it. What he was meditating on was the agreeable fact that money which he had been trying so vainly to recover from Doctor Twist would not be a dead loss after all. He would write it off as part of the working expenses of this little venture. He beamed happily at Mr. Molloy.

"Healthward Ho is on the telephone," he said. "Go and speak to Doctor Twist now and ask him to come over here at once." He hesitated for a moment, then came bravely to a decision. After all whatever the cost in petrol, oil and depreciation of tyres, it was for a good object. More working expenses. "I will send my car for him," he said.

If you wish to accumulate, you must inevitably speculate, felt Mr. Carmody.

★ 7 ★

A Crowded Night

I

THE strange depression which had come upon Pat in the shop of Chas. Bywater did not yield, as these grey moods generally do, to the curative influence of time. The following morning found her as gloomy as ever—indeed, rather gloomier, for shortly after breakfast the *Noblesse Oblige* spirit of the Wyverns had sent her on a reluctant visit to an old retainer who lived—if you could call it that—in one of the smaller and stuffier houses in Budd Street. Pensioned off after cooking for the Colonel for eighteen years, this female had retired to bed and stayed there, and there was a legend in the family, though neither by word nor look did she ever give any indication of it, that she enjoyed seeing Pat.

Bedridden ladies of advanced age seldom bubble over with fun and *joie de vivre*. This one's attitude towards life seemed to have been borrowed from her favourite light reading, the works of the Prophet Jeremiah, and Pat, as she emerged into the sunshine after some eighty minutes of her society, was feeling rather like Jeremiah's younger sister.

The sense of being in a world unworthy of her—a world cold and unsympathetic and full of an inferior grade of human being—had now become so oppressive that she was compelled to stop on her way home and linger on the old bridge which spanned the Skirme. From the days of her childhood this sleepy, peaceful spot had always been a haven when things went wrong. She was gazing down into the slow-moving water and waiting for it to exercise its old spell, when she heard her name spoken and turned to see Hugo.

"What ho," said Hugo, pausing beside her. His manner was genial and unconcerned. He had not met her since that embarrassing scene in the lobby of the Hotel Lincoln, but he was a man on whom the memory of past embarrassments sat lightly. "What do you think you're doing, young Pat?"

Pat found herself cheering up a little. She liked Hugo. The sense of being all alone in a bleak world left her.

"Nothing in particular," she said. "Just looking at the water."

"Which in its proper place," agreed Hugo, "is admirable stuff. I've been doing a bit of froth-blowing at the Carmody Arms. Also buying cigarettes and other necessaries. I say, have you heard about my Uncle Lester's brain coming unstuck? Absolutely. He's quite *non compos*. Belfry one seething mass of bats. He's taken to climbing ladders in the small hours after swallows' nests. However, shelving that for the moment, I'm very glad I ran into you this morning, young Pat. I wish to have a serious talk with you about old John."

"John?"

"John."

"What about John?"

At this moment there whirred past, bearing in its interior a weedy, snub-nosed man with a waxed moustache, a large red automobile. Hugo suspending his remarks, followed it with astonished eyes.

"Good Lord!"

"What about Johnnie?"

"That was the Dex-Mayo," said Hugo. "And the gargoyle inside was that blighter Twist from Healthward Ho. Great Scott! The car must have been over there to fetch him."

"What's so remarkable about that?"

"What's so remarkable?" echoed Hugo, astounded. "What's remarkable about Uncle Lester deliberately sending his car twenty miles to fetch a man who could have come, if he had to come at all, by train at his own expense? My dear old thing, it's revolutionary. It marks an epoch. Do you know what I think has happened? You remember that dynamite explosion in the park when Uncle Lester nearly got done in?"

"I don't have much chance to forget it."

"Well, what I believe has happened is that the shock he got that day has completely changed his nature. It's a well-known thing. You hear of such cases all the time. Ronnie Fish was telling me about one only yesterday. There was a man he knew in London, a moneylender, a fellow who had a glass eye, and the only thing that enabled anyone to tell which of his eyes was which was that the glass one had rather a more human expression than the other. That's the sort of chap he was. Well, one day he was nearly konked in a railway accident, and he came out of hospital a different man. Slapped people on the back, patted children on the head, tore up I.O.U.s, and talked about it being everybody's duty to make the world a better place. Take it from me, young Pat, Uncle Lester's whole nature has undergone some sort of rummy change like that. That swallow's nest business must have been a preliminary symptom. Ronnie tells me that this moneylender with the glass eye . . ."

Pat was not interested in glass-eyed moneylenders.

"What were you saying about John?"

"I'll tell you what I'm going to do. I'm going home quick, so as to be among those present when he starts scattering the stuff. It's quite on the cards that I may scoop that five hundred yet. Once a tight-wad starts seeing the light . . ."

"You were saying something about John," said Pat, falling into step with him as he moved off. His babble irked her, making her wish that she could put the clock back a few years. Age, no doubt, has its compensations, but one of the drawbacks of becoming grown-up and sedate is that you have to abandon the childish practice of clumping your friends on the side of the head when they wander from the point. However, she was not too old to pinch her companion in the fleshy part of the arm, and she did so.

"Ouch!" said Hugo, coming out of his trance.

"What about John?"

Hugo massaged his arm tenderly. The look of a greyhound pursuing an electric hare died out of his eyes.

"Of course, yes. John. Glad you reminded me. Have you seen John lately?"

"No. I'm not allowed to go to the Hall, and he seems too busy to come and see me."

"It isn't so much being busy. Don't forget there's a war on. No doubt he's afraid of bumping into the parent."

"If Johnnie's scared of father . . ."

"There's no need to speak in that contemptuous tone. I am, and there are few more intrepid men alive than Hugo Carmody. The old Col., believe me, is a tough baby. If I ever see him, I shall run like a rabbit, and my biographers may make of it what they will. You, being his daughter and having got accustomed to his ways, probably look on him as something quite ordinary and harmless, but even you will admit that he's got eyebrows which must be seen to be believed."

"Oh, never mind father's eyebrows. Go on about Johnnie."

"Right ho. Well, then, look here, young Pat," said Hugo, earnestly, "in re the aforesaid John, I want to ask you a favour. I understand he proposed to you that night at the Mustard Spoon."

"Well?"

"And you slipped him the mitten."

"Well?"

"Oh, don't think I'm blaming you," Hugo assured her. "If you don't want him, you don't. Nothing could be fairer than that. But what I'm asking you to do now is to keep clear of the poor chap. If you happen to run into him, that can't be helped, but be a sport and do your best to avoid him. Don't unsettle him. If you come buzzing round, stirring memories of the past and arousing thoughts of Auld Lang Syne and what not, that'll unsettle him. It'll take his mind off his job and . . . well . . . unsettle him. And, providing he isn't unsettled, I have strong hopes that we may get old John off this season. Do I make myself clear?"

Pat kicked viciously at an inoffensive pebble, whose only fault was that it happened to be within reach at the moment.

"I suppose what you're trying to break to me in your rambling, woollen-headed way is that Johnnie is mooning round that Molloy girl? I met her just now in Bywater's, and she told me she was staying at the Hall."

"I wouldn't call it mooning," said Hugo thoughtfully, speaking like a man who is an expert in these matters and can appraise subtle values. "I wouldn't say it had quite reached the mooning stage yet. But I have hopes. You see, John is a bloke whom nature intended for a married man. He's a confirmed settler-down, the sort of chap who . . ."

"You needn't go over all that again. I had the pleasure of hearing your views on the subject that night in the lobby of the hotel."

"Oh, you did hear?" said Hugo, unabashed. "Well, don't you think I'm right?"

"If you mean do I approve of Johnnie marrying Miss Molloy, I certainly do not."

"But if you don't want him . . ."

"It has nothing to do with my wanting him or not wanting him. I don't like Miss Molloy."

"Why not?"

"She's flashy."

"I would have said smart."

"I wouldn't." Pat, with an effort, recovered a certain measure of calm. Wrangling, she felt, was beneath her. As she could not hit Hugo with the basket in which she had carried two pounds of tea, a bunch of roses and a seed cake to her bedridden pensioner, the best thing to do was to preserve a ladylike composure. "Anyway, you're probably taking a lot for granted. Probably Johnnie isn't in the least attracted by her. Has he ever given any sign of it?"

"Sign?" Hugo considered. "It depends what you mean by sign. You know what old John is. One of these strong, silent fellows who looks on all occasions like a stuffed frog."

"He doesn't."

"Pardon me," said Hugo firmly. "Have you ever seen a stuffed frog? Well, I have. I had one for years when I was a kid. And John has exactly the same power of expressing emotion. You can't go by what he says or the way he looks. You have to keep an eye out for much subtler bits of evidence. Now, last night he was explaining the rules of cricket to this girl and answering all her questions on the subject, and, as he didn't at any point in the proceeding punch her on the nose, one is entitled to deduce, I consider, that he must be strongly attracted by her. Ronnie thinks so, too. So what I'm asking you to do . . ."

"Good-bye," said Pat. They had reached the gate of the little drive that led to her house, and she turned sharply.

"Eh?"

"Good-bye."

"But just a moment," insisted Hugo. "Will you . . ."

At this point he stopped in mid-sentence and began to walk quickly up the road; and Pat, puzzled to conjecture the reason for so abrupt a departure, received illumination a moment later when she saw her father coming down the drive. Colonel Wyvern had been dealing murderously with snails in the shadow of a bush, and the expression on his face seemed to indicate that he would be glad to extend the treatment to Hugo.

He gazed after that officious young man with a steely eye. The second post had arrived a short time before, and it had included among a number of bills and circulars a letter from his lawyer, in which the latter regretfully gave it as his opinion that an action against Mr. Lester Carmody in the matter of that dynamite business would not lie. To bring such an action would, in the judgment of Colonel Wyvern's lawyer, be a waste both of time and money.

The communication was not calculated to sweeten the Colonel's temper, nor did the spectacle of his daughter in apparently pleasant conversation with one of the enemy help to cheer him up.

"What were you talking about to that fellow?" he demanded. It was rare for Colonel Wyvern to be the heavy father, but there are times when heaviness in a father is excusable. "Where did you meet him?"

His tone disagreeably affected Pat's already harrowed nerves, but she replied to the questions equably.

"I met him on the bridge. We were talking about John."

"Well, kindly understand that I don't want you to hold any communication whatsoever with that young man or his cousin John or his infernal uncle or any of that Hall gang. Is that clear?"

Her father was looking at her as if she were a snail which he had just found eating one of his lettuce-leaves, but Pat still contrived with some difficulty to preserve a pale, saintlike calm.

"Quite clear."

"Very well, then."

There was a silence.

"I've known Johnnie fourteen years," said Pat in a small voice.

"Quite long enough," grunted Colonel Wyvern.

Pat walked on into the house and up the stairs to her room. There, having stamped on the basket and reduced it to a state where it would never again carry seed cake to ex-cooks, she sat on her bed and stared, dry-eyed, at her reflection in the mirror.

What with Dolly Molloy and Hugo and her father, the whole aspect of John Carroll seemed to be changing for her. No longer was she able to think of him as Poor Old Johnnie. He had the glamour now of something unattainable and greatly to be desired. She looked back at a night, some centuries ago, when a fool of a girl had refused the offer of this superman's love, and shuddered to think what a mess of things girls can make.

And she had no one to confide in. The only person who could have understood and sympathized with her was Hugo's glass-eyed moneylender. He knew what it was to change one's outlook.

II

Mr. Alexander (Chimp) Twist stood with his shoulders against the mantelpiece in Mr. Carmody's study and, twirling his waxed moustache thoughtfully, listened with an expressionless face to Soapy Molloy's synopsis of the events which had led up to his being at the Hall that morning. Dolly reclined in a deep arm-chair. Mr. Carmody was not present, having stated that he would prefer to leave the negotiations entirely to Mr. Molloy.

Through the open window the sounds and scents of summer poured in, but it is unlikely that Chimp Twist was aware of them. He was a man who believed in concentration, and his whole attention now was taken up by the remarkable facts which his old acquaintance and partner was placing before him.

The latter's conversation on the telephone some two hours ago had left Chimp Twist with an open mind. He was hopeful, but cautiously hopeful. Soapy had insisted that there was a big thing on, but he had reserved his enthusiasm until he should learn the details. The thing, he felt, might seem big to Soapy, but to Alexander Twist no things were big things unless he could see in advance a substantial profit for A. Twist in them.

Mr. Molloy, concluding his story, paused for reply. The visitor gave his moustache a final twirl, and shook his head.

"I don't get it," he said.

Mrs. Molloy straightened herself militantly in her chair. Of all masculine defects, she liked slowness of wit least; and she had never been a great admirer of Mr. Twist.

"You poor, nut-headed swozzie," she said with heat. "What don't you get? It's simple enough, isn't it? What's bothering you?"

"There's a catch somewhere. Why isn't this guy Carmody able to sell the things?"

"It's the law, you poor fish. Soapy explained all that."

"Not to me he didn't," said Chimp. "A lot of words fluttered out of him, but they didn't explain anything to me. Do you mean to say there's a law in this country that says a man can't sell his own property?"

"It isn't his own property." Dolly's voice was shrill with

exasperation. "The things belong in the family and have to be kept there. Does that penetrate, or have we got to use a steam drill? Listen here. Old George W. Ancestor starts one of these English families going—way back in the year G.X. something. He says to himself, 'I can't last forever, and when I go then what? My son Freddie is a good boy, handy with the battle-axe and okay at mounting his charger, but he's like all the rest of these kids—you can't keep him away from the hock-shop as long as there's anything in the house he can raise money on. It begins to look like the moment I'm gone my collection of old antiques can kiss itself good-bye.' And then he gets an idea. He has a law passed saying that Freddie can use the stuff as long as he lives but he can't sell it. And Freddie, when his time comes, he hands the law on to his son Archibald, and so on, down the line till you get to this here now Carmody. The only way this Carmody can realize on all these things is to sit in with somebody who'll pinch them and then salt them away somewheres, so that after the cops are out of the house and all the fuss has quieted down they can get together and do a deal."

Chimp's face cleared.

"Now I'm hep," he said. "Now I see what you're driving at. Why couldn't Soapy have put it like that before? Well, then, what's the idea? I sneak in and swipe the stuff. Then what?"

"You salt it away."

"At Healthward Ho?"

"No!" said Mr. Molloy.

"No!" said Mrs. Molloy.

It would have been difficult to say which spoke with the greater emphasis, and the effect was to create a rather embarrassing silence.

"It isn't that we don't trust you, Chimpie," said Mr. Molloy, when this silence had lasted some little time.

"Oh?" said Mr. Twist, rather distantly.

"It's simply that this bimbo Carmody naturally don't want the stuff to go out of the house. He wants it where he can keep an eye on it."

"How are you going to pinch it without taking it out of the house?"

"That's all been fixed. I was talking to him about it this morning after I 'phoned you. Here's the idea. You get the stuff and pack it away in a suitcase. . . ."

"Stuff that there's only enough of so's you can put it all in a suitcase is a hell of a lot of use to anyone," commented Mr. Twist disparagingly.

Dolly clutched her temples. Mr. Molloy brushed his hair back from his forehead with a despairing gesture.

"Sweet potatoes!" moaned Dolly. "Use your bean, you poor sap, use your bean. If you had another brain you'd just have one. A thing hasn't got to be the size of the Singer Building to be valuable, has it? I suppose if someone offered you a diamond you'd turn it down because it wasn't no bigger than a hen's egg."

"Diamond?" Chimp brightened. "Are there diamonds?"

"No, there aren't. But there's pictures and things, any one of them worth a packet. Go on, Soapy. Tell him."

Mr. Molloy smoothed his hair and addressed himself to his task once more.

"Well, it's like this, Chimpie," he said. "You put the stuff in a suitcase and you take it down into the hall where there's a closet under the stairs. . . ."

"We'll show you the closet," interjected Dolly.

"Sure we'll show you the closet," said Mr. Molloy generously. "Well, you put the suitcase in this closet and you leave it lay there. The idea is that later on I give old man Carmody my cheque and he hands it over and we take it away."

"He thinks Soapy owns a museum in America," explained Dolly. "He thinks Soapy's got all the money in the world."

"Of course, long before the time comes for giving any cheques, we'll have got the stuff away."

Mr. Chimp digested this.

"Who's going to buy it when you do get it away?" he asked.

"Oh, gee!" said Dolly. "You know as well as I do there's dozens of people on the other side who'll buy it."

"And how are you going to get it away? If it's in a closet in Carmody's house and Carmody has the key . . .?"

"Now there," said Mr. Molloy, with a deferential glance at his wife, as if requesting her permission to re-open a delicate subject, "the madam and I had a kind of an argument. I wanted to wait till a chance came along sort of natural, but Dolly's all for quick action. You know what women are. Impetuous."

"If you'd care to know what we're going to do," said Mrs. Molloy definitely, "we're not going to hang around waiting for any chances to come along sort of natural. We're going to slip a

couple of knock-out drops in old man Carmody's port one night
after dinner and clear out with the stuff while . . ."

"Knock-out drops?" said Chimp, impressed. "Have you got
any knock-out drops?"

"Sure we've got knock-out drops. Soapy never travels without
them."

"The madam always packs them in their little bottle first thing
before even my clean collars," said Mr. Molloy proudly. "So you
see, everything's all arranged, Chimpie."

"Yeah?" said Mr. Twist, "and how about me?"

"How do you mean, how about you?"

"It seems to me," pointed out Mr. Twist, eyeing his business
partner in rather an unpleasant manner with his beady little eyes,
"that you're asking me to take a pretty big chance. While you're
doping the old man I'll be twenty miles away at Healthward Ho.
How am I to know you won't go off with the stuff and leave me to
whistle for my share?"

It is only occasionally that one sees a man who cannot believe
his ears, but anybody who had been in Mr. Carmody's study at
this moment would have been able to enjoy that interesting
experience. A long minute of stunned and horrified amazement
passed before Mr. Molloy was able to decide that he really had
heard correctly.

"Chimpie! You don't suppose we'd double-cross you?"

"Ee-magine!" said Mrs. Molloy.

"Well, mind you don't," said Mr. Twist coldly. "But you
can't say I'm not taking a chance. And now, talking turkey for a
moment, how do we share?"

"Equal shares, of course, Chimpie."

"You mean half for me and half for you and Dolly?"

Mr. Molloy winced as if the mere suggestion had touched an
exposed nerve.

"No, no, no, Chimpie! You get a third, I get a third, and the
madam gets a third."

"Not on your life!"

"What!"

"Not on your life. What do you think I am?"

"I don't know," said Mrs. Molloy acidly. "But, whatever it is,
you're the only one of it."

"Is that so?"

"Yes, that is so."

"Now, now, now," said Mr. Molloy, intervening. "Let's not get personal. I can't figure this thing out, Chimpie. I can't see where your kick comes in. You surely aren't suggesting that you should ought to have as much as I and the wife put together?"

"No, I'm not. I'm suggesting I ought to have more."

"What!"

"Sixty-forty's my terms."

A feverish cry rang through the room, a cry that came straight from a suffering heart. The temperamental Mrs. Molloy was very near the point past which a sensitive woman cannot be pushed.

"Every time we get together on one of these jobs," she said, with deep emotion, "we always have this same fuss about the divvying up. Just when everything looks nice and settled you start this thing of trying to hand I and Soapy the nub end of the deal. What's the matter with you that you always want the earth? Be human, why can't you, you poor lump of Camembert."

"I'm human all right."

"You've got to prove it to me."

"What makes you say I'm not human?"

"Well, look in the glass and see for yourself," said Mrs. Molloy offensively.

The pacific Mr. Molloy felt it time to call the meeting to order once more.

"Now, now, now! All this isn't getting us anywheres. Let's stick to business. Where do you get that sixty-forty stuff, Chimp?"

"I'll tell you where I get it. I'm going into this thing as a favour, aren't I? There's no need for me to sit in at this game at all, is there? I've got a good, flourishing, respectable business of my own, haven't I? A business that's on the level. Well, then."

Dolly sniffed. Her husband's soothing intervention had failed signally to diminish her animosity.

"I don't know what your idea was in starting that Healthward Ho joint," she said, "but I'll bet my diamond sunburst it isn't on the level."

"Certainly it's on the level. A man with brains can always make a good living without descending to anything low and crooked. That's why I say that if I go into this thing it will simply be because I want to do a favour to two old friends."

"Old what?"

"Friends was what I said," repeated Mr. Twist. "If you don't like my terms, say so and we'll call the deal off. It'll be all right

by me. I'll simply get along back to Healthward Ho and go on
running my good, flourishing, respectable business. Come to
think of it, I'm not any too sold on this thing, anyway. I was
walking in my garden this morning and a magpie come up to me
as close as that."

Mrs. Molloy expressed the view that this was tough on the
magpie, but wanted to know what the bird's misfortune in
finding itself so close to Mr. Twist that it could not avoid taking
a good, square look at him had to do with the case.

"Well, I'm superstitious, same as everyone else. I saw the new
moon through glass, what's more."

"Oh, stop stringing the beads and talk sense," said Dolly
wearily.

"I'm talking sense all right. Sixty per cent. or I don't come in.
You wouldn't have asked me to come in if you could have done
without me. Think I don't know that? Sixty's moderate. I'm
doing all the hard work, aren't I?"

"Hard work?" Dolly laughed bitterly. "Where do you get the
idea it's going to be hard work? Everybody'll be out of the house
on the night of this concert thing they're having down in the
village, there'll be a window left open, and you'll just walk in and
pack up the stuff. If that's hard, what's easy? We're simply
handing you slathers of money for practically doing nothing."

"Sixty," said Mr. Twist. "And that's my last word."

"But, Chimpie. . . ." pleaded Mr. Molloy.

"Sixty."

"Have a heart!"

"Sixty."

"It isn't as though . . ."

"Sixty."

Dolly threw up her hands despairingly.

"Oh, give it him," she said. "He won't be happy if you don't.
If a guy's middle name is Shylock, where's the use wasting time
trying to do anything about it?"

III

Mrs. Molloy's prediction that on the night of Rudge's annual
dramatic and musical entertainment the Hall would be completely
emptied of its occupants was not, as it happened, literally fulfilled.

A wanderer through the stable yard at about the hour of ten would have perceived a light in an upper window: and had he taken the trouble to get a ladder and climb up and look in would have beheld John Carroll seated at his table, busy with a pile of accounts.

In an age so notoriously avid of pleasure as the one in which we live it is rare to find a young man of such sterling character that he voluntarily absents himself from a village concert in order to sit at home and work: and, contemplating John, one feels quite a glow. It was not as if he had been unaware of what he was missing. The vicar, he knew, was to open the proceedings with a short address: the choir would sing old English glees: the Misses Vivien and Alice Pond-Pond, were down on the programme for refined coon songs: and, in addition to other items too numerous and fascinating to mention, Hugo Carmody and his friend Mr. Fish would positively appear in person and render that noble example of Shakespeare's genius, the Quarrel Scene from *Julius Caesar*. Yet John Carroll sat in his room, working. England's future cannot be so dubious as the pessimists would have us believe while her younger generation is made of stuff like this.

John was finding in his work these days a good deal of consolation. There is probably no better corrective of the pangs of hopeless love than real, steady application to the prosaic details of an estate. The heart finds it difficult to ache its hardest while the mind is busy with such items as Sixty-one pounds, eight shillings and fivepence, due to Messrs. Truby and Gaunt for Fixing Gas Engine, or the claim of the Country Gentlemen's Association for eight pounds eight and fourpence for seeds. Add drains, manure, and feed of pigs, and you find yourself immediately in an atmosphere where Romeo himself would have let his mind wander. John, as he worked, was conscious of a distinct easing of the strain which had been on him since his return to the Hall. And if at intervals he allowed his eyes to stray to the photograph of Pat on the mantelpiece, that was the sort of thing that might happen to any young man, and could not be helped.

It was seldom that visitors penetrated to this room of his— indeed, he had chosen to live above the stables in preference to inside the house for this very reason, and on Rudge's big night he had looked forward to an unbroken solitude. He was surprised, therefore, as he checked the account of the Messrs. Vanderschoot

& Son for bulbs, to hear footsteps on the stairs. A moment later, the door had opened and Hugo walked in.

John's first impulse, as always when his cousin paid him a visit, was to tell him to get out. People who, when they saw Hugo, immediately told him to get out generally had the comfortable feeling that they were doing the right and sensible thing. But to-night there was in his demeanour something so crushed and forlorn that John had not the heart to pursue this admirable policy.

"Hullo," he said. "I thought you were down at the concert."

Hugo uttered a short, bitter laugh: and, sinking into a chair, stared bleakly before him. His eyelids, like those of the Mona Lisa, were a little weary. He looked like the hero of a Russian novel debating the advisability of murdering a few near relations before hanging himself in the barn.

"I was," he said. "Oh yes, I was down at the concert all right."

"Have you done your bit already?"

"I have. They put Ronnie and me on just after the Vicar's Short Address."

"Wanted to get the worst over quick, eh?"

Hugo raised a protesting hand. There was infinite sadness in the gesture.

"Don't mock, John. Don't jeer. Don't jibe and scoff. I'm a broken man. I came here for sympathy. And a drink. Have you got anything to drink."

"There's some whisky in that cupboard."

Hugo heaved himself from the chair, looking more Russian than ever. John watched his operations with some concern.

"Aren't you mixing it pretty strong?"

"I need it strong." The unhappy man emptied his glass, refilled it, and returned to the chair. "In fact, it's a point verging very much on the moot whether I ought to have put any water in it at all."

"What's the trouble?"

"This isn't bad whisky," said Hugo, becoming a little brighter.

"I know it isn't. What's the matter?"

The momentary flicker of cheerfulness died out. Gloom once more claimed Hugo for its own.

"John, old man," he said. "We got the bird."

"Yes?"

"Don't say 'Yes?' like that, as if you had expected it," said Hugo, hurt. "The thing came on me as a stunning blow. I thought we were going to be a riot. Of course, mind you, we came on much too early. It was criminal to bill us next to opening. An audience needs carefully warming up for an intellectual act like ours."

"What happened?"

Hugo rose and renewed the contents of his glass.

"There is a spirit creeping into the life of Rudge-in-the-Vale," he said, "which I don't like to see. A spirit of lawlessness and licence. Disruptive influences are at work. Would a Rudge audience have given me the bird a few years ago? Not a chance!"

"But you've never tried them with the Quarrel Scene from *Julius Caesar* before. Everybody has a breaking point."

The argument was specious, but Hugo shook his head.

"In the good old days I could have done Hamlet's Soliloquy, and the hall would have rung with hearty cheers. It's just this modern lawlessness and Bolshevism. There was a very tough collection of the Budd Street element standing at the back, who should never have been let in. They started straight away chi-yiking the vicar during his short address. I didn't think anything of it at the time. I merely supposed that they wanted him to cheese it and let the entertainment start. I thought that directly Ronnie and I came on we should grip them. But we were barely a third of the way through when there were loud cries of 'Rotten!' and 'Get off!' "

"I see what that meant. You hadn't gripped them."

"I was never so surprised in my life. Mark you, I'll admit that Ronnie was pretty bad. He kept foozling his lines and saying 'Oh, sorry!' and going back and repeating them. You can't get the best out of Shakespeare that way. The fact is, poor old Ronnie is feeling a little low just now. He got a letter this morning from his man, Bessemer, in London, a fellow who has been with him for years and has few equals as a trouser-presser, springing the news out of an absolutely clear sky that he's been secretly engaged for weeks and is just going to get married and leave Ronnie. Naturally, it has upset the poor chap badly. With a thing like that on his mind, he should never have attempted an exacting part like Brutus in the Quarrel Scene."

"Just what the audience thought, apparently. What happened after that?"

"Well, we buzzed along as well as we could, and we had just got to that bit about digesting the venom of your spleen though it do split you, when the proletariat suddenly started bunging vegetables."

"Vegetables?"

"Turnips, mostly, as far as I could gather. Now, do you see the significance of that, John?"

"How do you mean, the significance?"

"Well, obviously these blighters had come prepared. They had meant to make trouble right along. If not, why would they have come to a concert with their pockets bulging with turnips?"

"They probably knew by instinct that they would need them."

"No. It was simply this bally Bolshevism one reads so much about."

"You think these men were in the pay of Moscow?"

"I shouldn't wonder. Well, that took us off. Ronnie got rather a beefy whack on the side of the head and exited rapidly. And I wasn't going to stand out there doing the Quarrel Scene by myself, so I exited, too. The last I saw, Chas. Bywater had gone on and was telling Irish dialect stories with a Swedish accent."

"Did they throw turnips at him?"

"Not one. That's the sinister part of it. That's what makes me so sure the thing was an organised outbreak and all part of this Class War you hear about. Chas. Bywater, in spite of the fact that his material was blue round the edges, goes like a breeze and gets off without a single turnip, whereas Ronnie and I . . . well," said Hugo, a hideous grimness in his voice, "this has settled one thing. I've performed for the last time for Rudge-in-the-Vale. Next year when they come to me and plead with me to help out with the programme, I shall reply 'Not after what has occurred!' Well, thanks for the drink. I'll be buzzing along." Hugo rose and wandered somnambulistically to the table. "What are you doing?"

"Working."

"Working?"

"Yes, working."

"What at?"

"Accounts. Stop fiddling with those papers, curse you."

"What's this thing?"

"That," said John, removing it from his listless grasp and

putting it out of reach in a drawer, "is the diagram of a thing called an Alpha Separator. It works by centrifugal force and can separate two thousand seven hundred and twenty-four quarts of milk in an hour. It has also a Holstein butter-churner attachment, and a boiler which at seventy degrees centigrade destroys the obligatory and optional bacteria."

"Yes?"

"Positively."

"Oh? Well, damn it, anyway," said Hugo.

IV

Hugo crossed the strip of gravel which lay between the stable-yard and the house, and, having found in his trouser-pocket the key of the back door, proceeded to let himself in. His objective was the dining-room. He was feeling so much better after the refreshment of which he had just partaken that reason told him he had found the right treatment for his complaint. A few more swift ones from the cellarette in the dining-room and the depression caused by the despicable behaviour of the Budd Street Bolshevists might possibly leave him altogether.

The passage leading to his goal was in darkness, but he moved steadily forward. Occasionally a chair would dart from its place to crack him over the shin, but he was not to be kept from the cellarette by trifles like that. Soon his fingers were on the handle of the door, and he flung it open and entered. And it was at this moment that there came to his ears an odd noise.

It was not the noise itself that was odd. Feet scraping on gravel always make that unmistakable sound. What impressed itself on Hugo as curious was the fact that on the gravel outside the dining-room window feet at this hour should be scraping at all. His hand had been outstretched to switch on the light, but now he paused. He waited, listening. And presently in the oblong of the middle of the three large windows he saw dimly against the lesser darkness outside a human body. It was insinuating itself through the opening and what Hugo felt about this body was that he liked its bally cheek.

Hugo Carmody was no poltroon. Both physically and morally he possessed more than the normal store of courage. At Cambridge he had boxed for his University in the light-weight division and

once, in London, the petty cash having run short, he had tipped
a cloak-room attendant with an aspirin tablet. Moreover, although
it was his impression that the few drops of whisky which he had
drunk in John's room had but scratched the surface, their
effect in reality had been rather pronounced. "In some diatheses,"
an eminent physician has laid down, "whisky is not immediately
pathogenic. In other cases the spirit in question produces marked
cachexia." Hugo's cachexia was very marked indeed. He would
have resented keenly the suggestion that he was fried, boiled, or
even sozzled, but he was unquestionably in a definite condition of
cachexia.

In a situation, accordingly, in which many house-holders might
have quailed, he was filled with gay exhilaration. He felt able and
willing to chew the head off any burglar that ever packed a
centrebit. Glowing with cachexia and the spirit of adventure, he
switched on the light and found himself standing face to face
with a small, weedy man beneath whose snub nose there nestled a
waxed moustache.

"Stand ho!" said Hugo jubilantly, falling at once into the vein
of the Quarrel Scene.

In the bosom of the intruder many emotions were competing
for precedence, but jubilation was not one of them. If Mr.
Twist had had a weak heart, he would by now have been lying on
the floor breathing his last, for few people can ever have had a
nastier shock. He stood congealed, blinking at Hugo.

Hugo, meanwhile, had made the interesting discovery that it
was no stranger who stood before him but an old acquaintance.

"Great Scott!" he exclaimed. "Old Doc. Twist! The beautiful,
tranquil thoughts bird!" He chuckled joyously. His was a
retentive memory, and he could never forget that this man had
once come within an ace of ruining that big deal in cigarettes over
at Healthward Ho, and had also callously refused to lend him a
tenner. Of such a man he could believe anything, even that he
combined with the duties of a physical culture expert a little
house-breaking and burglary on the side. "Well, well, well!"
said Hugo. "Remember March, the Ides of March remember!
Did not great Julius bleed for justice's sake? What villain
touched his body that did stab and not for justice? Answer me
that, you blighter, yes or no."

Chimp Twist licked his lips nervously. He was a little un-
certain as to the exact import of his companion's last words, but

almost any words would have found in him at this moment a distrait listener.

"Oh, I could weep my spirit from my eyes!" said Hugo.

Chimp could have done the same. With an intense bitterness he was regretting that he had ever ignored the advice of one of the most intelligent magpies in Worcestershire and allowed Mr. Molloy to persuade him into this rash venture. But he was a man of resource. He made an effort to mend matters. Soapy, in a similar situation, would have done it better, but Chimp, though not possessing his old friend's glib tongue and insinuating manners, did the best he could. "You startled me," he said, smiling a sickly smile.

"I bet I did," agreed Hugo cordially.

"I came to see your uncle."

"You what?"

"I came to see your uncle."

"Twist, you lie! And, what is more, you lie in your teeth."

"Now, see here . . .!" began Chimp, with a feeble attempt at belligerence.

Hugo checked him with a gesture.

"There is no terror, Cassius, in your threats, for I am armed so strong in honesty that they pass by me like the idle wind, which I respect not. Must I give way and room to your rash choler? Shall I be frighted when a madman stares? By the gods, you shall digest the venom of your spleen though it do split you. And what could be fairer than that?" said Hugo.

Mr. Twist was discouraged, but he persevered.

"I guess it looked funny to you, seeing me come in through a window. But, you see, I rang the front door bell and couldn't seem to make anyone hear."

"Away, slight man!"

"You want me to go away?" said Mr. Twist, with a gleam of hope.

"You stay where you are, unless you'd like me to lean a decanter of port up against your head," said Hugo. "And don't flicker," he added, awakening to another grievance against this unpleasant little man.

"Don't what?" inquired Mr. Twist, puzzled but anxious to oblige.

"Flicker. Your outline keeps wobbling, and I don't like it.

And there's another thing about you that I don't like. I've forgotten what it is for the moment, but it'll come back to me soon."

He frowned darkly: and for the first time it was borne in upon Mr. Twist that his young host was not altogether himself. There was a gleam in his eyes which, in Mr. Twist's opinion, was far too wild to be agreeable.

"I know," said Hugo, having reflected. "It's your moustache."

"My moustache?"

"Or whatever it is that's broken out on your upper lip. I dislike it intensely. When Caesar lived," said Hugo querulously, "he durst not thus have moved me. And the worst thing of all is that you should have taken a quiet, harmless country house and called it such a beastly, repulsive name as Healthward Ho. Great Scott!" exclaimed Hugo. "I knew there was something I was forgetting. All this while you ought to have been doing bending and stretching exercises!"

"Your uncle, I guess, is still down at the concert thing in the village?" said Mr. Twist, weakly endeavouring to change the conversation.

Hugo started. A look of the keenest suspicion flashed into his eyes.

"Were you at that concert?" he said sternly.

"Me? No."

"Are you sure, Twist? Look me in the face."

"I've never been near any concert."

"I strongly suspect you," said Hugo, "of being one of the ringleaders in that concerted plot to give me the bird. I think I recognized you."

"Not me."

"You're sure?"

"Sure."

"Oh? Well, that doesn't alter the cardinal fact that you are the bloke who makes poor, unfortunate fat men do bending and stretching exercises. So do a few now yourself."

"Eh?"

"Bend!" said Hugo. "Stretch!"

"Stretch?"

"And bend," said Hugo, insisting on full measure. "First bend, then stretch. Let me see your chest expand and hear the tinkle of buttons as you burst your waistcoat asunder."

Mr. Twist was now definitely of opinion that the gleam in the young man's eyes was one of the most unpleasant and menacing things he had ever encountered. Transferring his gaze from this gleam to the other's well-knit frame, he decided that he was in the presence of one who, whether his singular request was due to weakness of intellect or to alcohol, had best be humoured.

"Get on with it," said Hugo.

He settled himself in a chair and lighted a cigarette. His whole manner was suggestive of the blasé nonchalance of a Sultan about to be entertained by the court acrobat. But, though his bearing was nonchalant, that gleam was still in his eyes, and Chimp Twist hesitated no longer. He bent, as requested—and then, having bent, stretched. For some moments he jerked his limbs painfully in this direction and in that, while Hugo, puffing smoke, surveyed him with languid appreciation.

"Now tie yourself into a reef knot," said Hugo.

Chimp gritted his teeth. A sorrow's crown of sorrow is remembering happier things, and there came back to him the recollection of mornings when he had stood at his window and laughed heartily at the spectacle of his patients at Healthward Ho being hounded on to these very movements by the vigilant Sergeant-Major Flannery. How little he had supposed that there would ever come a time when he would be compelled himself to perform these exercises. And how little he had guessed at the hideous discomfort which they could cause to a man who had let his body muscles grow stiff.

"Wait," said Hugo, suddenly.

Mr. Twist was glad to do so. He straightened himself, breathing heavily.

"Are you thinking beautiful thoughts?"

Chimp Twist gulped.

"Yes," he said, with a strong effort.

"Beautiful, tranquil thoughts?"

"Yes."

"Then carry on."

Chimp resumed his calisthenics. He was aching in every joint now, but into his discomfort there had shot a faint gleam of hope. Everything in this world has its drawbacks and its advantages. With the drawbacks to his present situation he had instantly become acquainted, but now at last one advantage presented itself to his notice—the fact, to wit, that the staggerings and totterings

inseparable from a performance of the kind with which he was
entertaining his limited but critical audience had brought him
very near to the open window.

"How are the thoughts?" asked Hugo. "Still beautiful?"

Chimp said they were, and he spoke sincerely. He had
contrived to put a space of several feet between himself and his
persecutor, and the window gaped invitingly almost at his
side.

"Yours," said Hugo, puffing smoke meditatively, "has been a
very happy life, Twist. Day after day you have had the privilege
of seeing my Uncle Lester doing just what you're doing now, and
it must have beaten a circus hollow. It's funny enough even when
you do it, and you haven't anything like his personality and appeal.
If you could see what a priceless ass you look it would keep you
giggling for weeks. I know," said Hugo, receiving an inspiration,
"do the one where you touch your toes without bending the
knees."

In all human affairs the semblance of any given thing is bound
to vary considerably with the point of view. To Chimp Twist, as
he endeavoured to comply with this request, it seemed incredible
that what he was doing could strike anyone as humorous. To
Hugo, on the other hand, it appeared as if the entertainment had
now reached its apex of wholesome fun. As Mr. Twist's purple
face came up for the third time, he abandoned himself whole-
heartedly to mirth. He rocked in his chair, and, rashly trying to
inhale cigarette smoke at the same time. found himself suddenly
overcome by a paroxysm of coughing.

It was the moment for which Chimp Twist had been waiting.
There is, as Ronnie Fish would have observed in the village Hall
an hour or so earlier if the audience had had the self-restraint to
let him get as far as that, a tide in the affairs of men which, taken
at the flood, leads on to fortune. Chimp did not neglect the
opportunity which Fate had granted him. With an agile bound
he was at the window, and, rendered supple, no doubt, by his
recent exercises, leaped smartly through it.

He descended heavily on the dog Emily. Emily, wandering out
for a last stroll before turning in, had just paused beneath the
window to investigate a smell which had been called to her attention on the gravel. She was trying to make up her mind
whether it was rats or the ghost of a long-lost bone when the
skies suddenly started raining heavy bodies on her.

V

Emily was a dog who, as a rule, took things as they came, her guiding motto in life being the old Horatian *Nil Admirari*, but she could lose her poise. She lost it now. A startled oath escaped her, and for a brief instant she was completely unequal to the situation. In this instant, Chimp, equally startled but far too busy to stop, had disengaged himself and was vanishing into the darkness.

A moment later Hugo came through the window. His coughing fit had spent itself, and he was now in good voice again. He was shouting.

At once Emily became herself again. All her sporting blood stirred in answer to these shouts. She forgot her agony. Her sense of grievance left her. Recognizing Hugo, she saw all things clearly, and realized in a flash that here at last was the burglar for whom she had been waiting ever since her conversation with that wire-haired terrier over at Webleigh Manor.

John had taken her to lunch there one day, and fraternizing with the Webleigh dog under the table, she had immediately noticed in his manner something aloof and distinctly patronizing. It had then come out in conversation that they had had a burglary at the Manor a couple of nights ago, and the wire-haired terrier, according to his own story, had been the hero of the occasion. He spoke with an ill-assumed off-handedness of barking and bitings and chasings in the night, and, though he did not say it in so many words, gave Emily plainly to understand that it took an unusual dog to grapple with such a situation, and that in a similar crisis she herself would inevitably be found wanting. Ever since that day she had been longing for a chance to show her mettle, and now it had come. Calling instructions in a high voice, she raced for the bushes into which Chimp had disappeared. Hugo, a bad third, brought up the rear of the procession.

Chimp, meanwhile, had been combining with swift movement some very rapid thinking. Fortune had been with him in the first moments of this dash for safety, but now, he considered, it had abandoned him, and he must trust to his native intelligence to see him through. He had not anticipated dogs. Dogs altered the whole complexion of the affair. To a go-as-you-please race across country with Hugo he would have trusted himself, but Hugo in collaboration with a dog was another matter. It became now a question not of speed but of craft; and he looked about him, as he ran, for a hiding-place, for some shelter from this canine and human storm which he had unwittingly aroused.

And Fortune, changing sides again, smiled upon him once more. Emily, who had been going nicely, attempted very in-judiciously at this moment to take a short cut and became in-volved in a bush. And Chimp, accelerating an always active brain, perceived a way out. There was a low stone wall immediately in front of him, and beyond it, as he came up, he saw the dull gleam of water.

It was not an ideal haven, but he was in no position to pick and choose. The interior of the tank from which the gardeners drew ammunition for their watering-cans had, for one who from child-hood had always disliked bathing, a singularly repellent air. Those dark, oily-looking depths suggested the presence of frogs, newts and other slimy things that work their way down a man's back and behave clammily around his spine. But it was most certainly a place of refuge.

He looked over his shoulder. An agitated crackling of branches announced that Emily had not yet worked clear, and Hugo had apparently stopped to render first aid. With a silent shudder Chimp stepped into the tank and, lowering himself into the depths, nestled behind a water-lily.

Hugo was finding the task of extricating Emily more difficult than he had anticipated. The bush was one of those thorny, adhesive bushes, and it twined itself lovingly in Emily's hair. Bad feeling began to rise, and the conversation took on an acrimonious tone.

"Stand still!" growled Hugo. "Stand still, you blighted dog."

"Push," retorted Emily. "Push, I tell you! Push, not pull. Don't you realize that all the while we're wasting time here that fellow's getting away?"

"Don't wriggle, confound you. How can I get you out if you keep wriggling?"

"Try a lift in an upwards direction. No, that's no good. Stop pushing and pull, I tell you. Pull not push. Now, when I say '*To* you. . . .'"

Something gave. Hugo staggered back. Emily sprang from his grasp. The chase was on again.

But now all the zest had gone out of it. The operations in the bush had occupied only a bare couple of minutes, but they had been enough to allow the quarry to vanish. He had completely disappeared. Hugo, sitting on the wall of the tank and trying to recover his breath, watched Emily as she darted to and fro, inspecting paths and drawing shrubberies, and knew that he had failed. It was a bitter moment, and he sat and smoked moodily. Presently even Emily gave the thing up. She came back to where Hugo sat, her tongue lolling, and disgust written all over her expressive features. There was a silence. Emily thought it was all Hugo's fault, Hugo thought it was Emily's. A stiffness had crept into their relations once again, and when at length Hugo, feeling a little more benevolent after three cigarettes, reached down and scratched Emily's head, the latter drew away coldly.

"Damn fool!" she said.

Hugo started. Was it some sound, some distant stealthy foot-step, that had caused his companion to speak? He stared into the night.

"Fathead!" said Emily. "Can't even pull somebody out of a bush."

She laughed mirthlessly, and Hugo, now keenly on the alert, rose from his seat and gazed this way and that. And then, moving softly away from him at the end of the path, he saw a dark figure.

Instantly, Hugo Carmody became once more the man of action. With a stern shout he dashed along the path. And he had not gone half a dozen feet when the ground seemed suddenly to give way under him.

This path, as he should have remembered, knowing the terrain as he did, was a terrace path, set high above the shrub-beries below. It was a simple enough matter to negotiate it in daylight and at a gentle stroll, but to race successfully along it in the dark required a Blondin. Hugo's third stride took him well into the abyss. He clutched out desperately, grasped only cool Worcestershire night air, and then, rolling down the slope, struck his head with great violence against a tree which seemed to have been put there for the purpose.

When the sparks had cleared away and the firework exhibition was over, he rose painfully to his feet.

A voice was speaking from above—the voice of Ronald Overbury Fish.

"Hullo!" said the voice. "What's up?"

VI

Weighed down by the burden of his many sorrows, Ronnie Fish had come to this terrace path to be alone. Solitude was what he desired, and solitude was what he supposed he had got until, abruptly, without any warning but a wild shout, the companion of his School and University days had suddenly dashed out from empty space and apparently attempted to commit suicide. Ronnie was surprised. Naturally no fellow likes getting the bird at a village concert, but Hugo, he considered, in trying to kill himself was adopting extreme measures. He peered down, going so far in his natural emotion as to remove the cigarette-holder from his mouth.

"What's up?" he asked again.

Hugo was struggling dazedly up the bank.

"Was that you, Ronnie?"

"Was what me?"

"That."

"Which?"

Hugo approached the matter from another angle.

"Did you see anyone?"

"When?"

"Just now. I thought I saw someone on the path. It must have been you."

"It was. Why?"

"I thought it was somebody else."

"Well it wasn't."

"I know, but I thought it was."

"Who did you think it was?"

"A fellow called Twist."

"Twist?"

"Yes, Twist."

"Why?"

"I've been chasing him."

"Chasing Twist?"

"Yes. I caught him burgling the house."

They had been walking along, and now reached a spot where the light, freed from overhanging branches, was stronger. Mr. Fish became aware that his friend had sustained injuries.

"I say," he said, "you've hurt your head."

"I know I've hurt my head, you silly ass."

"It's bleeding, I mean."

"Bleeding?"

"Bleeding."

Blood is always interesting. Hugo put a hand to his wound, took it away again, inspected it.

"By Jove! I'm bleeding."

"Yes, bleeding. You'd better go in and have it seen to."

"Yes." Hugo reflected. "I'll go and get old John to fix it. He once put six stitches in a cow."

"What cow?"

"One of the cows. I forget its name."

"Where do we find this John?"

"He's in his room over the stables."

"Can you walk it all right?"

"Oh, yes, rather."

Ronnie, relieved, lighted a cigarette, and approached an aspect of the affair which had been giving him food for thought.

"I say, Hugo, have you been having a few drinks or anything?"

"What do you mean?"

"Well, buzzing about the place after non-existent burglars."

"They weren't non-existent. I tell you I caught this man Twist . . ."

"How do you know it was Twist?"

"I've met him."

"Who? Twist?"

"Yes."

"Where?"

"He runs a place called Healthward Ho near here."

"What's Healthward Ho?"

"It's a place where fellows go to get fit. My uncle was there."

"And Twist runs it?"

"Yes."

"And you think this—dash it, this pillar of society was burgling the house?"

"I caught him, I tell you."

"Who? Twist?"

"Yes."

"Well, where is he, then?"

"I don't know."

"Listen, old man," said Ronnie gently. "I think you'd better be pushing along and getting that bulb of yours repaired."

He remained gazing after his friend, as he disappeared in the direction of the stable-yard, with much concern. He hated to think of good old Hugo getting into a mental state like this, though of course, it was only what you could expect if a man lived in the country all the time. He was still brooding when he heard footsteps behind him and looked round and saw Mr. Lester Carmody approaching.

Mr. Carmody was in a condition which in a slimmer man might have been called fluttering. He, like John, had absented himself from the festivities in the village, wishing to be on the spot when Mr. Twist made his entry into the house. He had seen Chimp get through the dining-room window and had instantly made his way to the front hall, proposing to wait there and see the precious suitcase duly deposited in the cupboard under the stairs. He had waited, but no Chimp had appeared. And then there had come to his ears barkings and shoutings and uproar in the night. Mr. Carmody, like Othello, was perplexed in the extreme.

"Ah, Carmody," said Mr. Fish.

He waved a kindly cigarette-holder at his host. The latter regarded him with tense apprehension. Was his guest about to announce that Mr. Twist, caught in the act, was now under lock and key? For some reason or other, it was plain, Hugo and this unspeakable friend of his had returned at an unexpectedly early hour from the village, and Mr. Carmody feared the worst.

"I've got a bit of bad news for you, Carmody," said Mr. Fish. "Brace up, my dear fellow."

Mr. Carmody gulped.

"What—what—what . . ."

"Poor old Hugo. Gone clean off his mental axis."

"What! What do you mean?"

"I found him just now running round in circles and dashing his head against trees. He said he was chasing a burglar. Of course there wasn't anything of the sort on the premises. For, mark this, my dear Carmody: according to his statement, which I carefully checked, the burglar was a most respectable fellow named Twist, who runs a sort of health place near here. You know him, I believe?"

"Slightly," said Mr. Carmody. "Slightly."

"Well, would a man in that position go about burgling houses? Pure delusion of course."

Mr. Carmody breathed a deep sigh. Relief had made him feel a little faint.

"Undoubtedly," he said. "Hugo was always weak-minded from a boy."

"By the way," said Mr. Fish, "did you by any chance get up at five in the morning the other day and climb a ladder to look for swallow's nests?"

"Certainly not."

"I thought as much. Hugo said he saw you. Delusion again. The whole truth of the matter is, my dear Carmody, living in the country has begun to soften poor old Hugo's brain. You must act swiftly. You don't want a gibbering nephew about the place. Take my tip and send him away to London at the earliest possible moment."

It was rare for Lester Carmody to feel gratitude for the advice which this young man gave him so freely, but he was grateful now. He perceived clearly that a venture like the one on which he and his colleagues had embarked should never have been undertaken while the house was full of infernal, interfering young men. Such was his emotion that for an instant he almost liked Mr. Fish.

"Hugo was saying that you wished him to become your partner in some commercial enterprise," he said.

"A night-club. The Hot Spot. Situated just off Bond Street, in the heart of London's pleasure-seeking area."

"You were going to give him a half-share for five hundred pounds, I believe?"

"Five hundred was the figure."

"He shall have a cheque immediately," said Mr. Carmody. "I will go and write it now. And tomorrow you shall take him to London. The best trains are in the morning. I quite agree with you about his mental condition. I am very much obliged to you for drawing it to my notice."

"Don't mention it, Carmody," said Mr. Fish graciously. "Only too glad, my dear fellow. Always a pleasure, always a pleasure."

VII

John had returned to his work and was deep in it when Hugo and his wounded head crossed his threshold. He was startled and concerned.

"Good heavens!" he cried. "What's been happening?"

"Fell down a bank and bumped the old lemon against a tree," said Hugo, with the quiet pride of a man who has had an accident. "I looked in to see if you had got some glue or something to stick it up with."

John, as became one who thought nothing of putting stitches in cows, exhibited a cool efficiency. He bustled about, found water and cotton wool and iodine, and threw in sympathy as a make-weight. Only when the operation was completed did he give way to a natural curiosity.

"How did it happen?"

"Well, it started when I found that bounder Twist burgling the house."

"Twist?"

"Yes, Twist. The Healthward Ho bird."

"You found Doctor Twist burgling the house?"

"Yes, and I made him do bending and stretching exercises. And in the middle he legged it through the window, and Emily and I chivvied him about the garden. Then he disappeared, and I saw him again at the end of that path above the shrubberies, and I dashed after him and took a toss and it wasn't Twist at all, it was Ronnie."

John forbore to ask further questions. This incoherent tale satisfied him that his cousin, if not delirious, was certainly on the borderland. He remembered the whole-heartedness with which Hugo had drowned his sorrows only a short while back in this very room, and he was satisfied that what the other needed was rest.

"You'd better go to bed," he said. "I think I've fixed you up pretty well, but perhaps you had better see the doctor to-morrow."

"Doc. Twist?"

"No, not Doctor Twist," said John soothingly. "Doctor Bain, down in the village."

"Something ought to be done about the man Twist," argued Hugo. "Somebody ought to pop it across him."

"If I were you I'd just forget all about Twist. Put him right out of your mind."

"But are we going to sit still and let perishers with waxed moustaches burgle the house whenever they feel inclined and not do a thing to bring their grey hairs in sorrow to the grave?"

"I wouldn't worry about it, if I were you. I'd just go off and have a nice long sleep."

Hugo raised his eyebrows, and, finding that the process caused exquisite agony to his wounded head, quickly lowered them again. He looked at John with cold disapproval, pained at this evidence of supineness in a member of a proud family.

"Oh?" he said. "Well, bung-ho, then!"

"Good night."

"Give my love to the Alpha Separator and all the little Separators."

"I will," said John.

He accompanied his cousin down the stairs and out into the stable-yard. Having watched him move away and feeling satisfied that he could reach the house without assistance, he felt in his pocket for the materials for the last smoke of the day, and was filling his pipe when Emily came round the corner.

Emily was in great spirits.

"Such larks!" said Emily. "One of those big nights. Burglars dashing to and fro, people falling over banks and butting their heads against trees, and everything bright and lively. But let me tell you something. A fellow like your cousin Hugo is no use whatever to a dog in any real emergency. He's not a force. A broken reed. You should have seen him. He . . ."

"Stop that noise and get to bed," said John.

"Right ho," said Emily. "You'll be coming soon, I suppose?"

She charged up the stairs, glad to get to her basket after a busy evening. John lighted his pipe, and began to meditate. Usually he smoked the last pipe of the day to the accompaniment of thoughts about Pat, but now he found his mind turning to this extraordinary delusion of Hugo's that he had caught Doctor Twist, of Healthward Ho, burgling the house.

John had never met Doctor Twist, but he knew that he was

the proprietor of a flourishing health-cure establishment and assumed him to be a reputable citizen; and the idea that he had come all the way from Healthward Ho to burgle Rudge Hall was so bizarre that he could not imagine by what weird mental processes his cousin had been led to suppose that he had seen him. Why Doctor Twist, of all people? Why not the vicar or Chas. Bywater?

Footsteps sounded on the gravel, and he was aware of the subject of his thoughts returning. There was a dazed expression on Hugo's face, and in his hand there fluttered a small oblong slip of paper.

"John," said Hugo, "look at this and tell me if you see what I see. Is it a cheque?"

"Yes."

"For five hundred quid, made out to me and signed by Uncle Lester?"

"Yes."

"Then there *is* a Santa Claus!" said Hugo reverently. "John, old man, it's absolutely uncanny. Directly I got into the house just now Uncle Lester called me to his study, handed me this cheque, and told me that I could go to London with Ronnie to-morrow and help him start that night-club. You remember me telling you about Ronnie's night-club, the Hot Spot, situated just off Bond Street in the heart of London's pleasure-seeking area? Or did I? Well, anyway, he is starting a night-club there, and he offered me a half-share if I'd put up five hundred. By the way, Uncle Lester wants you to go to London to-morrow, too."

"Me. Why?"

"I fancy he's got the wind up a bit about this burglary business to-night. He said something about wanting you to go and see the insurance people—to bump up the insurance a trifle, I suppose. He'll explain. But, listen, John. It really is the most extraordinary thing, this. Uncle Lester starting to unbelt, I mean, and scattering money all over the place. I was absolutely right when I told Pat this morning . . ."

"Have you seen Pat?"

"Met her this morning on the bridge. And I said to her . . ."

"Did she—er—ask after me?"

"No."

"No?" said John hollowly.

"Not that I remember. I brought your name into the talk, and we had a few words about you, but I don't recollect her asking after you." Hugo laid a hand on his cousin's arm. "It's no use, John. Be a man! Forget her. Keep plugging away at that Molloy girl. I think you're beginning to make an impression. I think she's softening. I was watching her narrowly last night, and I fancied I saw a tender look in her eyes when they fell on you. I may have been mistaken, but that's what I fancied. A sort of shy, filmy look. I'll tell you what it is, John. You're much too modest. You underrate yourself. Keep steadily before you the fact that almost anybody can get married if they only plug away at it. Look at this man Bessemer, for instance, Ronnie's man that I told you about. As ugly a devil as you would wish to see outside the House of Commons, equipped with number sixteen feet and a face more like a walnut than anything. And yet he has clicked. The moral of which is that no one need ever lose hope. You may say so yourself that you have no chance with this Molloy girl, that she will not look at you. But consider the case of Bessemer. Compared with him, you are quite good-looking. His ears alone . . ."

"Good night," said John.

He knocked out his pipe and turned to the stairs. Hugo thought his manner abrupt.

VIII

Sergeant-Major Flannery, that able and conscientious man, walked briskly up the main staircase of Healthward Ho. Outside a door off the second landing he stopped and knocked.

A loud sneeze sounded from within.

"Cub!" called a voice.

Chimp Twist, propped up with pillows, was sitting in bed, swathed in a woollen dressing-gown. His face was flushed, and he regarded his visitor from under swollen eyelids with a moroseness which would have wounded a more sensitive man. Sergeant-Major Flannery stood six feet two in his boots: he had a round, shiny face at which it was agony for a sick man to look, and Chimp was aware that when he spoke it would be in a rolling, barrack-square bellow which would go clean through him like a red-hot bullet through butter. One has to be in rude health and at the top of one's form to bear up against the Sergeant-Major Flannerys of this world.

"Well?" he muttered thickly.

He broke off to sniff at a steaming jug which stood beside his bed, and the Sergeant-Major, gazing down at him with the offensive superiority of a robust man in the presence of an invalid, fingered his waxed moustache. The action intensified Chimp's dislike. From the first he had been jealous of that moustache. Until it had come into his life he had always thought highly of his own fungoid growth, but one look at this rival exhibit had taken all the heart out of him. The thing was long and blond and bushy, and it shot heavenwards into two glorious needle-point ends, a shining zareba of hair quite beyond the scope of any mere civilian. Non-army men may grow moustaches and wax them and brood over them and be fond and proud of them, but to obtain a waxed moustache in the deepest and holiest sense of the words you have to be a Sergeant-Major.

"Oo-er!" said Mr. Flannery. "That's a nasty cold you've got."

Chimp, as if to endorse this opinion, sneezed again.

"A nasty feverish cold," proceeded the Sergeant Major in the tones in which he had once been wont to request squads of recruits to number off from the right. "You ought to do something about that cold."

"I am doing sobthig about it," growled Chimp, having recourse to the jug once more.

"I don't mean sniffing at jugs, sir. You won't do yourself no good sniffing at jugs, Mr. Twist. You want to go to the root of the matter, if you understand the expression. You want to attack it from the stummick. The stummick is the seat of the trouble. Get the stummick right and the rest follows natural."

"Wad do you wad?"

"There's some say quinine and some say a drop of camphor on a lump of sugar and some say cinnamon, but you can take it from me the best thing for a nasty feverish cold in the head is taraxacum and hops. There is no occasion to damn my eyes, Mr. Twist. I am only trying to be 'elpful. You send out for some taraxacum and hops, and before you know where you are . . ."

"Wad do you wad?"

"I'm telling you. There's a gentleman below—a gentleman who's called," said Sergeant-Major Flannery, making his mean-

ng clearer. "A gentleman," being still more precise, "who's
called at the front door in a nortermobile. He wants to see
you."

"Well, he can't."

"Says his name's Molloy."

"Molloy?"

"That's what he *said*," replied Mr. Flannery, as one declining
to be quoted or to accept any responsibility.

"Oh? All right. Send him up."

"Taraxacum and hops," repeated the Sergeant-Major, pausing
at the door.

He disappeared, and a few moments later returned, ushering in
Soapy. He left the two old friends together, and Soapy approached
the bed with rather an awestruck air.

"You've got a cold," he said.

Chimp sniffed—twice. Once with annoyance and once at the
jug.

"So would you have a code if you'd been sitting up to your
neck in water for half an hour last night and had to ride home
tweddy biles wriggig wet on a motor-cycle."

"Says which?" exclaimed Soapy, astounded.

Chimp related the saga of the previous night, touching disparagingly on Hugo and saying some things about Emily which
it was well she could not hear.

"And that leds me out," he concluded.

"No, no!"

"I'm through."

"Don't say that."

"I do say thad."

"But, Chimpie, we've got it all fixed for you to get away with
the stuff to-night."

Chimp stared at him incredulously.

"To-night? You thig I'm going out to-night with this code
of mine, to clibe through windows and be run off my legs
by . . ."

"But, Chimpie, there's no danger of that now. We've got everything set. That guy Hugo and his friend are going to London this
morning, and so's the other fellow. You won't have a thing to do
but walk in."

"Oh?" said Chimp.

He relapsed into silence, and took a thoughtful sniff at the jug.

This information, he was bound to admit, did alter the complexion of affairs. But he was a business man.

"Well, if I do agree to go out and risk exposing this nasty, feverish code of mine to the night air, which is the worst thig a man can do—ask any doctor . . ."

"Chimpie!" cried Mr. Molloy in a stricken voice. His keen intuition told him what was coming.

". . . I don't do it on any sigsdy-forty basis. Sigsdy-five—thirty-five is the figure."

Mr. Molloy had always been an eloquent man—without a natural turn for eloquence you cannot hope to traffic successfully in the baser varieties of oil stocks—but never had he touched the sublime heights of oratory to which he soared now. Even the first few words would have been enough to melt most people. Nevertheless, when at the end of five minutes he paused for breath, he knew that he had failed to grip his audience.

"Sigsdy-five—thirty-five," said Chimp firmly. "You need me, or you wouldn't have brought me into this. If you could have worked the job by yourself, you'd never have tode me a word about it."

"I can't work it by myself. I've got to have an alibi. I and the wife are going to a theatre to-night in Birmingham."

"That's what I'm saying. You can't get alog without me. And that's why it's going to be sigsdy-five—thirty-five."

Mr. Molloy wandered to the window and looked hopelessly out over the garden.

"Think what Dolly will say when I tell her," he pleaded.

Chimp replied ungallantly that Dolly and what she might say meant little in his life. Mr. Molloy groaned hollowly.

"Well, I guess if that's the way you feel . . ."

Chimp assured him it was.

"Then I suppose that's the way we'll have to fix it."

"All right," said Chimp. "Then I'll be there somewheres about eleven, or a little later, maybe. And you needn't bother to leave any window opud this time. Just have a ladder laying around and I'll bust the window of the picture-gallery, where the stuff is. It'll be more trouble, but I dode bide takid a bidder trouble to make thigs look more natural. You just see thad thad ladder's where I can fide it, and then you can leave all the difficud part of it to me."

"Difficult!"

"Difficud was what I said," returned Chimp. "Suppose I trip over somethig id the dark? Suppose I slip on the stairs? Suppose the ladder breaks? Suppose that dog gets after me again? That dog's not goig to London, is it? Well, then! Besides, considering that I may quide ligely get pneumonia and pass in my checks . . . What did you say?"

Mr. Molloy had not spoken. He had merely sighed wistfully.

★ 8 ★

Two on a Moat

I

ALTHOUGH anxious thought for the comfort of his juniors was not habitually one of Lester Carmody's outstanding qualities, in planning his nephew John's expedition to London he had been considerateness itself. John, he urged, must on no account dream of trying to make the double journey in a single day. Apart from the fatigue inseparable from such a performance, he was a young man, and young men, Mr. Carmody pointed out, are always the better for a little relaxation and an occasional taste of the pleasures which a metropolis has to offer. Let John have a good dinner in London, go to a theatre, sleep comfortably at a first-class hotel and return at his leisure on the morrow.

Nevertheless, in spite of his uncle's solicitude, nightfall found the latter hurrying back into Worcestershire in the Widgeon Seven. He did not admit that he was nervous, yet there had undoubtedly come upon him something that resembled uneasiness. He had been thinking a good deal during his ride to London about the peculiar behaviour of his cousin Hugo on the previous night. The supposition that Hugo had found Doctor Twist of Healthward Ho trying to burgle Rudge Hall was, of course, too absurd for consideration, but it did seem possible that he had surprised some sort of an attempt upon the house. Rambling and incoherent as his story had been, it had certainly appeared to rest upon that substratum of fact, and John had protested rather earnestly to his uncle against being sent to London, on an errand which could have been put through much more simply by letter, at a time when burglars were in the neighbourhood.

Mr. Carmody had laughed at his apprehensions. It was most unlikely, he pointed out, that Hugo had ever seen a marauder at all. But assuming that he had done so, and that he had surprised and pursued him about the garden, was it reasonable to suppose that the man would return on the very next night? And if, finally, he did return, the mere absence of John would make very little difference. Unless he proposed to patrol the grounds all night, John, sleeping as he did over the stable-yard, could not be of much help, and even without him Rudge Hall was scarcely in a state of defencelessness. Sturgis, the butler, it was true, must, on account of age and flat feet, be reckoned a non-combatant, but apart from Mr. Carmody himself the garrison, John must recollect, included the intrepid Thomas G. Molloy, a warrior at the very mention of whose name Bad Men in Western mining-camps had in days gone by trembled like aspens.

It was all very plausible, yet John, having completed his business in London, swallowed an early dinner and turned the head of the Widgeon Seven homewards.

It is often the man with the smallest stake in a venture who has its interests most deeply at heart. His uncle Lester John had always suspected of a complete lack of interest in the welfare of Rudge Hall; and, as for Hugo, that urban-minded young man looked on the place as a sort of penitentiary, grudging every moment he was compelled to spend within its ancient walls. To John it was left to regard Rudge in the right Carmody spirit, the spirit of that Nigel Carmody who had once held it for King Charles against the forces of the Commonwealth. Where Rudge was concerned, John was fussy. The thought of intruders treading its sacred floors appalled him. He urged the Widgeon Seven forward at its best speed and reached Rudge as the clock over the stables was striking eleven.

The first thing that met his eye as he turned in at the stable-yard was the door of the garage gaping widely open and empty space in the spot where the Dex-Mayo should have stood. He ran the two-seater in, switched off the engine and the lights, and, climbing down stiffly, proceeded to ponder over this phenomenon. The only explanation he could think of was that his uncle must have ordered the car out after dinner on an expedition of some kind. To Birmingham, probably. The only place you ever went to from Rudge after nightfall was Birmingham.

John thought he could guess what must have happened. He did not often read the Birmingham papers himself, but the *Post* came to the house every morning: and he seemed to see

Miss Molloy, her appetite for entertainment whetted rather than satisfied by the village concert, finding in its columns the announcement that one of the musical comedies of her native land was playing at the Prince of Wales. No doubt she had wheedled his uncle into taking herself and her father over there, with the result that here the house was without anything in the shape of protection except butler Sturgis, who had been old when John was a boy.

A wave of irritation passed over John. Two long drives in the Widgeon Seven in a single day had induced even in his whip-cord body a certain measure of fatigue. He had been looking forward to tumbling into bed without delay, and this meant that he must remain up and keep vigil till the party's return. Well, at least he would rout Emily out of her slumbers.

"Hullo?" said Emily sleepily, in answer to his whistle. "Yes?"

"Come down," called John.

There was a scrabbling on the stairs. Emily bounded out, full of life.

"Well, well, well!" she said. "You back?"

"Come along."

"What's up? More larks?"

"Don't make such a beastly noise," said John. "Do you know what time it is?"

They walked out together and proceeded to make a slow circle of the house. And gradually the magic of the night began to soften John's annoyance. The grounds of Rudge Hall, he should have remembered, were at their best at this hour and under these conditions. Shy little scents were abroad which did not trust themselves out in the daytime, and you needed still-ness like this really to hear the soft whispering of the trees.

London had been stiflingly hot, and this sweet coolness was like balm. Emily had disappeared into the darkness, which probably meant that she would clump back up the stairs at two in the morning having rolled in something unpleasant and ruin his night's repose by leaping on his chest, but he could not bring himself to worry about it. A sort of beatific peace was upon him. It was almost as though an inner voice were whispering to him that he was on the brink of some wonderful experience. And what experience the immediate future could hold except the possible washing of Emily when she finally decided to come home he was unable to imagine.

Moving at a leisurely pace, he worked round to the back of the house again and stepped off the grass on to the gravel outside the stable-yard. And as his shoes grated in the warm silence a splash of white suddenly appeared in the blackness before him.

"Johnnie?"

He came back on his heels as if he had received a blow. It was the voice of Pat, sounding in the warm silence like moonlight made audible.

"Is that you, Johnnie?"

John broke into a little run. His heart was jumping, and all the happiness which had been glowing inside him had leaped up into a roaring flame. That mysterious premonition had meant something, after all. But he had never dreamed it could mean anything so wonderful as this.

II

The night was full of stars, but overhanging trees made the spot where they stood a little island of darkness in which all that was visible of Pat was a faint gleaming of white. John stared at her dumbly. Only once in his life before could he remember having felt as he felt now, and that was one raw November evening at school at the close of the football match against Marlborough when, after battling wearily through a long half hour to preserve the slenderest of all possible leads, he had heard the referee's whistle sound through the rising mists and had stood up, bruised and battered and covered with mud, to the realisation that the game was over and won. He had had his moments since then, but never again till now had he felt that strange, almost awful ecstasy.

Pat, for her part, appeared composed.

"That mongrel of yours is a nice sort of watchdog," she said. "I've been flinging tons of gravel at your window and she hasn't uttered a sound."

"Emily's gone away somewhere."

"I hope she gets bitten by a rabbit," said Pat. "I'm off that hound for life. I met her in the village a little while ago and she practically cut me dead."

There was a pause.

"Pat!" said John, thickly.

"I thought I'd come up and see how you were getting on. It was such a lovely night, I couldn't go to bed. What were you doing, prowling round?"

It suddenly came home to John that he was neglecting his vigil. The thought caused him no remorse whatever. A thousand burglars with a thousand jemmies could break into the Hall and he would not stir a step to prevent them.

"Oh, just walking."

"Were you surprised to see me?"

"Yes."

"We don't see much of each other nowadays."

"I didn't know. . . . I wasn't sure you wanted to see me."

"Good gracious! What made you think that?"

"I don't know."

Silence fell upon them again. John was harassed by a growing consciousness that he was failing to prove himself worthy of this golden moment which the Fates had granted to him. Was this all he was capable of—stiff, halting words which sounded banal even to himself? A night like this deserved, he felt, something better. He saw himself for an instant as he must be appearing to a girl like Pat, a girl who had been everywhere and met all sorts of men—glib, dashing men; suave, ingratiating men; men of poise and *savoir faire* who could carry themselves with a swagger. An aching humility swept over him.

And yet she had come here to-night to see him. The thought a little restored his self-respect, and he was trying with desperate search in the unexplored recesses of his mind to discover some remark which would show his appreciation of that divine benevolence, when she spoke again.

"Johnnie, let's go out on the moat."

John's heart was singing like one of the morning stars. The suggestion was not one which he would have made himself, for it would not have occurred to him, but now that it had been made, he saw how super-excellent it was. He tried to say so, but words would not come to him.

"You don't seem very enthusiastic," said Pat. "I suppose you think I ought to be at home and in bed?"

"No."

"Perhaps you want to go to bed?"

"No."

"Well, come on then."

They walked in silence down the yew-hedged path that led to the boat-house. The tranquil beauty of the night wrapped them about as in a garment. It was very dark here, and even the gleam of white that was Pat had become indistinct.

"Johnnie?"

"Yes?"

He heard her utter a little exclamation. Something soft and scented stumbled against him, and for an instant he was holding her in his arms. The next moment he had very properly released her again, and he heard her laugh.

"Sorry," said Pat. "I stumbled."

John did not reply. He was incapable of speech. That swift moment of contact had had the effect of clarifying his mental turmoil. Luminously now he perceived what was causing his lack of eloquence. It was the surging, choking desire to kiss Pat, to reach out and snatch her up in his arms and hold her there.

He stopped abruptly.

"What's the matter?"

"Nothing," said John.

Prudence, the kill-joy, had whispered in his ear. He visualised Prudence as a pale-faced female with down-drawn lips and mild, warning stare who murmured thinly "Is it wise?" Before her whisper primitive emotions fled, abashed. The caveman in John fled back into the dim past whence he had come. Most certainly, felt the twentieth-century John, it would not be wise. Very clearly Pat had shown him, that night in London, that all that she could give him was friendship, and to gratify the urge of some distant ancestor who ought to have been ashamed of himself he had been proposing to shatter the delicate crystal of this friendship into fragments. He shivered at the narrowness of escape.

He had read stories. In stories girls drew their breath in sharply and said "Oh, why must you spoil everything?" He decided not to spoil everything. Walking warily, he reached the little gate that led to the boathouse steps and opened it with something of a flourish.

"Be careful," he said.

"What of?" said Pat. It seemed to John that she spoke a trifle flatly.

"These steps are rather tricky."

"Oh?" said Pat.

III

He followed her into the punt, oppressed once more by a feeling that something had gone wrong with what should have been the most wonderful night of his life. Girls are creatures of moods, and Pat seemed now to have fallen into one of odd aloofness. She said nothing as he pushed the boat out, and remained silent as it slid through the water with a little tinkling ripple, bearing them into a world of stars and coolness, where everything was still and the trees stood out against the sky as if carved from cardboard.

"Are you all right?" said John, at last.

"Splendid, thanks," Pat's mood seemed to have undergone another swift change. Her voice was friendly again. She nestled into the cushions. "This is luxury. Do you remember the old days when there was nothing but the weed-boat?"

"They were pretty good days," said John wistfully.

"They were, rather," said Pat.

The spell of the summer night held them silent again. No sound broke the stillness but the slap of tiny waves and the rhythmic dip and splash of the paddle. Then with a dry flittering a bat wheeled overhead, and out somewhere by the little island where the birds nested something leaped noisily in the water. Pat raised her head.

"A pike?"

"Must have been."

Pat sat up and leaned forward.

"That would have excited father," she said. "I know he's dying to get out here and have another go at the pike. Johnnie, I do wish somebody could do something to stop this absurd feud between him and Mr. Carmody. It's too silly. I know father would be all over Mr. Carmody if only he would make some sort of advance. After all, he did behave very badly. He might at least apologise."

John did not reply for a moment. He was thinking that whoever tried to make his uncle apologise for anything had a whole-time job on his hands. Obstinate was a mild word for the squire of Rudge. Pigs bowed as he passed, and mules could have taken his correspondence course.

"Uncle Lester's a peculiar man."

"But he might listen to you."

"He might," said John doubtfully.

"Well, will you try? Will you go to him and say that all father wants is for him to admit he was in the wrong? Good heavens! It isn't asking much of a man to admit that when he's nearly murdered somebody."

"I'll try."

"Hugo says Mr. Carmody has gone off his head, but he can't have gone far enough off not to be able to see that father has a perfect right to be offended at being grabbed round the waist and used as a dug-out against dynamite explosions."

"I think Hugo's off his head," said John. "He was running round the garden last night, dashing himself against trees. He said he was chasing a burglar."

Pat was not to be diverted into a discussion of Hugo's mental deficiencies.

"Well, will you do your best, Johnnie? Don't just let things slide as if they didn't matter. I tell you, it's rotten for me. Father found me talking to Hugo the other day and behaved like something out of a super-film. He seemed sorry there wasn't any snow, so that he couldn't drive his erring daughter out into it. If he knew I was up here to-night he would foam with fury. He says I mustn't speak to you or Hugo or Mr. Carmody or Emily—not that I want to speak to Emily, the little blighter— nor your ox nor your ass nor anything that is within your gates. He's put a curse on the Hall. It's one of those comprehensive curses, taking in everything from the family to the mice in the kitchen, and I tell you I'm jolly well fed up. This place has always been just like a home to me, and you . . ."

John paused in the act of dipping his paddle into the water.

". . . and you have always been just like a brother . . ."

John dug the paddle down with a vicious jerk.

". . . and if father thinks it doesn't affect me to be told I mustn't come here and see you, he's wrong. I suppose most girls nowadays would just laugh at him, but I can't. It isn't his being angry I'd mind—it would hurt his feelings so frightfully if I let him down and went fraternizing with the enemy. So I have come here on the sly, and if there's one thing in the world I hate it's doing things on the sly. So do reason with that old pig of an uncle of yours, Johnnie. Talk to him like a mother."

"Pat," said John fervently, "I don't know how it's going to be done, but if it can be done I'll do it.'"

"That's the stuff! You're a funny old thing, Johnnie. In some ways you're so slow, but I believe when you really start out to do anything you generally put it through."

"Slow?" said John, stung. "How do you mean, slow?"

"Well, don't you think you're slow?"

"In what way?"

"Oh, just slow."

In spite of the fact that the stars were shining bravely, the night was very dark, much too dark for John to be able to see Pat's face: but he got the impression that, could he have seen it, he would have discovered that she was smiling that old mocking smile of hers. And somehow, though in the past he had often wilted meekly and apologetically beneath this smile, it filled him now with a surge of fury. He plied the paddle wrathfully, and the boat shot forward.

"Don't go so fast," said Pat.

"I thought I was slow," retorted John, sinking back through the years to the repartee of school days.

Pat gurgled in the darkness.

"Did I wound you, Johnnie? I'm sorry. You aren't slow. It's just Prudence, I expect."

Prudence! John ceased to paddle. He was tingling all over, and there had come upon him a strange breathlessness.

"How do you mean, prudence?"

"Oh, just prudence. I can't explain."

Prudence! John sat and stared through the darkness in a futile effort to see her face. A water-rat swam past, cleaving a fan-shaped trail. The stars winked down at him. In the little island a bird moved among the reeds. Prudence! Was she referring . . .? Had she meant . . .? Did she allude . . .?

He came to life and dug the paddle into the water. Of course she wasn't. Of course she hadn't. Of course she didn't. In that little episode on the path, he had behaved exactly as he should have behaved. If he had behaved as he should not have behaved, if he had behaved as that old flint-axe and bearskin John of the Stone Age would have had him behave, he would have behaved unpardonably. The swift intake of the breath and the "Oh, why must you spoil everything?"—that was what would have been the result of listening to the advice of a bounder of an

ancestor who might have been a social success in his day but
certainly didn't understand the niceties of modern civilization.

Nevertheless, he worked with unnecessary vigour at the paddle,
calling down another rebuke from his passenger.

"Don't race along like that. Are you trying to hint that you
want to get this over as quickly as you can and send me home
to bed?"

"No," was all John could find to say.

"Well, I suppose I ought to be thinking of bed. I'll tell you
what. Take me out into the Skirme and down as far as the bridge
and drop me there. Or is that too big a programme? You're
probably tired."

John had motored two hundred miles that day, but he had
never felt less tired. His view was that he wished they could row
on for ever.

"All right," he said.

"Push on, then," said Pat. "Only do go slowly. I want to
enjoy this. I don't want to whizz by all the old landmarks. How
far to Ghost Corner?"

"It's just ahead."

"Well, take it easy."

The moat proper was a narrow strip of water which encircled
the Hall and had been placed there by the first Carmody in the
days when householders believed in making things difficult for
their visitors. With the gradual spread of peace throughout the
land its original purpose had been forgotten, and later members
of the family had broadened it and added to it and tinkered with
it and sprinkled it with little islands with the view of converting
it into something resembling as nearly as possible an ornamental
lake. Apparently it came to an end at the spot where a mass
of yew-trees stood forbiddingly in a gloomy row; that haunted
spot which Pat as a child had named Ghost Corner: but if you
approached this corner intrepidly you found there a narrow
channel. Which navigated, you came into a winding stream which
led past meadows and under bridges to the upper reaches of
the Skirme.

"How old were you, Johnnie, when you were first brave
enough to come past Ghost Corner at night all by yourself?"
asked Pat.

"Sixteen."

"I bet you were much more than that."

"I did it on my sixteenth birthday."

Pat stretched out a hand and the branches brushed her fingers.

"I wouldn't do it even now," she said. "I know perfectly well a skinny arm covered with black hair would come out of the yews and grab me. There's something that looks like a skinny arm hovering at the back of your neck now, Johnnie. What made you such a hero that particular day?"

"You had betted me I wouldn't, if you remember."

"I don't remember. Did I?"

"Well, you egged me on with taunts."

"And you went and did it? What a good influence I've been in your life, haven't I? Oh, dear! It's funny to think of you and me as kids on this very bit of water and here we are again now, old and worn and quite different people, and the water's just the same as ever."

"I'm not different."

"Yes, you are."

"What makes you say I'm different?"

"Oh, I don't know."

John stopped paddling. He wanted to get to the bottom of this.

"Why do you say I'm different?"

"Those white things through the trees there must be geese."

John was not interested in geese.

"I'm not different at all," he said, "I . . ." He broke off. He had been on the verge of saying that he had loved her then and that he loved her still—which, he perceived, would have spoiled everything. "I'm just the same," he concluded lamely.

"Then why don't you sport with me on the green as you did when you were a growing lad? Here you have been back for days, and to-night is the first glimpse I get of you. And, even so, I had to walk a mile and fling gravel at your window. In the old days you used to live on my doorstep. Do you think I've enjoyed being left all alone all this time?"

John was appalled. Put this way, the facts did seem to point to a callous negligence on his part. And all the while he had been supposing his conduct due to delicacy and a sense of what was fitting and would be appreciated. In John's code, it was the duty of a man who has told a girl he loves her and been informed that she does not love him to efface himself, to crawl into the background, to pass out of her life till the memory of his crude audacity shall have been blotted out by time. Why, half the big game shot in Africa owed their untimely end, he understood, to this tradition.

"I didn't know. . . ."

"What?"

"I didn't know you wanted to see me."

"Of course I wanted to see you. Look here, Johnnie. I'll tell you what. Are you doing anything to-morrow?"

"No."

"Then get out that old rattletrap of yours and gather me up at my place, and we'll go off and have a regular picnic like we used to do in the old days. Father is lunching out. You could come at about one o'clock. We could get out to Wenlock Edge in an hour. It would be lovely there if this weather holds up. What do you say?"

John did not immediately say anything. His feelings were too deep for words. He urged the boat forward, and the Skirme received it with that slow, grave, sleepy courtesy which made it for right-thinking people the best of all rivers.

"Will you?"

"Will I!"

"All right. That's splendid. I'll expect you at one."

The Skirme rippled about the boat, chuckling softly to itself. It was a kindly, thoughtful river, given to chuckling to itself like an old gentleman who likes seeing young people happy.

"We used to have some topping picnics in the old days," said Pat dreamily.

"We did," said John.

"Though why on earth you ever wanted to be with a beastly bossy, consequential, fractious kid like me, goodness knows."

"You were fine," said John.

The Old Bridge loomed up through the shadows. John had steered the boat shorewards, and it brushed against the reeds with a sound like the blowing of fairy bugles.

Pat scrambled out and bent down to where he sat, holding to the bank.

"I'm not nearly so beastly now, Johnnie," she said in a whisper. "You'll find that out some day, perhaps, if you're very patient. Good-night, Johnnie, dear. Don't forget to-morrow."

She flitted away into the darkness, and John, releasing his hold on the bank and starting up as if he had had an electric shock, was carried out into midstream. He was tingling from head to foot. It could not have happened, of course, but for a moment he had suddenly received the extraordinary impression that Pat had kissed him.

"Pat!" he called, choking.

There came no answer out of the night—only the sleepy chuckling of the Skirme as it pottered on to tell its old friend the Severn about it.

"Pat!"

John drove the paddle forcefully into the water, and the Skirme, ceasing to chuckle, uttered two loud gurgles of protest as if resenting treatment so violent. The nose of the boat bumped against the bank, and he sprang ashore. He stood there, listening. But there was nothing to hear. Silence had fallen on an empty world.

A little sound came to him in the darkness. The Skirme was chuckling again.

★ 9 ★

Knock-Out Drops

I

JOHN woke late next day, and in the moment between sleeping and waking was dimly conscious of a feeling of extraordinary happiness. For some reason, which he could not immediately analyse, the world seemed suddenly to have become the best of all possible worlds. Then he remembered, and sprang out of bed with a shout.

Emily, lying curled up in her basket, her whole appearance that of a dog who has come home with the milk, raised a drowsy head. Usually it was her custom to bustle about and lend a hand while John bathed and dressed, but this morning she did not feel equal to it. Deciding that it was too much trouble even to tell him about the man she had seen in the grounds last night, she breathed heavily twice and returned to her slumbers.

Having dressed and come out into the open, John found that he had missed some hours of what appeared to be the most perfect morning in the world's history. The stable-yard was a well of sunshine: light breezes whispered in the branches of the cedars: fleecy clouds swam in a sea of blue: and from the direction of the home farm there came the soothing crooning of fowls. His happiness swelled into a feeling of universal benevolence towards all created things. He looked upon the birds and found them all that birds should be: the insects which hummed in the sunshine were, he perceived, a quite superior brand of insect: he even felt fraternal towards a wasp which came flying about his face. And when the Dex-Mayo rolled across the bridge of the moat and Bolt, applying the brakes, drew up at his side, he thought he had never seen a nicer-looking chauffeur.

"Good morning, Bolt," said John, effusively.

"Good morning, sir."

"Where have you been off to so early?"

"Mr. Carmody sent me to Worcester, sir, to leave a bag for him at Shrub Hill station. If you're going into the house, Mr. John, perhaps you wouldn't mind giving him the ticket?"

John was delighted. It was a small kindness that the chauffeur was asking, and he wished it had been in his power to do something for him on a bigger scale. However, the chance of doing even small kindnesses was something to be grateful for on a morning like this. He took the ticket and put it in his pocket.

"How are you, Bolt?"

"All right, thank you, sir."

"How's Mrs. Bolt?"

"She's all right, Mr. John."

"How's the baby?"

"The baby's all right."

"And the dog?"

"The dog's all right, sir."

"That's splendid," said John. "That's great. That's fine. That's capital. I'm delighted."

He smiled a radiant smile of cheeriness and goodwill, and turned towards the house. However much the heart may be uplifted, the animal in a man insists on demanding breakfast, and though John was practically pure spirit this morning, he was not blind to the fact that a couple of eggs and a cup of coffee would be no bad thing. As he reached the door, he remembered that Mrs. Bolt had a canary and that he had not inquired after that, but decided that the moment had gone by. Later on, perhaps. He opened the back door and made his way to the morning-room, where eggs abounded and coffee could be had for the asking. Pausing only to tickle a passing cat under the ear and make chirruping noises to it, he went in.

The morning-room was empty, and there were signs that the rest of the party had already breakfasted. John was glad of it. Genially disposed though he felt towards his species to-day, he relished the prospect of solitude. A man who is about to picnic on Wenlock Edge in perfect weather with the only girl in the world wants to meditate, not to make conversation.

So thoroughly had his predecessors breakfasted that he found, on inspecting the coffee-pot, that it was empty. He rang the bell.

"Good morning, Sturgis," he said affably, as the butler appeared. "You might give me some more coffee, will you ?"

The butler of Rudge Hall was a little man with snowy hair who had been placidly withering in Mr. Carmody's service for the last twenty years. John had known him ever since he could remember, and he had always been just the same—frail and venerable and kindly and dried-up. He looked exactly like the Good Old Man in a touring melodrama company.

"Why, Mr. John! I thought you were in London."

"I got back late last night. And very glad," said John heartily, "to be back. How's the rheumatism, Sturgis ?"

"Rather troublesome, Mr. John."

John was horrified. Could these things be on such a day as this ?

"You don't say so ?"

"Yes, Mr. John. I was awake the greater portion of the night."

"You must rub yourself with something and then go and lie down and have a good rest. Where do you feel it mostly ?"

"In the limbs, Mr. John. It comes on in sharp twinges."

"That's bad. By Jove, yes, that's bad. Perhaps this fine weather will make it better."

"I hope so, Mr. John."

"So do I, so do I," said John earnestly. "Tell me, where is everybody ?"

"Mr. Hugo and the young gentleman went up to London."

"Of course, yes. I was forgetting."

"Mr. Molloy and Miss Molloy finished their breakfast some little time ago, and are now out in the garden."

"Ah, yes. And my uncle ?"

"He is up in the picture-gallery with the policeman, Mr. John."

John stared.

"With the what ?"

"With the policeman, Mr. John, who's come about the burglary."

"Burglary ?"

"Didn't you hear, Mr. John, we had a burglary last night ?"

The world being constituted as it is, with Fate waiting round almost every corner with its sand-bag, it is not often that we are permitted to remain for long undisturbed in our moods of exaltation. John came down to earth swiftly.

"Good heavens!"

"Yes, Mr. John. And if you could spare the time to allow me . . ."

Remorse gripped John. He felt like a sentinel who, falling asleep at his post, has allowed the enemy to creep past him in the night.

"I must go up and see about this."

"Very good, Mr. John. But if I might have a word . . ."

"Some other time, Sturgis."

He ran up the stairs to the picture-gallery. Mr. Carmody and Rudge's one policeman were examining something by the window, and John, in the brief interval which elapsed before they became aware of his presence, was enabled to see the evidence of the disaster. Several picture-frames, robbed of their contents, gaped at him like blank windows. A glass case containing miniatures had been broken and rifled. The Elizabethan salt-cellar presented to Amyas Carmody by the Virgin Queen herself was no longer in its place.

"Gosh!" said John.

Mr. Carmody and his companion turned.

"John! I thought you were in London."

"I came back last night."

"Did you see or observe or hear anything of this business?" asked the policeman.

Constable Mould was one of the slowest-witted men in Rudge and he had eyes like two brown puddles filmed over with scum, but he was doing his best to look at John keenly.

"No."

"Why not?"

"I wasn't here."

"You said you were, sir," Constable Mould pointed out cleverly.

"I mean, I wasn't anywhere near the house," replied John impatiently. "Immediately I arrived I went out for a row on the moat."

"Then you did not see or observe anything?"

"No."

Constable Mould, who had been licking the tip of his pencil

and holding a note-book in readiness, subsided disappointedly.

"When did this happen?" asked John.

"It is impossible to say," replied Mr. Carmody. "By a most unfortunate combination of circumstances the house was virtually empty from almost directly after dinner. Hugo and his friend, as you know, left for London yesterday morning. Mr. Molloy and his daughter took the car to Birmingham to see a play. And I myself retired to bed early with a headache. The man could have effected an entrance without being observed almost any time after eight o'clock. No doubt he actually did break in shortly before midnight."

"How did he get in?"

"Undoubtedly through this window by means of a ladder."

John perceived that the glass of the window had been cut out.

"Another most unfortunate thing," proceeded Mr. Carmody, "is that the objects stolen, though so extremely valuable, are small in actual size. The man could have carried them off without any inconvenience. No doubt they are miles away by this time, possibly even in London."

"Was this here stuff insured?" asked Constable Mould.

"Yes. Curiously enough, the reason my nephew here went to London yesterday was to increase the insurance. You saw to that matter, John?"

"Oh, yes." John spoke absently. Like everybody else who has ever found himself on the scene of a recently committed burglary, he was looking about for clues. "Hullo!"

"What is the matter?"

"Did you see this?"

"Certainly I saw it," said Mr. Carmody.

"I saw it first," said Constable Mould.

"The man must have cut his finger getting in."

"That's what I thought," said Constable Mould.

The combined Mould-Carmody-John discovery was a blood-stained finger-print on the woodwork of the window-sill: and, like so many things in this world, it had at first sight the air of being much more important than it really was. John said he considered it valuable evidence, and felt damped when Mr. Carmody pointed out that its value was decreased by the fact that it was not easy to search through the whole of England for a man with a cut finger.

"I see," said John.

Constable Mould said he had seen it right away.

"The only thing to be done, I suppose," said Mr. Carmody resignedly, "is to telephone to the police in Worcester. Not that they will be likely to effect anything, but it is as well to observe the formalities. Come downstairs with me, Mould."

They left the room, the constable, it seemed to John, taking none too kindly to the idea that there were higher powers in the world of detection than himself. His uncle, he considered, had shown a good deal of dignity in his acceptance of the disaster. Many men would have fussed and lost their heads, but Lester Carmody remained calm. John thought it showed a good spirit.

He wandered about the room, hoping for more and better clues. But the difficulty confronting the novice on these occasions is that it is so hard to tell what is a clue and what is not. Probably, if he only knew, there were clues lying about all over the place, shouting to him to pick them up. But how to recognize them? Sherlock Holmes can extract a clue from a wisp of straw or a flake of cigar-ash. Doctor Watson has to have it taken out for him and dusted and exhibited clearly with a label attached. John was forced reluctantly to the conclusion that he was essentially a Doctor Watson. He did not rise even to the modest level of a Scotland Yard Bungler.

He awoke from a reverie to find Sturgis at his side.

II

"Ah, Sturgis," said John absently.

He was not particularly pleased to see the butler. The man looked as if he were about to dodder, and in moments of intense thought one does not wish to have doddering butlers around one.

"Might I have a word, Mr. John?"

John supposed he might, though he was not frightfully keen about it. He respected Sturgis's white hairs, but the poor old ruin had horned in at an unfortunate moment.

"My rheumatism was very bad last night, Mr. John."

John recognised the blunder he had made in being so sympathetic just now. At the time, feeling, as he had done, that all mankind were his little brothers, to inquire after and display a keen interest in Sturgis's rheumatism had been a natural and, one might say, unavoidable act. But now he regretted it. He required every cell in his brain for this very delicate business of clue-hunting, and it was maddening to be compelled to call a number of them off duty to attend to gossip about a butler's swollen joints. A little coldly he asked Sturgis if he had ever tried Christian Science.

"It kept me awake a very long time, Mr. John."

"I read in a paper the other day that bee-stings sometimes have a good effect."

"Bee-stings, sir?"

"So they say. You get yourself stung by bees, and the acid or whatever it is in the sting draws out the acid or whatever it is in you."

Sturgis was silent for awhile, and John supposed he was about to ask if he could direct him to a good bee. Such, however, was not the butler's intention. It was Sturgis the old retainer with the welfare of Rudge Hall nearest his heart—not Sturgis the sufferer from twinges in the limbs, who was present now in the picture-gallery.

"It is very kind of you, Mr. John," he said, "to interest yourself, but what I wished to have a word with you about was this burglary of ours last night."

This was more the stuff. John became heartier.

"A most mysterious affair, Sturgis. The man apparently climbed in through this window, and no doubt escaped the same way."

"No, Mr. John. That's what I wished to have a word with you about. He went away down the front stairs."

"What! How do you know?"

"I saw him, Mr. John."

"You saw him?"

"Yes, Mr. John. Owing to being kept awake by my rheumatism."

The remorse which had come upon John at the moment when he had first heard the news of the burglary was as nothing to the remorse which racked him now. Just because this fine old man had one of those mild, goofy faces and bleated like a sheep when he talked, he had dismissed him without further thought as a dodderer. And all the time the splendid old fellow, who could not help his face and was surely not to be blamed if age had affected his vocal chords, had been the God from the Machine, sent from heaven to assist him in getting to the bottom of this outrage. There is no known case on record of a man patting a butler on the head, but John at this moment came very near to providing one.

"You saw him!"

"Yes, Mr. John."

"What did he look like?"

"I couldn't say, Mr. John, not really definite."

"Why couldn't you?"

"Because I did not really see him."

"But you said you did."

"Yes, Mr. John, but only in a manner of speaking."

John's new-born cordiality waned a little. His first estimate, he felt, had been right. This was doddering, pure and simple.

"How do you mean, only in a manner of speaking?"

"Well, it was like this, Mr. John . . ."

"Look here," said John. "Tell me the whole thing right from the start."

Sturgis glanced cautiously at the door. When he spoke, it was in a lowered voice, which gave his delivery the effect of a sheep bleating with cotton-wool in its mouth.

"I was awake with my rheumatism last night, Mr. John, and at last it come on so bad I felt I really couldn't hardly bear it no longer. I lay in bed, thinking, and after I had thought for quite some time, Mr. John, it suddenly crossed my mind that Mr. Hugo had once remarked, while kindly interesting himself in my little trouble, that a glassful of whisky, drunk without water, frequently alleviated the pain."

John nodded. So far, the story bore the stamp of truth. A glassful of neat whisky was just what Hugo would have recommended for any complaint, from rheumatism to a broken heart.

"So I thought in the circumstances that Mr. Carmody would not object if I tried a little. So I got out of bed and put on my overcoat, and I had just reached the head of the stairs, it being my intention to go to the cellarette in the dining-room, when what should I hear but a noise."

"What sort of noise?"

"A sort of sneezing noise, Mr. John. As it might be somebody sneezing."

"Yes? Well?"

"I was stottled."

"Stottled? Oh, yes, I see. Well?"

"I remained at the head of the stairs. For quite a while I remained at the head of the stairs. Then I crope . . ."

"You what?"

"I crope to the door of the picture-gallery."

"Oh, I see. Yes?"

"Because the sneezing seemed to have come from there. And then I heard another sneeze. Two or three sneezes, Mr. John. As if whoever was in there had got a nasty cold in the head. And then I heard footsteps coming towards the door."

"What did you do?"

"I went back to the head of the stairs again, sir. If anybody had told me half an hour before that I could have moved so quick I wouldn't have believed him. And then out of the door came a man carrying a bag. He had one of those electric torches. He went down the stairs, but it was only when he was at the bottom that I caught even a glimpse of his face."

"But you did then?"

"Yes, Mr. John, for just a moment. And I was stottled."

"Why? You mean he was somebody you knew?"

The butler lowered his voice again.

"I could have sworn, Mr. John, it was that Doctor Twist who came over here the other day from Healthward Ho."

"Doctor Twist!"

"Yes, Mr. John. I didn't tell the policeman just now, and I wouldn't tell anybody but you, because after all it was only a glimpse, as you might say, and I couldn't swear to it, and there's defamation of character to be considered. So I didn't mention it to Mr. Mould when he was inquiring of me. I said I'd heard nothing, being in my bed at the time. Because, apart from defamation of character and me not being prepared to swear on oath, I wasn't sure how Mr. Carmody would like the idea of my going to the dining-room cellarette even though in agonies of pain. So I'd be much obliged if you would not mention it to him, Mr. John."

"I won't."

"Thank you, sir."

"You'd better leave me to think this over, Sturgis."

"Very good, Mr. John."

"You were quite right to tell me."

"Thank you, Mr. John. Are you coming downstairs to finish your breakfast, sir?"

John waved away the material suggestion.

"No. I want to think."

"Very good, Mr. John."

Left alone, John walked to the window and frowned meditatively out. His brain was now working with a rapidity and clearness which the most professional of detectives might have envied. For the first time since his cousin Hugo had come to him to have his head repaired he began to realize that there might have been something, after all, in that young man's rambling story. Taken in conjunction with what Sturgis had just told him, Hugo's weird tale of finding Doctor Twist burgling the house became significant.

This Twist, now. After all, what about him? He had come from nowhere to settle down in Worcestershire, ostensibly in order to conduct a health-farm. But what if that health-farm were a mere blind for more dastardly work? After all, it was surely a commonplace that your scientific criminal invariably adopted some specious cover of respectability for his crimes. . . .

Into the radius of John's vision there came Mr. Thomas G. Molloy, walking placidly beside the moat with his dashing daughter. It seemed to John as if he had been sent at just this moment for a purpose. What he wanted above all things was a keen-minded, sensible man of the world with whom to discuss these suspicions of his, and who was better qualified for this rôle than Mr. Molloy? Long since he had fallen under the spell of the other's magnetic personality, and had admired the breadth of his intellect. Thomas G. Molloy was, it seemed to him, the ideal confidant.

He left the room hurriedly, and ran down the stairs.

III

Mr. Molloy was still strolling beside the moat when John arrived. He greeted him with his usual bluff kindliness. Soapy, like John some half-hour earlier, was feeling amiably disposed towards all mankind this morning.

"Well, well, well!" said Soapy. "So you're back? Did you have a pleasant time in London?"

"All right, thanks. I wanted to see you. . . ."

"You've heard about this unfortunate business last night?"

"Yes. It was about that. . . ."

"I have never been so upset by anything in my life," said Mr. Molloy. "By pure bad luck Dolly here and myself went over to Birmingham after dinner to see a show, and in our absence the outrage must have occurred. I venture to say," went on Mr. Molloy, a stern look creeping into his eyes, "that if only I'd been on the spot the thing could never have happened. My hearing's good, and I'm pretty quick on a trigger, Mr. Carroll —pretty quick, let me tell you. It would have taken a right smart burglar to have gotten past me."

"You bet it would," said Dolly. "Gee! It's a pity. And the man didn't leave a single trace, did he?"

"A finger-print—or it may have been a thumb-print—on the sill of the window, honey. That was all. And I don't see what good that's going to do us. You can't round up the population of England and ask to see their thumbs."

"And outside of that not so much as a single trace. Isn't it too bad! From start to finish not a soul set eyes on the fellow."

"Yes they did," said John. "That's what I came to talk to you about. One of the servants heard a noise and came out and saw him going down the staircase."

If he had failed up to this point to secure the undivided attention of his audience, he had got it now. Miss Molloy seemed suddenly to become all eyes, and so tremendous was the joy and relief of Mr. Molloy that he actually staggered.

"Saw him?" exclaimed Miss Molloy.

"Sus-saw him?" echoed her father, scarcely able to speak in his delight.

"Yes, Do you by any chance know a man named Twist?"

"Twist?" said Mr. Molloy, still speaking with difficulty. He wrinkled his forehead. "Twist? Do I know a man named Twist, honey?"

"The name seems kind of familiar," admitted Miss Molloy.

"He runs a place called Healthward Ho about twenty miles from here. My uncle stayed there for a couple of weeks. It's a place where people go to get into condition—a sort of health-farm, I suppose you would call it."

"Of course, yes. I have heard Mr. Carmody speak of his friend Twist. But . . ."

"Apparently he called here the other day—to see my uncle, I suppose, and this servant I'm speaking about saw him and is convinced that he was the burglar."

"Improbable, surely?" Mr. Molloy seemed still to be having a little trouble with his breath. "Surely not very probable? This man Twist, from what you tell me, is a personal friend of your uncle. Why, therefore . . . Besides, if he owns a prosperous business . . ."

John was not be be put off the trail by mere superficial argument. Doctor Watson may be slow at starting, but, once started, he is a bloodhound for tenacity.

"I've thought of all that. I admit it did seem curious at first. But if you come to look into it you can see that the very thing a burglar who wanted to operate in these parts would do is to start some business that would make people unsuspicious of him."

Mr. Molloy shook his head.

"It sounds far-fetched to me."

John's opinion of his sturdy good sense began to diminish.

"Well, anyhow," he said in his solid way, "this servant is sure he recognised Twist, and one can't do any harm by going over there and having a look at the man. I've got quite a good excuse for seeing him. My uncle's having a dispute about his bill, and I can say I came over to discuss it."

"Yes," said Mr. Molloy in a strained voice. "But—"

"Sure you can," said Miss Molloy, with sudden animation. "Smart of you to think of that. You need an excuse, if you don't want to make this Twist fellow suspicious."

"Exactly," said John.

He looked at the girl with something resembling approval.

"And there's another thing," proceeded Miss Molloy, warming to her subject. "Don't forget that this bird, if he's the man that did the burgling last night, has a cut finger or thumb. If you find this Twist is going around with sticking-plaster on him, why then that'll be evidence."

John's approval deepened.

"That's a great idea," he agreed. "What I was thinking was that I wanted to find out if Twist has a cold in the head."

"A kuk-kuk-kuk . . .?" said Mr. Molloy.

"Yes. You see, the burglar had. He was sneezing all the time, my informant tells me."

"Well, say, this begins to look like the goods," cried Miss Molloy gleefully. "If this fellow has a cut thumb *and* a cold in the head, there's nothing to it. It's all over except tearing off the false whiskers and saying 'I am Hawkshaw, the Detective!' Say, listen. You get that little car of yours out and you and I will go right over to Healthward Ho, now. You see, if I come along that'll make him all the more unsuspicious. We'll tell him I'm a girl with a brother that's been whooping it up a little too hearty for some time past, and I want to make inquiries with the idea of putting him where he can't get the stuff for awhile. I'm sure you're on the right track. This bird Twist is the villain of the piece, I'll bet a million dollars. As you say, a fellow that wanted to burgle houses in these parts just naturally would settle down and pretend to be something respectable. You go and get that car out, Mr. Carroll, and we'll be off right away."

John reflected. Filled though he was with the enthusiasm of the chase, he could not forget that his time to-day was ear-marked for other and higher things than the investigation of the mysterious Doctor Twist of Healthward Ho.

"I must be back here by a quarter to one," he said.

"Why?"

"I must."

"Well, that's all right. We're not going to spend the week-end with this guy. We're simply going to take a look at him. As soon as we've done that, we come right home and turn the thing over to the police. It's only twenty miles. You'll be back here again before twelve."

"Of course," said John. "You're perfectly right. I'll have the car out in a couple of minutes."

He hurried off. His views concerning Miss Molloy now were definitely favourable. She might not be the sort of girl he could ever like, she might not be the sort of girl he wanted staying at the Hall, but it was idle to deny that she had her redeeming qualities. About her intelligence, for instance, there was, he felt, no doubt whatsoever.

And yet it was with regard to this intelligence that Soapy Molloy was at this very moment entertaining doubts of the gravest kind. His eyes were protruding a little, and he uttered an odd, strangled sound.

"It's all right, you poor sap," said Dolly, meeting his shocked gaze with a confident unconcern.

Soapy found speech.

"All right? You say it's all right? How's it all right? If you hadn't pulled all that stuff . . ."

"Say, listen!" said Dolly urgently. "Where's your sense? He would have gone over to see Chimp anyway, wouldn't he? Nothing we could have done would have headed him off from that, would it? And he'd have noticed Chimp had a cut finger, without my telling him, wouldn't he? All I've done is to make him think I'm on the level and working in cahoots with him."

"What's the use of that?"

"I'll tell you what use it is. I know what I'm doing. Listen, Soapy, you just race into the house and get those knock-out drops and give them to me. And make it snappy," said Dolly.

As when on a day of rain and storm there appears among the clouds a tiny gleam of blue, so now, at those magic words "knock-out drops", did there flicker into Mr. Molloy's sombre face a faint suggestion of hope.

"Don't you worry, Soapy. I've got this thing well in hand. When we've gone, you jump to the 'phone and get Chimp on the wire and tell him this guy and I are on our way over. Tell him I'm bringing the kayo drops and I'll slip them to him as soon as I arrive. Tell him to be sure to have something to drink handy and to see that this bird gets a taste of it."

"I get you, pettie!" Mr. Molloy's manner was full of a sort of awe-struck reverence, like that of some humble adherent of Napoleon listening to his great leader outlining plans for a forthcoming campaign; but nevertheless it was tinged with doubt. He had always admired his wife's broad, spacious out-look, but she was apt sometimes, he considered, in her fresh young enthusiasm, to overlook details. "But, pettie," he said, "is this wise? Don't forget you're not in Chicago now. I mean, supposing you do put this fellow to sleep, he's going to wake up pretty soon, isn't he? And when he does won't he raise an awful holler?"

"I've got that all fixed. I don't know what sort of staff Chimp keeps over at that joint of his, but he's probably got assistants and all like that. Well, you tell him to tell them that there's a young lady coming over with a brother that wants looking after, and this brother has got to be given a sleeping-draught and locked away somewhere to keep him from getting violent and doing somebody an injury. That'll get him out of the way long enough for us to collect the stuff and clear out. It's rapid action now, Soapy. Now that Chimp has gummed the game by letting himself be seen we've got to move quick. We've got to make our getaway to-day. So don't you go off wandering about the fields picking daisies after I've gone. You stick round that 'phone, because I'll be calling you before long. See?"

"Honey," said Mr. Molloy devoutly, "I always said you were the brains of the firm, and I always will say it. I'd never have thought of a thing like this myself in a million years."

IV

It was about an hour later that Sergeant-Major Flannery, seated at his ease beneath a shady elm in the garden of Healthward Ho, looked up from the novelette over which he had been relaxing his conscientious mind and became aware that he was in the presence of Youth and Beauty. Towards him, across the lawn, was walking a girl who, his experienced eye assured him at a single glance, fell into that limited division of the Sex which is embraced by the word Pippin. Her willowy figure was clothed in some clinging material of a beige colour, and her bright hazel eyes, when she came close enough for them to be seen, touched in the Sergeant-Major's susceptible bosom a ready chord. He rose from his seat with easy grace, and his hand, falling from the salute, came to rest on the western section of his waxed moustache.

"Nice morning, Miss," he bellowed.

It seemed to Sergeant-Major Flannery that this girl was gazing upon him as on some wonderful dream of hers that had unexpectedly come true, and he was thrilled. It was unlikely, he felt, that she was about to ask him to perform some great knightly service for her, but if she did he would spring smartly to attention and do it in a soldierly manner while she waited. Sergeant-Major Flannery was pro-Dolly from the first moment of their meeting.

"Are you one of Doctor Twist's assistants?" asked Dolly.

"I am his only assistant, Miss. Sergeant-Major Flannery is the name."

"Oh? Then you look after the patients here?"

"That's right, Miss."

"Then it is you who will be in charge of my poor brother?" She uttered a little sigh, and there came into her hazel eyes a look of pain.

"Your brother, Miss? Are you the lady . . ."

"Did Doctor Twist tell you about my brother?"

"Yes, Miss. The fellow who's been . . ."

He paused, appalled. Only by a hair's-breadth had he stopped himself from using in the presence of this divine creature the hideous expression "mopping it up a bit".

"Yes," said Dolly. "I see you know about it."

"All I know about it, Miss," said Sergeant-Major Flannery, "is that the doctor had me into the orderly-room just now and said he was expecting a young lady to arrive with her brother, who needed attention. He said I wasn't to be surprised if I found myself called for to lend a hand in a rough-house, because this bloke—because this patient was apt to get verlent."

"My brother does get very violent," sighed Dolly. "I only hope he won't do you an injury."

Sergeant-Major Flannery twitched his banana-like fingers and inflated his powerful chest. He smiled a complacent smile.

"He won't do *me* an injury, Miss. I've had experience with . . ." Again he stopped just in time, on the very verge of shocking his companion's ears with the ghastly noun "souses" . . . "with these sort of nervous cases," he amended. "Besides, the doctor says he's going to give the gentleman a little sleeping-draught, which'll keep him as you might say 'armless till he wakes up and finds himself under lock and key."

"I see. Yes, that's a very good idea."

"No sense in troubling trouble till trouble troubles you, as the saying is, Miss," agreed the Sergeant-Major. "If you can do a thing in a nice, easy, tactful manner without verlence, then why use verlence? Has the gentleman been this way long, Miss?"

"For years."

"You ought to have had him in a home sooner."

"I have put him into dozens of homes. But he always gets out. That's why I'm so worried."

"He won't get out of Healthward Ho, Miss."

"He's very clever."

It was on the tip of Sergeant-Major Flannery's tongue to point out that other people were clever, too, but he refrained, not so much from modesty as because at this moment he swallowed some sort of insect. When he had finished coughing he found that his companion had passed on to another aspect of the matter.

"I left him alone with Doctor Twist. I wonder if that was safe."

"Quite safe, Miss," the Sergeant-Major assured her. "You can see the window's open and the room's on the ground floor. If there's trouble and the gentleman starts any verlence, all the doctor's got to do is to shout for 'elp and I'll get to the spot at the double and climb in and lend a hand."

His visitor regarded him with a shy admiration.

"It's such a relief to feel that there's someone like you here, Mr. Flannery. I'm sure you are wonderful in any kind of an emergency."

"People have said so, Miss," replied the Sergeant-Major, stroking his moustache and smiling another quiet smile.

"But what's worrying me is what's going to happen when my brother comes to after the sleeping-draught and finds that he is locked-up. That's what I meant just now when I said he was so clever. The last place he was in they promised to see that he stayed there, but he talked them into letting him out. He said he belonged to some big family in the neighbourhood and had been shut up by mistake."

"He won't get round *me* that way, Miss."

"Are you sure?"

"Quite sure, Miss. If there's one thing you get used to in a place like this, it's artfulness. You wouldn't believe how artful some of these gentlemen can be. Only yesterday that Admiral Sir Rigby-Rudd toppled over in my presence after doing his bending and stretching exercises and said he felt faint and he was afraid it was his heart and would I go and get him a drop of brandy. Anything like the way he carried on when I just poured half a bucketful of cold water down his back instead, you never heard in your life. I'm on the watch all the time, I can tell you, Miss. I wouldn't trust my own mother if she was in here, taking the cure. And it's no use arguing with them and pointing out to them that they came here voluntarily of their own free will, and are paying big money to be exercised and kept away from wines, spirits, and rich food. They just spend their whole time thinking up ways of being artful."

"Do they ever try to bribe you?"

"No, Miss," said Mr. Flannery, a little wistfully. "I suppose they take a look at me and think—and see that I'm not the sort of fellow that would take bribes."

"My brother is sure to offer you money to let him go.'"

"How much—how much good," said Sergeant-Major Flannery carefully, "does he think that's going to do him?"

"You wouldn't take it, would you?"

"Who, me, Miss? Take money to betray my trust, if you understand the expression?"

"Whatever he offers you, I will double. You see, it's so very important that he is kept here, where he will be safe from temptation, Mr. Flannery," said Dolly, timidly, "I wish you would accept this."

The Sergeant-Major felt a quickening of the spirit as he gazed upon the rustling piece of paper in her hand.

"No, no, miss," he said, taking it. "It really isn't necessary."

"I know. But I would rather you had it. You see, I'm afraid my brother may give you a lot of trouble."

"Trouble's what I'm here for, Miss," said Mr. Flannery bravely. "Trouble's what I draw my salary for. Besides, he can't give much trouble when he's under lock and key, as the saying is. Don't you worry, Miss. We're going to make this brother of yours a different man. We . . ."

"Oh!" cried Dolly.

A head and shoulders had shot suddenly out of the study window—the head and shoulders of Doctor Twist. The voice of Doctor Twist sounded sharply above the droning of bees and insects.

"Flannery!"

"On the spot, sir."

"Come here, Flannery. I want you."

"You stay here, Miss," counselled Sergeant-Major Flannery paternally. "There may be verlence."

V

There were, however, when Dolly made her way to the study some five minutes later, no signs of anything of an exciting and boisterous nature having occurred recently in the room. The table was unbroken, the carpet unruffled. The chairs stood in their places, and not even a picture-glass had been cracked. It was evident that the operations had proceeded according to plan, and that matters had been carried through in what Sergeant-Major Flannery would have termed a nice, easy, tactful manner.

"Everything jake?" inquired Dolly.

"Uh-huh," said Chimp, speaking, however, in a voice that quavered a little.

Mr. Twist was the only object in the room that looked in any way disturbed. He had turned an odd greenish colour, and from time to time he swallowed uneasily. Although he had spent a lifetime outside the law, Chimp Twist was essentially a man of peace and accustomed to look askance at any by-product of his profession that seemed to him to come under the heading of rough stuff. This doping of respectable visitors, he considered, was distinctly so to be classified; and only Mr. Molloy's urgency over the telephone wire had persuaded him to the task. He was nervous and apprehensive, in a condition to start at sudden noises.

"What happened?"

"Well, I did what Soapy said. After you left us the guy and I talk back and forth for awhile, and then I agreed to knock a bit off the old man's bill, and then I said 'How about a little drink?' and then we have a little drink, and then I slip the stuff you gave me in while he wasn't looking. It didn't seem like it was going to act at first."

"It don't. It takes a little time. You don't feel nothing till you jerk your head or move yourself, and then it's like as if somebody has beaned you one with an iron girder or something. So they tell me," said Dolly.

"I guess he must have jerked his head, then. Because all of a sudden he went down and out," Chimp gulped. "You—you don't think he's . . . I mean, you're sure this stuff . . . ?"

Dolly had nothing but contempt for these masculine tremors.

"Of course. Do you suppose I go about the place croaking people? He's all right."

"Well, he didn't look it. If I'd been a life-insurance company I'd have paid up on him without a yip."

"He'll wake up with a headache in a little while, but outside of that he'll be as well as he ever was. Where have you been all your life that you don't know how kayo drops act?"

"I've never had occasion to be connected with none of this raw work before," said Chimp virtuously. "If you'd of seen him when he slumped down on the table, you wouldn't be feeling so good yourself, maybe. If ever I saw a guy that looked like he was qualified to step straight into a coffin, he was him."

"Aw, be yourself, Chimp!"

"I'm being myself all right, all right."

"Well, then, for Pete's sake, be somebody else. Pull yourself together, why can't you? Have a drink."

"Ah!" said Mr. Twist, struck with the idea.

His hand was still shaking, but he accomplished the delicate task of mixing a whisky and soda without disaster.

"What did you with the remains?" asked Dolly, interested.

Mr. Twist, who had been raising the glass to his lips, lowered it again. He disapproved of levity of speech at such a moment.

"Would you kindly not call him 'the remains'," he begged. "It's all very well for you to be so easy about it all and to pull this stuff about him doing nothing but wake up with a headache, but what I'm asking myself is, will he wake up at all?"

"Oh, cut it out! Sure, he'll wake up."

"But will it be in this world?"

"You drink that up, you poor dumb-bell, and then fix yourself another," advised Dolly. "And make it a bit stronger next time. You seem to need it."

Mr. Twist did as directed, and found the treatment beneficial.

"You've nothing to grumble at," Dolly proceeded, still looking on the bright side. "What with all this excitement and all, you seem to have lost that cold of yours."

"That's right," said Chimp, impressed. "It does seem to have got a whole lot better."

"Pity you couldn't have got rid of it a little earlier. Then e wouldn't have had all this trouble. From what I can make of , you seem to have roused the house by sneezing your head off, nd a bunch of the help come and stood looking over the banisters t you."

Chimp tottered.

"You don't mean somebody saw me last night?"

"Sure they saw you. Didn't Soapy tell you that over the ire?"

"I could hardly make out all Soapy was saying over the wire. ay! What are we going to do?"

"Don't you worry. We've done it. The only difficult part is ver. Now that we've fixed the remains. . . ."

"Will you please . . .!"

"Well, call him what you like. Now that we've fixed that uy the thing's simple. By the way, what did you do with im?"

"Flannery took him upstairs."

"Where to?"

"There's a room on the top floor. Must have been a nursery r something, I guess. Anyway, there's bars to the window."

"How's the door?"

"Good solid oak. You've got to hand it to the guys who uilt these old English houses. They knew their groceries. Vhen they spit on their hands and set to work to make a door, hey made one. You couldn't push that door down, not if you vas an elephant."

"Well, that's all right, then. Now, listen, Chimp. Here's the w-down. We . . ." She broke off. "What's that?"

"What's what?" asked Mr. Twist, starting violently.

"I thought I heard someone outside in the corridor. Go and ook."

With an infinite caution born of alarm, Mr. Twist crept across he floor, reached the door and flung it open. The passage was mpty. He looked up and down it, and Dolly, whose fingers ad hovered for an instant over the glass which he had left n the table, sat back with an air of content.

"My mistake," she said. "I thought I heard something."

Chimp returned to the table. He was still much perturbed.

"I wish I'd never gone into this thing," he said with a sudden ush of self-pity. "I felt all along, what with seeing that magpie nd the new moon through glass. . . ."

"Now, listen!" said Dolly vigorously. "Considering you'v
stood Soapy and me up for practically all there is in thi
thing except a little small change, I'll ask you kindly, i
you don't mind, not to stand there beefing and expectin
me to hold your hand and pat you on the head and
be a second mother to you. You came into this busines
because you wanted to. You're getting sixty-five per cent
of the gross. So what's biting you? You're all right—s
far."

It was in Mr. Twist's mind to inquire of his companio
precisely what she meant by this expression, but more urgen
matters claimed his attention. More even than the exact in
terpretation of the phrase "so far", he wished to know what th
next move was.

"What happens now?" he asked.

"We go back to Rudge."

"And collect the stuff?"

"Yes. And then make our getaway."

No programme could have outlined more admirably Mr
Twist's own desires. The mere contemplation of it heartene
him. He snatched his glass from the table and drained it with
gesture almost swashbuckling.

"Soapy will have doped the old man by this time, eh?"

"That's right."

"But suppose he hasn't been able to?" said Mr. Twist with
return of his old nervousness. "Suppose he hasn't had a
opportunity?"

"You can always find an opportunity of doping people. Yo
ought to know that."

The implied compliment pleased Chimp.

"That's right," he chuckled.

He nodded his head complacently. And immediately some
thing which may have been an iron girder or possibly the ceiling
and the upper parts of the house seemed to strike him on th
base of the skull. He had been standing by the table, and now
crumpling at the knees, he slid gently down to the floor. Dolly
regarding him, recognized instantly what he had meant jus
now when he had spoken of John appearing like a total loss t
his life-insurance company. The best you could have said o
Alexander Twist at this moment was that he looked peaceful
She drew in her breath a little sharply, and then, being a woma

t heart, took a cushion from the arm-chair and placed it beneath
is head.

Only then did she go to the telephone and in a gentle voice
.sk the operator to connect her with Rudge Hall.

"Soapy?"

"Hello!"

The promptitude with which the summons of the bell
aad been answered brought a smile of approval to her lips.
Soapy, she felt, must have been sitting with his head on the
eceiver.

"Listen, sweetie."

"I'm listening, pettie!"

"Everything's set."

"Have you fixed that guy?"

"Sure, precious. And Chimp, too."

"How's that? Chimp?"

"Sure. We don't want Chimp around, do we, with that sixty-
five—thirty-five stuff of his? I just slipped a couple of drops
into his high-ball and he's gone off as peaceful as a lamb. Say,
wait a minute," she added, as the wire hummed with Mr.
Molloy's low-voiced congratulations. "Hello!" she said, returning.

"What were you doing, honey? Did you hear somebody?"

"No. I caught sight of a bunch of lilies in a vase, and I just
slipped across and put one of them in Chimp's hand. Made it
seem more sort of natural. Now listen, Soapy. Everything's
clear for you at your end now, so go right ahead and clean up.
I'm going to beat it in that guy Carroll's runabout, and I haven't
much time, so don't start talking about the weather or nothing.
I'm going to London, to the Belvedere. You collect the stuff
and meet me there. Is that all straight?"

"But, pettie!"

"Now what?"

"How am I to get the stuff away?"

"For goodness sake! You can drive a car, can't you? Old
Carmody's car was outside the stable-yard when I left. I guess
it's there still. Get the stuff and then go and tell the chauffeur
that old Carmody wants to see him. Then, when he's gone,
climb in and drive to Birmingham. Leave the car outside
the station and take a train. That's simple enough, isn't
it?"

There was a long pause. Admiration seemed to have deprived Mr. Molloy of speech.

"Honey," he said at length, in a hushed voice, "when it comes to the real smooth stuff you're there every time. Let me just tell you . . ."

"All right, baby," said Dolly. "Save it till later, I'm in a hurry."

★ 10 ★

Activity of Soapy Molloy

I

SOAPY MOLLOY replaced the receiver, and came out of the telephone-cupboard glowing with the resolve to go right ahead and clean up as his helpmeet had directed. Like all good husbands, he felt that his wife was an example and an inspiration to him. Mopping his fine forehead, for it had been warm in the cupboard with the door shut, he stood for awhile and mused, sketching out in his mind a plan of campaign.

The prudent man, before embarking on any enterprise which may at a moment's notice necessitate his skipping away from a given spot like a scalded cat, will always begin by preparing his lines of retreat. Mr. Molloy's first act was to go to the stable-yard in order to ascertain with his own eyes that the Dex-Mayo was still there.

It was. It stood out on the gravel, simply waiting for someone to spring to its wheel and be off.

So far, so good. But how far actually was it? The really difficult part of the operations, Mr. Molloy could not but recognize, still lay before him. The knock-out drops nestled in his waistcoat pocket all ready for use, but in order to bring about the happy ending it was necessary for him, like some conjuror doing a trick, to transfer them thence to the interior of Mr. Lester Carmody. And little by little, chilling his enthusiasm, there crept upon Soapy the realization that he had not a notion how the deuce this was to be done.

The whole question of administering knock-out drops to a fellow-creature is a very delicate and complex one. So much depends on the co-operation of the party of the second part. Before you can get anything in the nature of action, your victim must first be induced to start drinking something. At Healthward Ho, Soapy had gathered from the recent telephone conversation,

167

no obstacles had arisen. The thing had been, apparently, from the start a sort of jolly carousal. But at Rudge Hall, it was plain, matters were not going to be nearly so simple.

When you are a guest in a man's house, you cannot very well go about thrusting drinks on your host at half-past eleven in the morning. Probably Mr. Carmody would not think of taking liquid refreshment till lunch-time, and then there would be a butler in and out of the room all the while. Besides, lunch would not be for another two hours or more, and the whole essence of this enterprise was that it should be put through swiftly and at once.

Mr. Molloy groaned in spirit. He wandered forth into the garden, turning the problem over in his mind with growing desperation, and had just come to the conclusion that he was mentally unequal to it, when, reaching the low wall that bordered the moat, he saw a sight which sent the blood coursing joyously through his veins once more—a sight which made the world a thing of sunshine and bird-song again.

Out in the middle of the moat lay the punt. In the punt sat Mr. Carmody. And in Mr. Carmody's hand was a fishing-rod.

Æsthetically considered, wearing as he did a pink shirt and a slouch hat which should long ago have been given to the deserving poor, Mr. Carmody was not much of a spectacle, but Soapy, eyeing him, felt that he had never beheld anything lovelier. He was not a fisherman himself, but he knew all about fishermen. They became, he was aware, when engaged on their favourite pursuit, virtually monomaniacs. Earthquakes might occur in their immediate neighbourhood, dynasties fall and pestilences ravage the land, but they would just go on fishing. As long as the bait held out, Lester Carmody, sitting in that punt, was for all essential purposes as good as if he had been crammed to the brim with the finest knockout drops. It was as though he were in another world.

Exhilaration filled Soapy like a tonic.

"Any luck?" he shouted.

"Wah, wah, wah," replied Mr. Carmody inaudibly.

"Stick to it," cried Soapy. " 'Atta-boy!"

With an encouraging wave of the hand he hurried back to the house. The problem which a moment before had seemed to defy solution had now become so simple and easy that a child

~ould have negotiated it—any child, that is to say, capable of
_ulding a hatchet and endowed with sufficient strength to break a
cupboard door with it.

"I'm telling the birds, telling the bees," sang Soapy gaily,
charging into the hall, "Telling the flowers, telling the trees how
I love you . . ."

"Sir?" said Sturgis respectfully, suddenly becoming manifest
out of the infinite.

Soapy gazed at the butler blankly, his wild woodnotes dying
away in a guttural gurgle. Apart from the embarrassment which
always comes upon a man when caught singing, he was feeling,
as Sturgis himself would have put it, stottled. A moment before,
the place had been completely free from butlers, and where this
one could have come from was more than he could understand.
Rudge Hall's old retainer did not look the sort of man who
would pop up through traps, but there seemed no other explanation of his presence.

And then, close to the cupboard door, Soapy espied another
door, covered with green baize. This, evidently, was the Sturgis
bolt-hole.

"Nothing," he said.

"I thought you called, sir."

"No."

"Lovely day, sir."

"Beautiful," said Soapy.

He gazed bulgily at this inconvenient old fossil. Once more,
shadows had fallen about his world, and he was brooding again
on the deep gulf that is fixed between artistic conception and
detail-work.

The broad artistic conception of breaking open the cupboard
door and getting away with the swag while Mr. Carmody,
anchored out on the moat, dabbled for bream or dibbled for
chub or sniggled for eels or whatever weak-minded thing it is
that fishermen do when left to themselves in the middle of a
sheet of water, was magnificent. It was bold, dashing, big in
every sense of the word. Only when you came to inspect it in
detail did it occur to you that it might also be a little noisy.

That was the fatal flaw—the noise. The more Soapy examined
the scheme, the more clearly did he see that it could not be
carried through in even comparative quiet. And the very first
blow of the hammer or axe or chisel selected for the operation

must inevitably bring Methuselah's little brother popping through that green baize door, full of inquiries.

"Hell!" said Soapy.

"Sir?"

"Nothing," said Soapy. "I was just thinking."

He continued to think, and to such effect that before long he had begun to see daylight. There is no doubt that in time of stress the human mind has an odd tendency to take off its coat and roll up its sleeves and generally spread itself in a spasm of unwonted energy. Probably if this thing had been put up to Mr. Molloy as an academic problem over the nuts and wine after dinner, he would have had to confess himself baffled. Now, however, with such vital issues at stake, it took him but a few minutes to reach the conclusion that what he required, as he could not break open a cupboard door in silence, was some plausible reason for making a noise.

He followed up this line of thought. A noise of smashing wood. In what branch of human activity may a man smash wood blamelessly? The answer is simple. When he is doing carpentering. What sort of carpentering? Why, making something. What? Oh, anything. Yes, but what? Well, say for example a rabbit-hutch. But why a rabbit-hutch? Well, a man might very easily have a daughter who, in her girlish, impulsive way, had decided to keep pet rabbits, mightn't he? There actually were pet rabbits on the Rudge Hall estate, weren't there? Certainly there were. Soapy had seen them down at one of the lodges.

The thing began to look good. It only remained to ascertain whether Sturgis was the right recipient for this kind of statement. The world may be divided broadly into two classes—men who will believe you when you suddenly inform them at half-past eleven on a summer morning that you propose to start making rabbit-hutches, and men who will not. Sturgis looked as if he belonged to the former and far more likeable class. He looked, indeed, like a man who would believe anything.

"Say!" said Soapy.

"Sir?"

"My daughter wants me to make her a rabbit-hutch."

"Indeed, sir?"

Soapy felt relieved. There had been no incredulity in the other's gaze—on the contrary, something that looked very much

ike a sort of senile enthusiasm. He had the air of a butler who
as heard good news from home.

"Have you got such a thing as a packing-case or a sugar-box
r something like that? And a hatchet?"

"Yes, sir."

"Then fetch them along."

"Very good, sir."

The butler disappeared through his green baize door, and
Soapy, to fill in the time of waiting, examined the cupboard.
t appeared to be a very ordinary sort of cupboard, the kind that
resolute man can open with one well-directed blow. Soapy
elt complacent. Though primarily a thinker, it pleased him to
eel that he could be the man of action when the occasion called.

There was a noise of bumping without. Sturgis reappeared,
acking-case in one hand, hatchet in the other, looking like
Noah taking ship's stores aboard the Ark.

"Here they are, sir."

"Thanks."

"I used to keep roberts when I was a lad, sir," said the butler.
Oh, dear, yes. Many's the robert I've made a pet of in my time.
Roberts and white mice, those were what I was fondest of. And
ewts in a little aquarium."

He leaned easily against the wall, beaming, and Soapy, with
eep concern, became aware that the Last of the Great Victorians
roposed to make this thing a social gathering. He appeared to
e regarding Soapy as the nucleus of a salon.

"Don't let me keep you," said Soapy.

"You aren't keeping me, sir," the butler assured him. "Oh,
o, sir, you aren't keeping me. I've done my silver. It will be a
leasure to watch you, sir. Quite likely I can give you a hint
r two if you've never made a robert-hutch before. Many's
he hutch I've made in my time. As a lad, I was very handy at
aat sort of thing."

A dull despair settled upon Soapy. It was plain to him now
nat he had unwittingly delivered himself over into the clutches
f a bore who had probably been pining away for someone on
hom to pour out his wealth of stored-up conversation. Words
ad begun to flutter out of this butler like bats out of a barn.
He had become a sort of human Topical Talk on rabbits. He
as speaking of rabbits he had known in his hot youth—their
anners, customs and the amount of lettuce they had consumed

per diem. To a man interested in rabbits but too lazy to loo
the subject up in the Encyclopaedia the narrative would hav
been enthralling. It induced in Soapy a feverishness that touche
the skirts of homicidal mania. The thought came into his min
that there are other uses to which a hatchet may be put beside
the making of rabbit-hutches. England trembled on the verg
of being short one butler.

Sturgis had now become involved in a long story of his earl
manhood, and even had Soapy been less distrait he might hav
found it difficult to enjoy it to the full. It was about an acquaint
ance of his who had kept rabbits, and it suffered in lucidit
from his unfortunate habit of pronouncing rabbits 'roberts
combined with the fact that by a singular coincidence the ac
quaintance had been a Mr. Roberts. Roberts, it seemed, ha
been deeply attached to roberts. In fact, his practice of keepin
roberts in his bedroom had led to trouble with Mrs. Robert
and in the end Mrs. Roberts had drowned the roberts in th
pond and Roberts, who thought the world of his roberts an
not quite so highly of Mrs. Roberts, had never forgiven her.

Here Sturgis paused, apparently for comment.

"Is that so?" said Soapy, breathing heavily.

"Yes, sir."

"In the pond?"

"In the pond, sir."

Like some Open Sesame, the word suddenly touched a chor
in Soapy's mind.

"Say, listen," he said. "All the while we've been talking
was forgetting that Mr. Carmody is out there on the pond."

"The moat, sir?"

"Call it what you like. Anyway, he's there, fishing, and h
told me to tell you to take him out something to drink."

Immediately, Sturgis, the lecturer, with a change almo
startling in its abruptness, became Sturgis, the butler, onc
more. The fanatic rabbit-gleam died out of his eyes.

"Very good, sir."

"I should hurry. His tongue was hanging out when I le
him."

For an instant the butler wavered. The words had recalle
to his mind a lop-eared doe which he had once owned, whos
habit of putting out its tongue and gasping had been the cause c
some concern to him in the late 'seventies. But he recovere

himself. Registering a mental resolve to seek out this new-made friend of his later and put the complete facts before him, he passed through the green baize door.

Soapy, alone at last, did not delay. With all the pent up energy which had been accumulating within him during a quarter of an hour which had seemed a lifetime, he swung the hatchet and brought it down. The panel splintered. The lock snapped. The door swung open.

There was an electric switch inside the cupboard. He pressed it down and was able to see clearly. And, having seen clearly, he drew back, his lips trembling with half-spoken words of the regrettable kind which a man picks up in the course of a lifetime spent in the less refined social circles of New York, Philadelphia and Chicago.

The cupboard contained an old rain-coat, two hats, a rusty golf-club, six croquet balls, a pamphlet on stock-breeding, three umbrellas, a copy of the Parish Magazine for the preceding November, a shoe, a mouse, and a smell of apples, but no suit-case.

That much Soapy had been able to see in the first awful, disintegrating instant.

No bag, box, portmanteau or suitcase of any kind or description whatsoever.

II

Hope does not readily desert the human breast. After the first numbing impact of any shock, we most of us have a tendency to try to persuade ourselves that things may not be so bad as they seem. Some explanation, we feel, will be forthcoming shortly, putting the whole matter in a different light. And so, after a few moments during which he stood petrified, muttering some of the comments which on the face of it the situation seemed to demand, Soapy cheered up a little.

He had had, he reflected, no opportunity of private speech with his host this morning. If Mr. Carmody had decided to change his plans and deposit the suitcase in some other hiding-place he might have done so in quite good faith without Soapy's knowledge. For all he knew, in mentally labelling Mr. Carmody a fat, pop-eyed, crooked, swindling, pie-faced, double-crossing

Judas, he might be doing him an injustice. Feeling calmer though still anxious, he left the house and started towards the moat.

Half-way down the garden, he encounted Sturgis, returning with an empty tray.

"You must have misunderstood Mr. Carmody, sir," said the butler, genially, as one rabbit-fancier to another. "He says he did not ask for any drink. But he came ashore and had it. If you're looking for him, you will find him in the boathouse."

And in the boathouse Mr. Carmody was, lolling at his ease on the cushions of the punt, sipping the contents of a long glass.

"Hullo," said Mr. Carmody. "There you are."

Soapy descended the steps. What he had to say was not the kind of thing a prudent man shouts at long range.

"Say!" said Soapy in a cautious undertone. "I've been trying to get a word with you all the morning. But that darned policeman was around all the time."

"Something on your mind?" said Mr. Carmody affably. "I've caught two perch, a bream and a grayling," he added, finishing the contents of his glass with a good deal of relish.

Such was the condition of Soapy's nervous system that he very nearly damned the perch, the bream and the grayling, in the order named. But he checked himself in time. If ever, he felt, there was a moment when diplomacy was needed, this was it.

"Listen," he said, "I've been thinking."

"Yes?"

"I've been wondering if, after all, that closet you were going to put the stuff in is a safe place. Somebody might be apt to take a look in it. Maybe," said Soapy, tensely, "that occurred to you?"

"What makes you think that?"

"It just crossed my mind."

"Oh? I thought perhaps you might have been having a look in that cupboard yourself."

Soapy moistened his lips, which had become uncomfortably dry.

"But you locked it, surely?" he said.

"Yes, I locked it," said Mr. Carmody. "But it struck me that after you had got the butler out of the way by telling him to bring me a drink, you might have thought of breaking the door open."

In the silence which followed this devastating remark there suddenly made itself heard an odd, gurgling noise like a leaking cistern, and Soapy, gazing at his host, was shocked to observe that he had given himself up to an apoplectic spasm of laughter. Mr. Carmody's rotund body was quivering like a jelly. His eyes were closed, and he was rocking himself to and fro. And from his lips proceeded those hideous sounds of mirth.

The hope which until this moment had been sustaining Soapy had never been a strong, robust hope. From birth it had been an invalid. And now, as he listened to this laughter, the poor, sickly thing coughed quietly and died.

"Oh dear!" said Mr. Carmody, recovering. "Very funny. Very funny."

"You think it's funny, do you?" said Soapy.

"I do," said Mr. Carmody sincerely. "I wish I could have seen your face when you looked in that cupboard."

Soapy had nothing to say. He was beaten, crushed, routed, and he knew it. He stared out hopelessly on a bleak world. Outside the boathouse the sun was still shining, but not for Soapy.

"I've seen through you all along, my man," proceeded Mr. Carmody, with ungenerous triumph. "Not from the very beginning, perhaps, because I really did suppose for a while that you were what you professed to be. The first thing that made me suspicious was when I cabled over to New York to make inquiries about a well-known financier named Thomas G. Molloy and was informed that no such person existed."

Soapy did not speak. The bitterness of his meditations precluded words. His eyes were fixed on the trees and flowers on the other side of the water, and he was disliking these very much. Nature had done its best for the scene, and he thought Nature a washout.

"And then," proceeded Mr. Carmody, "I listened outside the study window while you and your friends were having your little discussion. And I heard all I wanted to hear. Next time you have one of these board-meetings of yours, Mr. Molloy, I suggest that you close the window and lower your voices."

"Yeah?" said Soapy.

It was not, he was forced himself to admit, much of a retort, but it was the best he could think of. He was in the depths, and men who are in the depths seldom excel in the matter of rapier-like repartee.

"I thought the matter over, and decided that my best plan was to allow matters to proceed. I was disappointed, of course, to discover that that cheque of yours for a million or two million or whatever it was would not be coming my way. But," said Mr. Carmody philosophically, "there is always the insurance money. It should amount to a nice little sum. Not what a man like you, accustomed to big transactions with Mr. Schwab and Pierpont Morgan, would call much, of course, but quite satis-factory to me."

"You think so?" said Soapy, goaded to speech. "You think you're going to clean up on the insurance?"

"I do."

"Then, say, listen, let me tell you something. The insurance company is going to send a fellow down to inquire, isn't it? Well, what's to prevent me spilling the beans?"

"I beg your pardon?"

"What's to keep me from telling him the burglary was a put-up job?"

Mr. Carmody smiled tranquilly.

"Your good sense, I should imagine. How could you make such a story credible without involving yourself in more un-pleasantness than I should imagine you would desire? I think I shall be able to rely on you for sympathetic silence, Mr. Molloy."

"Yeah?"

"I think so."

And Soapy, reflecting, thought so, too, For the process of beans-spilling to be enjoyable, he realized, the conditions have to be right.

"I am offering a little reward," said Mr. Carmody, gently urging the punt out into the open, "just to make everything seem more natural. One thousand pounds is the sum I am proposing to give for the recovery of this stolen property. You had better try for that. Well, I must not keep you here all the morning, chattering away like this. No doubt you have much to do."

The punt floated out into the sunshine, and the roof of the boathouse hid this fat, conscienceless man from Soapy's eyes. From somewhere out in the great open spaces beyond came the sound of a paddle, wielded with a care-free joyousness. Whatever might be his guest's state of mind, Mr. Carmody was plainly in the pink.

Soapy climbed the steps listlessly. The interview had left him weak and shaken. He brooded dully on this revelation of the inky depths of Lester Carmody's soul. It seemed to him that if this was what England's upper classes (who ought to be setting an example) were like, Great Britain could not hope to continue much longer as a first-class power, and it gave him in his anguish a little satisfaction to remember that in years gone by his ancestors had thrown off Britain's yoke. Beyond burning his eyebrows one Fourth of July, when a boy, with a maroon that exploded prematurely, he had never thought much about this affair before, but now he was conscious of a glow of patriotic fervour. If General Washington had been present at that moment Soapy would have shaken hands with him.

Soapy wandered aimlessly through the sunlit garden. The little spurt of consolation caused by the reflection that some hundred and fifty years previously the United States of America had severed relations with a country which was to produce a man like Lester Carmody had long since ebbed away, leaving emptiness behind it. He was feeling very low, and in urgent need of one of those largely advertised tonics which claim to relieve Anaemia, Brain-Fag, Lassitude, Anxiety, Palpitations, Faintness, Melancholia, Exhaustion, Neurasthenia, Muscular Limpness and Depression of Spirits. For he had got them all, especially brain-fag and melancholia; and the sudden appearance of Sturgis, fluttering towards him down the gravel path, provided nothing in the nature of a cure.

He felt that he had had all he wanted of the butler's conversation. Even of the most stimulating society enough is enough, and to Soapy about half a minute of Sturgis seemed a good medium dose for an adult. He would have fled, but there was nowhere to go. He remained where he was, making his expression as forbidding as possible. A motion-picture director could have read that expression like a book. Soapy was registering deep disinclination to talk about rabbits.

But for the moment, it appeared, Sturgis had put rabbits on one side. Other matters occupied his mind.

"I beg your pardon, sir," he said, "but have you seen Mr. John?"

"Mr. who?"

"Mr. John, sir."

So deep was Soapy's preoccupation that for a moment the name conveyed nothing to him.

"Mr. Carmody's nephew, sir. Mr. Carroll."

"Oh? Yes, he went off in his car with my daughter."

"Will he be gone long, do you think, sir?"

Soapy could answer that one.

"Yes," he said. "He won't be back for some time."

"You see, when I took Mr. Carmody his drink, sir, he told me to tell Bolt, the chauffeur, to give me the ticket."

"What ticket?" asked Soapy wearily.

The butler was only too glad to reply. He had feared that this talk of theirs might be about to end all too quickly, and these explanations helped to prolong it. And, now that he knew that there was no need to go on searching for John, his time was his own again.

"It was a ticket for a bag which Mr. Carmody sent Bolt to leave at the cloak-room at Shrub Hill station, in Worcester, this morning, sir. I now ascertain from Bolt that he gave it to Mr. John to give to Mr. Carmody."

"What!" cried Soapy

"And Mr. John has apparently gone off without giving it to him. However, no doubt it is quite safe. Did you make satisfactory progress with the hutch, sir?"

"Eh?"

"The robert-hutch, sir."

"What?"

A look of concern came into Sturgis's face. His companion's manner was strange.

"Is anything the matter, sir?"

"Eh?"

"Shall I bring you something to drink, sir?"

Few men ever became so distrait that this particular question fails to penetrate. Soapy nodded feverishly. Something to drink was precisely what at this moment he felt he needed most. Moreover, the process of fetching it would relieve him, for a time at least, of the society of a butler who seemed to combine in equal proportions the outstanding characteristics of a porous plaster and a gadfly.

"Yes," he replied.

"Very good, sir."

Soapy's mind was in a whirl. He could almost feel the brains inside his head heaving and tossing like an angry ocean. So that was what that smooth old crook had done with the stuff—stored it away in a Left Luggage office at a railway station! If circumstances had been such as to permit of a more impartial and detached attitude of mind, Soapy would have felt for Mr. Carmody's resource and ingenuity nothing but admiration. A Left Luggage office was an ideal place in which to store stolen property, as good as the innermost recesses of some Safe Deposit Company's deepest vault.

But, numerous as were the emotions surging in his bosom, admiration was not one of them. For a while he gave himself up almost entirely to that saddest of mental exercises, the brooding on what might have been. If only he had known that John had the ticket . . .!

But he was a practical man. It was not his way to waste time torturing himself with thoughts of past failures. The future claimed his attention.

What to do?

All, he perceived, was not yet lost. It would be absurd to pretend that things were shaping themselves ideally, but disaster might still be retrieved. It would be embarrassing, no doubt, to meet Chimp Twist after what had occurred, but a man who would win to wealth must learn to put up with embarrassments. The only possible next move was to go over to Healthward Ho, reveal to Chimp what had occurred, and with his co-operation recover the ticket from John.

Soapy brightened. Another possibility had occurred to him. If he were to reach Healthward Ho with the minimum of delay, it might be that he would find both Chimp and John still under the influence of those admirable drops, in which case a man of his resource would surely be able to insinuate himself into John's presence long enough to be able to remove a Left Luggage ticket from his person.

But if 'twere done, then, 'twere well 'twere done quickly. What he needed was the Dex-Mayo. And the Dex-Mayo was standing outside the stable-yard, waiting for him. He became a thing of dash and activity. For many years he had almost given up the exercise of running, but he ran now like the lissom athlete he had been in his early twenties.

And as he came panting round the back of the house the first thing he saw was the tail-end of the car disappearing into the stable-yard.

"Hi!" shouted Soapy, using for the purpose the last remains of his breath.

The Dex-Mayo vanished. And Soapy, very nearly a spent force now, arrived at the opening of the stable-yard just in time to see Bolt, the chauffeur, putting the key of the garage in his pocket after locking the door.

Bolt was a thing of beauty. He gleamed in the sunshine. He was wearing a new hat, his Sunday clothes, and a pair of yellow shoes that might have been bits chipped off the sun itself. There was a carnation in his buttonhole. He would have lent tone to a garden-party at Buckingham Palace.

He regarded Soapy with interest.

"Been having a little run, sir?"

"The car!" croaked Soapy.

"I've just put it away, sir. Mr. Carmody has given me the day off to attend the wedding of the wife's niece over at Upton Snodsbury."

"I want the car."

"I've just put it away, sir," said Bolt, speaking more slowly and with the manner of one explaining something to an untutored foreigner. "Mr. Carmody has given me the day off. Mrs. Bolt's niece is being married over at Upton Snodsbury. And she's got a lovely day for it," said the chauffeur, glancing at the sky with something as near approval as a chauffeur ever permits himself. "Happy the bride that the sun shines on, they say. Not that I agree altogether with these old sayings. I know that when I and Mrs. Bolt was married it rained the whole time like cats and dogs, and we've been very happy. Very happy indeed we've been, taking it by and large. I don't say we haven't had our disagreements, but, taking it one way and another . . ."

It began to seem to Soapy that the staffs of English country-houses must be selected primarily for their powers of conversation. Every domestic with whom he had come in contact in Rudge Hall so far had at his disposal an apparently endless flow of lively small-talk. The butler, if you let him, would gossip all day about rabbits, and here was the chauffeur apparently settling down to dictate his autobiography. And every moment was precious.

With a violent effort he contrived to take in a stock of breath.

"I want the car, to go to Healthward Ho. I can drive it."

The chauffeur's manner changed. Up till now he had been the cheery clubman meeting an old friend in the smoking-room and drawing him aside for a long, intimate chat, but at this shocking suggestion he froze. He gazed at Soapy with horrified incredulity.

"Drive the Dex-Mayo, sir?" he gasped.

"Over to Healthward Ho."

The crisis passed. Bolt swallowed convulsively and was himself once more. One must be patient, he realized, with laymen. They do not understand. When they come to a chauffeur and calmly propose that their vile hands shall touch his sacred steering-wheel they are not trying to be deliberately offensive. It is simply that they do not know.

"I'm afraid that wouldn't quite do, sir," he said with a faint, reproving smile.

"Do you think I can't drive?"

"Not the Dex-Mayo you can't, sir." Bolt spoke a little curtly, for he had been much moved and was still shaken. "Mr. Carmody don't like nobody handling his car but me."

"But I must go over to Healthward Ho. It's important. Business."

The chauffeur reflected. Fundamentally he was a kindly man, who liked to do his Good Deed daily.

"Well, sir, there's an old push-bike of mine lying in the stables. You could take that if you liked. It's a little rusty, not having been used for some time, but I daresay it would carry you as far as Healthward Ho."

Soapy hesitated for a moment. The idea of a twenty-mile journey on a machine which he had always supposed to have become obsolete during his knickerbocker days made him quail a little. Then the thought of his mission lent him strength. He was a desperate man, and desperate men must do desperate things.

"Fetch it out!" he said.

Bolt fetched it out, and Soapy, looking upon it, quailed again.

"Is that it?" he said dully.

"That's it, sir," said the chauffeur.

There was only one adjective to describe this push-bike— the adjective blackguardly. It had that leering air, shared by some parrots and the baser variety of cat, of having seen and being jauntily familiar with all the sin of the world. It looked low and furtive. Its handle-bars curved up instead of down, it had gaps in its spokes, and its pedals were naked and unashamed. A sans-culotte of a bicycle. The sort of bicycle that snaps at strangers.

"H'm!" said Soapy, ruminating.

"Yes," said Soapy, still ruminating.

Then he remembered again how imperative was the need of reaching Healthward Ho somehow.

"All right," he said, with a shudder.

He climbed on to the machine, and after one majestic wobble passed through the gates into the park, pedalling bravely. As he disappeared from view, there floated back to Bolt, standing outside the stable-yard, a single, agonized "Ouch!"

Chauffeurs do not laugh, but they occasionally smile. Bolt smiled. He had been bitten by that bicycle himself.

III

It was twenty minutes past one that butler Sturgis, dozing in his pantry, was jerked from slumber by the sound of the telephone bell. He had been hoping for an uninterrupted siesta, for he had had a perplexing and trying morning. First, on top of the most sensational night of his life, there had been all the nervous excitement of seeing policemen roaming about the place. Then the American gentleman, Mr. Molloy, had told him that Mr. Carmody wanted something to drink, and Mr. Carmody had denied having ordered it. Then Mr. Molloy had asked for a drink himself and had disappeared without waiting to get it. And, finally, there was the matter of the cupboard. Mr. Molloy, after starting to build a rabbit-hutch, had apparently suspended operations in favour of smashing in the door of the cupboard at the foot of the stairs. It was all very puzzling to Sturgis, and, like most men of settled habit, he found the process of being puzzled upsetting.

He went to the telephone, and a silver voice came to him over the wire.

"Is this the Hall? I want to speak to Mr. Carroll."

Sturgis recognized the voice.

"Miss Wyvern?"

"Yes. Is that Sturgis? I say, Sturgis, what has become of Mr. Carroll? I was expecting him here half an hour ago. Have you seen him about anywhere?"

"I have not seen him since shortly after breakfast, Miss. I understand that he went off in his little car with Miss Molloy."

"What!"

"Yes, Miss. Some time ago."

There was silence at the other end of the wire.

"With Miss Molloy?" said the silver voice flatly.

"Yes, Miss."

Silence again.

"Did he say when he would be back?"

"No, Miss. But I understand that he was not proposing to return till quite late in the day."

More silence.

"Oh?"

"Yes, Miss. Any message I can give him?"

"No, thank you. . . . No . . . No, it doesn't matter."

"Very good, Miss."

Sturgis returned to his pantry. Pat, hanging up the receiver, went out into her garden. Her face was set, and her lips compressed.

A snail crossed her path. She did not tread on it, for she had a kind heart, but she gave it a look. It was a look which, had it reached John, at whom it was really directed, would have scorched him.

She walked to the gate and stood leaning on it, staring straight before her.

★ 11 ★

John in Captivity

I

IT had been the opinion of Dolly Molloy, expressed during her conversation with Mr. Twist, that John, on awaking from his drugged slumber, would find himself suffering from a headache. The event proved her a true prophet.

John, as became one who prized physical fitness, had been all his life a rather unusually abstemious young man. But on certain rare occasions dotted through the years of his sojourn at Oxford he had permitted himself to relax. As for instance, the night of his twenty-first birthday . . . Boat-Race night in his freshman year . . . and, perhaps most notable of all, the night of the University football match in the season when he had first found a place in the Oxford team and had helped to win one of the most spectacular games ever seen at Twickenham. To celebrate each of these events he had lapsed from his normal austerity, and every time had woken on the morrow to a world full of greyness and horror and sharp, shooting pains. But never had he experienced anything to compare with what he was feeling now.

He was dimly conscious that strange things must have been happening to him, and that these things had ended by depositing him on a strange bed in a strange room, but he was at present in no condition to give his situation any sustained thought. He merely lay perfectly still, concentrating all his powers on the difficult task of keeping his head from splitting in half.

When eventually, moving with exquisite care, he slid from the bed and stood up, the first thing of which he became aware was that the sun had sunk so considerably that it was now shining almost horizontally through the barred window of the room. The air, moreover, which accompanied its rays through the window had that cool fragrance which indicates the approach of evening.

Poets have said some good things in their time about this particular hour of the day, but to John on this occasion it brought no romantic thoughts. He was merely bewildered. He had started out from Rudge not long after eleven in the morning, and here it was late afternoon.

He moved to the window, feeling like Rip van Winkle. And presently the sweet air, playing about his aching brow, restored him so considerably that he was able to make deductions and arrive at the truth. The last thing he could recollect was the man Twist handing him a tall glass. In that glass, it now became evident, must have lurked the cause of all his troubles. With an imbecile lack of the most elementary caution, inexcusable in one who had been reading detective stories all his life, he had allowed himself to be drugged.

It was a bitter thought, but he was not permitted to dwell on it for long. Gradually, driving everything else from his mind, there stole upon him the realization that unless he found something immediately to slake the thirst which was burning him up he would perish of spontaneous combustion. There was a jug on the wash-stand: and, tottering to it, he found it mercifully full to the brim. For the next few moments he was occupied, to the exclusion of all other mundane matters, with the task of seeing how much of the contents of this jug he could swallow without pausing for breath.

This done, he was at leisure to look about him and examine the position of affairs.

That he was a prisoner was proved directly he tested the handle of the door. And, as further evidence, there were those bars on the window. Whatever else might be doubtful, the one thing certain was that he would have to remain in this room until somebody came along and let him out.

His first reaction on making this discovery was a feeling of irritation at the silliness of the whole business. Where was the sense of it? Did this man Twist suppose that in the heart of peaceful Worcestershire he could immure a fellow for ever in an upper room of his house?

And then his clouded intellect began to function more nimbly. Twist's behaviour, he saw, was not so childish as he had supposed. It had been imperative for him to gain time in order to get away

with his loot; and, John realized, he had most certainly gained
it. And the longer he remained in this room, the more complete
would be the scoundrel's triumph.

John became active. He went to the door again and examined
it carefully. A moment's inspection showed him that nothing
was to be hoped for from that quarter. A violent application
of his shoulder did not make the solid oak so much as quiver.

He tried the window. The bars were firm. Tugging had no
effect on them.

There seemed to John only one course to pursue.

He shouted.

It was an injudicious move. The top of his head did not
actually come off, but it was a very near thing. By a sudden
clutch at both temples he managed to avert disaster in the nick
of time, and tottered weakly to the bed. There for some minutes
he remained while unseen hands drove red-hot rivets into his
skull.

Presently the agony abated. He was able to rise again and make
his way feebly to the jug, which he had now come to look on as
his only friend in the world.

He had just finished his second non-stop draught when
something attracted his notice out of the corner of his eye, and
he saw that in the window beside him were framed a head and
shoulders.

"Hoy!" observed the head in a voice like a lorry full of steel
girders passing over cobblestones. "I've brought you a cupper
tea."

II

The head was red in colour and ornamented halfway down
by a large and impressive moustache, waxed at the ends. The
shoulders were broad and square, the eyes prawn-like. The
whole apparition, in short, one could tell at a glance, was a
sample or first instalment of the person of a Sergeant-Major.
And unless he had dropped from heaven—which from John's
knowledge of Sergeant-Majors, seemed unlikely—the newcomer
must be standing on top of a ladder.

And such, indeed, was the case. Sergeant-Major Flannery,
though no acrobat, had nobly risked life and limb by climbing

to this upper window to see how his charge was getting on and to bring him a little refreshment.

"Take your cuppertea, young fellow," said Mr. Flannery.

The hospitality had arrived too late. In the matter of tea-drinking John was handicapped by the fact that he had just swallowed approximately a third of a jug of water. He regretted to be compelled to reject the contribution for lack of space. But as what he desired most at the moment was human society and conversation, he advanced eagerly to the window.

"Who are you?" he asked.

"Flannery's my name, young fellow."

"How did I get here?"

"In that room?"

"Yes."

"I put you there."

"You did, did you?" said John. "Open this door at once, damn you!"

The Sergeant-Major shook his head.

"Language!" he said reprovingly. "Profanity won't do you no good, young man. Cursing and swearing won't 'elp you. You just drink your cuppertea and don't let's have no nonsense. If you'd made a 'abit in the past of drinking more tea and less of the other thing, you wouldn't be in what I may call your present predicament."

"Will you open this door!"

"No, sir. I will not open that door. There aren't going to be no doors opened till your conduct and behaviour has been carefully examined in the course of a day or so and we can be sure there'll be no verlence."

"Listen," said John, curbing a desire to jab at this man through the bars with the tea-spoon. "I don't know who you are . . ."

"Flannery's the name, sir, as I said before. Sergeant-Major Flannery."

". . . but I can't believe you're in this business . . ."

"Indeed I am, sir. I am Doctor Twist's assistant."

"But this man is a criminal, you fool . . ."

Sergeant-Major Flannery seemed pained rather than annoyed.

"Come, come, sir. A little civility, if you please. This what I may call contumacious attitude isn't helping you. Surely you can see that for yourself? Always remember, sir, the voice with the smile wins."

"This fellow Twist burgled our house last night. And all the while you're keeping me shut up here he's getting away."

"Is that so, sir? What house would that be?"

"Rudge Hall."

"Never heard of it."

"It's near Rudge-in-the-Vale. Twenty miles from here. Mr. Carmody's place."

"Mr. Lester Carmody who was here taking the cure?"

"Yes. I'm his nephew."

"His nephew, eh?"

"Yes."

"Come, come!"

"What do you mean?"

"Is so 'appens," said Mr. Flannery, with quiet satisfaction, removing one hand from the window-bars in order to fondle his moustache, "that I've seen Mr. Carmody's nephew. Tallish, thinnish, pleasant-faced young fellow. He was over here to visit Mr. Carmody during the latter's temp'ry residence. I had him pointed out to me."

Painful though the process was, John felt compelled to grit his teeth.

"That was Mr. Carmody's other nephew."

"Other nephew, eh?"

"My cousin."

"Your cousin, eh?"

"His name's Hugo."

"Hugo, eh?"

"Good God!" cried John. "Are you a parrot?"

Mr. Flannery, if he had not been standing on a ladder, would no doubt have drawn himself up haughtily at this outburst. Being none too certain of his footing, he contented himself with looking offended.

"No, sir," he said with a dignity which became him well, "in reply to your question, I am not a parrot. I am a salaried assistant at Doctor Twist's health-establishment, detailed to look after the patients and keep them away from the cigarettes and see that they do their exercises in a proper manner. And, as I said to the young lady, I understand human nature and am a match for artfulness of any description. What's more, it was precisely this kind of artfulness on your part that the young lady warned me against. 'Be careful, Sergeant-Major,'

she said to me, clasping her 'ands in what I may call an agony
of appeal, 'that this poor, misguided young son of a what-not
don't come it over you with his talk about being the Lost Heir
of some family living in the near neighbourhood. Because he's
sure to try it on, you can take it from me, Sergeant-Major,'
she said. And I said to the young lady, 'Miss,' I said, 'he won't
come it over Egbert Flannery. Not him. I've seen too much of
that sort of thing, Miss,' I said. And the young lady said, 'Gawd's
strewth, Sergeant-Major,' she said, 'I wish there was more
men in the world like you, Sergeant-Major, because then it
would be a damn sight better place than it is, Sergeant-Major.' "
He paused. Then, realizing an omission, added the words, "She
said."

John clutched at his throbbing head.

"Young lady? What young lady?"

"You know well enough what young lady, sir. The young
lady what brought you here to leave you in our charge. That
young lady."

"That young lady?"

"Yes, sir. The one who brought you here."

"Brought me here?"

"And left you in our charge."

"Left me in your charge?"

"Come, come, sir!" said Mr. Flannery. "Are you a parrot?"

The adroit thrust made no impression on John. His mind was
too busy to recognize it for what it was—viz., about the cleverest
repartee ever uttered by a non-commissioned officer of His
Majesty's regular forces. A monstrous suspicion had smitten
him, with the effect almost of a physical blow. Suspicion?
It was more than a suspicion. If it was at Dolly Molloy's request
that he was now locked up in this infernal room, then, bizarre
as it might seem, Dolly Molloy must in some way be connected
with the nefarious activities of the man Twist. The links that
connected the two might be obscure, but as to the fact there
could be no doubt whatever.

"You mean . . ." he gasped.

"I mean your sister, sir, who brought you over here in her
car."

"What! That was my car."

"No, no, sir, that won't do. I saw her myself driving off
in it some hours ago. She waved her 'and to me," said Mr.

Flannery, caressing his moustache and allowing a note of tender sentiment to creep into his voice. "Yes, sir! She turned and waved her 'and.''

John made no reply. He was beyond speech. Trifling though it might seem to an insurance company in comparison with the loss of Rudge Hall's more valuable treasures, the theft of the two-seater smote him a blow from which he could not hope to rally. He loved his Widgeon Seven. He had nursed it, tended it, oiled it, watered it, watched over it in sickness and in health as if it had been a baby sister. And now it had gone.

"Look here!" he cried feverishly. "You must let me out of here. At once!"

"No, sir. I promised your sister . . ."

"She isn't my sister! I haven't got a sister! Good heavens, man, can't you understand . . ."

"I understand very well, sir. Artfulness! I was prepared for it." Sergeant-Major Flannery paused for an instant. "The young lady," he said dreamily, "was afraid, too, that you might try to bribe me. She warned me most particular."

John did not speak. His Widgeon Seven! Gone!

"Bribe me!" repeated Sergeant-Major Flannery, his eyes widening. It was evident that the mere thought of such a thing sickened this good man. "She said you would try to bribe me to let you go."

"Well, you can make your mind easy," said John between his teeth. "I haven't any money."

There was a moment's silence. Then Mr. Flannery said "Ho!" in a rather short manner. And silence fell again.

It was broken by the Sergeant-Major, in a moralising vein.

"It's a wonder to me," he said, and there was peevishness in his voice, "that a young fellow with a lovely sister like what you've got can bring himself to lower himself to the beasts of the field, as the saying is. Drink in moderation is one thing. Moping it up and becoming verlent and a nuisance to all is another. If you'd ever seen one of them lantern-slides showing what alcohol does to the liver of the excessive drinker maybe you'd have pulled up sharp while there was time. And not," said the Sergeant-Major, still with that oddly querulous note in his voice, "have wasted all your money on what could only do you 'arm. If you 'adn't of give in so to your self-indulgence and what I may call besottedness, you would now 'ave your pocket full of money to spend how you fancied." He sighed. "Your cuppertea's got cold," he said moodily.

"I don't want any tea."

"Then I'll be leaving you," said Mr. Flannery. "If you require anything, press the bell. Nobody'll take any notice of it."

He withdrew cautiously down the ladder: and, having paused at the bottom to shake his head reproachfully, disappeared from view.

John did not miss him. His desire for company had passed. What he wanted now was to be alone and to think. Not that there was any likelihood of his thoughts being pleasant ones. The more he contemplated the iniquity of the Molloy family, the deeper did the iron enter into his soul. If ever he set eyes on Thomas G. Molloy again . . .

He set eyes on him again, oddly enough, at this very moment. From where he stood, looking out through the bars of the window, there was visible to him a considerable section of the drive. And up the drive at this juncture, toiling painfully, came Mr. Molloy in person, seated on a bicycle.

As John craned his neck and glared down with burning eyes, the rider dismounted, and the bicycle, which appeared to have been waiting for the chance, bit him neatly in the ankle with its left pedal. John was too far away to hear the faint cry of agony which escaped the suffering man, but he could see his face. It was a bright crimson face, powdered with dust, and its features were twisted in anguish.

John went back to the jug and took another long drink. In the spectacle just presented to him he had found a faint, feeble glimmering of consolation.

★ 12 ★

Unpleasant Scene Between two old Friends

I

O N leaving John, Sergeant-Major Flannery's first act was to go to what he was accustomed to call the orderly-room and make his report. He reached it only a few minutes after its occupant's return to consciousness. Chimp Twist had opened his eyes and staggered to his feet at just about the moment when the Sergeant-Major was offering John the cup of tea.

Mr. Twist's initial discovery, like John's, was that he had a headache. He then set himself to try to decide where he was. His mind clearing a little, he was enabled to gather that he was in England . . . and, assembling the facts by degrees, in his study at Healthward Ho (formerly Graveney Court), Worcestershire. After that, everything came back to him, and he stood holding to the table with one hand and still grasping the lily with the other, and gave himself up to scorching reflections on the subject of the resourceful Mrs. Molloy.

He was still busy with these, when there was a forceful knock on the door and Sergeant-Major Flannery entered.

Chimp's grip of the table tightened. He held himself together like one who sees a match set to a train of gunpowder and awaits the shattering explosion. His visitor's lips had begun to move, and Chimp could guess how that parade-ground voice was going to sound to a man with a headache like his.

"H'rarp-h'm," began Mr. Flannery, clearing his throat, and Chimp with a sharp cry reeled to a chair and sank into it. The noise had hit him like a shell. He cowered where he sat, peering at the Sergeant-Major with haggard eyes.

"Oo-er!" boomed Mr. Flannery, noting these symptoms. "You aren't looking up to the mark, Mr. Twist."

Chimp dropped the lily, feeling the necessity of having both

192

ands free. He found he experienced a little relief if he put
he palms over his eyes and pressed hard.

"I'll tell you what it is, sir," roared the sympathetic Sergeant-
Major. "What's 'appened 'ere is that that nasty feverish cold
of yours has gone and struck inwards. It's left your 'ead and
as penetrated internally to your vitals. If only you'd have
ook taraxacum and hops like I told you . . ."

"Go away!" moaned Chimp, adding in a low voice what
eemed to him a suitable destination.

Mr. Flannery regarded him with mild reproach.

"There's nothing gained, Mr. Twist, by telling me to get to
Ell out of here. I've merely come for the single and simple
eason that I thought you would wish to know I've had a con-
ersation with the verlent case upstairs, and the way it looks
o me, sir, subject to your approval, is that it 'ud be best not
o let him out from under lock and key for some time to come.
Frue, 'e did not attempt anything in the nature of actual physical
ttack, being prevented no doubt by the fact that there was iron
ars between him and me, but his manner throughout was
eculiar not to say odd, and I recommend that all communica-
ions be conducted till further notice through the window."

"Do what you like," said Chimp faintly.

"It isn't what I like, sir," bellowed Mr. Flannery virtuously.
It's what you like and instruct, me being in your employment
nd only 'ere to carry out your orders smartly as you give them.
And there's one other matter, sir. As perhaps you are aware,
ne young lady went off in the little car . . ."

"Don't talk to me about the young lady."

"I was only about to say, Mr. Twist, that you will doubtless
e surprised to hear that for some reason or another, having started
o go off in the little car, the young lady apparently decided on
econd thoughts to continue her journey by train. She left the
ttle car at Lowick station, with instructions that it be returned
ere. I found that young Jakes, the station-master's son, outside
vith it a moment ago. Tooting the 'orn, he was, the young
ascal, and saying he wanted half a crown. Using my
wn discretion I clumped him on the head and gave him
xpence. You may reimburse me at your leisure and when
onvenient. Shall I take the little car and put it in the garridge,
r?"

Chimp gave eager assent to this proposition, as he would

have done to any proposition which appeared to carry with i
the prospect of removing this man from his presence.

"It's funny the young lady leaving the little car at the station
sir," mused Mr. Flannery in a voice that shook the chandelier
"I suppose she happened to reach there at a moment when
train was signalled and decided that she preferred not to over
tax her limited strength by driving to London. I fancy she mus
have had London as her objective."

Chimp fancied so, too. A picture rose before his eyes o
Dolly and Soapy revelling together in the metropolis, witl
the loot of Rudge Hall bestowed in some safe place where h
would never, never be able to get at it. The picture was s
vivid that he uttered a groan.

"Where does it catch you, sir?" asked Mr. Flannery solicitously
"Eh?"

"The pain, sir. The agony. You appear to be suffering. I
you take my advice, you'll get off to bed and put an 'ot-wate
bottle on your stummick. Lay it right across the abdomen, si
It may dror the poison out. I had an old aunt . . ."

"I don't want to hear about your aunt."

"Very good, sir. Just as you wish."

"Tell me about her some other time."

"Any time that suits you, sir," said Mr. Flannery agreeably
"Well, I'll be off and putting the little car in the garridge."

He left the room, and Chimp, withdrawing his hands from
his eyes, gave himself up to racking thought. A man recoverin
from knock-out drops must necessarily see things in a jaundice
light, but it is scarcely probable that, even had he been in robus
health, Mr. Twist's meditations would have been much pleasante
Condensed, they resolved themselves, like John's, into
passionate wish that he could meet Soapy Molloy again, if onl
for a moment.

And he had hardly decided that such a meeting was the onl
thing which life now had to offer, when the door opened agai
and the maid appeared.

"Mr. Molloy to see you, sir."

Chimp started from his chair.

"Show him in," he said in a tense, husky voice.

There was a shuffling noise without, and Soapy appeared i
the doorway.

II

The progress of Mr. Molloy across the threshold of Chimp Twist's study bore a striking resemblance to that of some spent runner breasting the tape at the conclusion of a more than usually gruelling Marathon race. His hair was disordered, his face streaked with dust and heat, and his legs acted so independently of his body that they gave him an odd appearance of moving in several directions at once. An unbiased observer, seeing him, could not but have felt a pang of pity for this wreck of what had once, apparently, been a fine, upstanding man.

Chimp was not an unbiased observer. He did not pity his old business partner. Judging from a first glance, Soapy Molloy seemed to him to have been caught in some sort of machinery and subsequently run over by several motor-lorries, and Chimp was glad of it. He would have liked to seek out the man in charge of that machinery and the drivers of those lorries and reward them handsomely.

"So here you are!" he said.

Mr. Molloy, navigating cautiously, backed and filled in the direction of the arm-chair. Reaching it after considerable difficulty, he gripped its sides and lowered himself with infinite weariness. A sharp exclamation escaped him as he touched the cushions. Then, sinking back, he closed his eyes and immediately went to sleep.

Chimp gazed down at him, seething with resentment that made his head ache worse than ever. That Soapy should have had the cold, callous crust to come to Healthward Ho at all after what had happened was sufficiently infuriating. That, having come, he should proceed without a word of explanation or apology to treat the study as a bedroom was more than Chimp could endure. Stooping down, he gripped his old friend by his luxuriant hair and waggled his head smartly from side to side several times.

The treatment proved effective. Soapy sat up.

"Eh?" he said, blinking.

"What do you mean, eh?"

"Which . . .? Why . . .? Where am I?"

"I'll tell you where you are."

"Oh!" said Mr. Molloy, intelligence returning.

He sank back among the cushions again. Now that the firs agony of contact was over he was finding their softness de lightful. In the matter of seats, a man who has ridden twent miles on an elderly push-bicycle becomes an exacting critic.

"Gee! I feel bad!" he murmured.

It was a natural remark, perhaps, for a man in his conditio: to make, but it had the effect of adding several degrees Fahrenhei to his companion's already impressive warmth. For som moments Chimp Twist, wrestling with his emotion, could fin no form of self-expression beyond a curious spluttering noise

"Yes, sir," proceeded Mr. Molloy, "I feel bad. All the way over here on a bicycle, Chimpie, that's where I've been. It': in the calf of the leg that it gets me principally. There and around the instep. And I wish I had a dollar for every bruise those darned pedals have made on me."

"And what about me?" demanded Chimp, at last ceasing to splutter.

"Yes, sir," said Mr. Molloy, wistfully, "I certainly wisl someone would come along and offer me even as much as fifty cents for every bruise I've gotten from the ankles upwards. They've come out on me like a rash or something."

"If you had my headache . . ."

"Yes, I've a headache, too," said Mr. Molloy. "It was the hot sun beating down on my neck that did it. There were times when I thought really I'd have to pass the thing up. Say, if you knew what I feel like . . ."

"And how about what I feel like?" shrilled Mr. Twist, quivering with self-pity. "A nice thing that was that wife o yours did to me! A fine trick to play on a business partner! Slipping stuff into my highball that laid me out cold. Is that any way to behave? Is that a system?"

Mr. Molloy considered the point.

"The madam is a mite impulsive," he admitted.

"And leaving me laying there and putting a lily in my hand!"

"That was her playfulness," explained Mr. Molloy. "Girls will have their bit of fun."

"Fun! Say . . ."

Mr. Molloy felt that it was time to point the moral.

"It was your fault, Chimpie. You brought it on yourself by acting greedy and trying to get the earth. If you hadn't tood us up for that sixty-five—thirty-five of yours, all this would never had happened. Naturally no high-spirited girl like the madam wasn't going to stand for nothing like that. But listen while I tell you what I've come about. If you're willing to can all that stuff and have a fresh deal and a square one this ime—one third to me, one third to you, and one third to the madam—I'll put you hep to something that'll make you feel good. Yes, sir, you'll go singing about the house."

"The only thing you could tell me that would make me feel good," replied Chimp, churlishly, "would be that you'd tumbled off of that bicycle of yours and broken your damned neck."

Mr. Molloy was pained.

"Is that nice, Chimpie?"

Mr. Twist wished to know if, in the circumstances and after what had occurred, Mr. Molloy expected him to kiss him. Mr. Molloy said No, but where was the sense of harsh words? Where did harsh words get anybody? When had harsh words ever paid any dividend?

"If you had a headache like mine, Chimpie," said Mr. Molloy, reproachfully, "you'd know how it felt to sit and listen to an old friend giving you the razz."

Chimp was obliged to struggle for awhile with a sudden return of his spluttering.

"A headache like yours? Where do you get that stuff? My headache's a darned sight worse than your headache."

"It couldn't be, Chimpie."

"If you want to know what a headache really is, you take some of those kayo drops you're so fond of."

"Well, putting that on one side," said Mr. Molloy, wisely forbearing to argue, "let me tell you what I've come here about. Chimpie, that guy Carmody has double-crossed us. He was on to us from the start."

"What!"

"Yes, sir. I had it from his own lips in person. And do you know what he done? He took that stuff out of the closet and sent his chauffeur over to Worcester to put it in the Left Luggage place at the depot there."

"What!"

"Yes, sir."

"Gee!" said Mr. Twist, impressed. "That was smooth. Then you haven't got it, do you mean?"

"No. I haven't got it."

Mr. Twist had never expected to feel anything in the nature of elation that day or for many days to come, but at these words something like ecstasy came upon him. He uttered a delighted laugh, which, owing to sudden agony in the head, changed to a muffled howl.

"So, after all your smartness," he said, removing his hands from his temples as the spasm passed, "you're no better off than what I am?"

"We're both sitting pretty, Chimpie, if we get together and act quick."

"How's that? Act how?"

"I'll tell you. This chauffeur guy left the stuff and brought home the ticket . . ."

". . . and gave it to old man Carmody, I suppose? Well, where does that get us?"

"No, sir! He didn't give it to old man Carmody. He gave it to that young Carroll fellow!" said Mr. Molloy.

The significance of the information was not lost upon Chimp. He stared at Mr. Molloy.

"Carroll?" he said. "You mean the bird upstairs?"

"Is he upstairs?"

"Sure he's upstairs. Locked in a room with bars on the window. You're certain he has the ticket?"

"I know he has. So all we've got to do now is get it off him."

"That's all?"

"That's all."

"And how," inquired Chimp, "do you propose to do it?"

Mr. Molloy made no immediate reply. The question was one which, in the intervals of dodging the pedals of his bicycle, he had been asking himself ever since he had left Rudge Hall. He had hoped that in the enthusiasm of the moment some spontaneous solution would leap from his old friend's lips, but it was plain that this was not to be.

"I thought maybe you would think of a way, Chimpie," he was compelled to confess.

"Oh? Me, eh?"

"You're smart," said Mr. Molloy, deferentially. "You've got a head. Whatever anyone's said about you, no one's ever denied that. You'll think of a way."

"I will, will I? And while I'm doing it, you'll just sit back,

I suppose, and have a nice rest? And all you're suggesting that I'm to get out of it . . ."

"Now, Chimpie!" quavered Mr. Molloy. He had feared this development.

". . . is a measly one third. Say, let me tell you . . ."

"Now, Chimpie," urged Mr. Molloy, with unshed tears in his voice, "let's not start all that over again. We settled the terms. Gentlemen's agreement. It's all fixed."

"Is it? Come down out of the clouds, you're scaring the birds. What I want now, if I'm going to do all the work and help you out of a tough spot, is seventy—thirty."

"Seventy—thirty!" echoed Mr. Molloy, appalled.

"And if you don't like it let's hear you suggest a way of getting that ticket off that guy upstairs. Maybe you'd like to go up and have a talk with him? If he's feeling anything like the way I felt when I came to after those kayo drops of yours, he'll be glad to see you. What does it matter to you if he pulls your head off and drops it out of window? You can only live once, so what the hell!"

Mr. Molloy gazed dismally before him. Never a very inventive man, his bicycle-ride had left him even less capable of inspiration than usual. He had to admit himself totally lacking in anything resembling a constructive plan of campaign. He yearned for his dear wife's gentle presence. Dolly was the bright one of the family. In a crisis like this she would have been full of ideas, each one a crackerjack.

"We can't keep him locked up in that room for ever," he said unhappily.

"We don't have to—not if you agree to my seventy—thirty."

"Have you thought of a way, then?"

"Sure I've thought of a way."

Mr. Molloy's depression became more marked than ever. He knew what this meant. The moment he gave up the riddle that miserable little Chimp would come out with some scheme which had been staring him in the face all along, if only he had had the intelligence to see it.

"Well?" said Chimp. "Think quick. And remember thirty's better than nothing. And don't say, when I've told you, that it's just the idea you've had yourself from the start."

Mr. Molloy urged his weary brain to one last spurt of activity, but without result. He was a specialist. He could sell shares in phantom oil-wells better than anybody on either side of the Atlantic, but there he stopped. Outside his speciality he was almost a total loss.

"All right, Chimpie," he sighed, facing the inevitable.

"Seventy—thirty?"

"Seventy—thirty. Though how I'm to break it to the madam. I don't know. She won't like it, Chimpie. It'll be a nasty blow for the madam."

"I hope it chokes her," said Chimp, unchivalrously. "Her and her lilies! Well, then. Here's what we do. When Flannery takes the guy his coffee and eggs tomorrow, there'll be something in the pot besides coffee. There'll be some of those kayo drops of yours. And then all we have to do is just simply walk upstairs and dig the ticket out of his clothes and there we are."

Mr. Molloy uttered an agonized cry. His presentiment had been correct.

"I'd have thought of that myself . . ." he wailed.

"Sure you would," replied Chimp, comfortably, "if you'd of had something that wasn't a hubbard squash or something where your head ought to be. Those just-as-good imitation heads never pay in the long run. What you ought to do is sell yours for what it'll fetch and get a new one. And next time," said Chimp, "make it a prettier one."

⋆ 13 ⋆

Mr. Molloy Speaks on the Telephone

I

THE dawn of what promised to be an eventful day broke greyly over Healthward Ho. By seven o'clock, however, the sun had forced its way through the mists and at eight precisely one of its rays, stealing in at an upper window, fell upon Sergeant-Major Flannery, lovely in sleep. He grunted, opened his eyes, and, realizing that another morning had arrived with all its manifold tasks and responsibilities, heaved himself out of bed and after a few soldierly setting-up exercises began his simple toilet. This completed, he made his way to the kitchen, where a fragrant smell of bacon and coffee announced that breakfast awaited him.

His companions in the feast, Rosa, the maid, and Mrs. Evans, the cook, greeted him with the respectful warmth due to a man of his position and gifts. However unpopular Mr. Flannery might be with the resident patients of Healthward Ho—and Admiral Sir James Rigby-Rudd, for one, had on several occasions expressed a wistful desire to skin him—he was always sure of a hearty welcome below stairs. Rosa worshipped his moustache, and Mrs. Evans found his conversation entertaining.

To-day, however, though the moustache was present in all its pristine glory, the conversation was lacking. Usually it was his custom, before so much as spearing an egg, to set things going brightly with some entertaining remark on the state of the weather or possibly the absorbing description of a dream which he had had in the night, but this morning he sat silent—or as nearly silent as he could ever be when eating.

"A penny for your thoughts, Mr. Flannery," said Mrs. Evans, piqued.

The Sergeant-Major started. It came to him that he had been remiss.

"I was thinking, ma'am," he said, poising a forkful of bacon, "of what I may call the sadness of life."

"Life is sad," agreed Mrs. Evans.

"Ah!" said Rosa, the maid, who, being a mere slip of a girl and only permitted to join in these symposia as a favour, should not have spoken at all.

"That verlent case upstairs," proceeded Mr. Flannery, swallowing the bacon and forking up another load. "Now, there's something that makes your heart bleed, if I may use the expression at the breakfast table. That young fellow, no doubt, started out in life with everything pointing to a happy and prosperous career. Good home, good education, everything. And just because he's allowed himself to fall into bad 'abits, there he is under lock and key, so to speak."

"Can he get out?" asked Rosa. It was a subject which she and the cook discussed in alarmed whispers far into the night.

Mr. Flannery raised his eyebrows.

"No, he cannot get out. And, if he did, you wouldn't have nothing to fear, not with me around."

"I'm sure it's a comfort feeling that you are around, Mr. Flannery," said Mrs. Evans.

"Almost the very words the young fellow's sister said to me when she left him here," rumbled Mr. Flannery complacently. "She said to me 'Sergeant-Major,' she said, 'it's such a relief to feel that there's someone like you 'ere, Sergeant-Major,' she said. 'I'm sure you're wonderful in any kind of an emergency, Sergeant-Major,' she said." He sighed. "It's thinking of 'er that brings home the sadness of it all to a man, if you understand me. What I mean, here's that beautiful young creature racked with anxiety, as the saying is, on account of this worthless brother of hers . . ."

"I didn't think she was so beautiful," said Rosa.

An awful silence followed these words, the sort of silence that would fall upon a Housekeeper's Room if, supposing such a thing possible, some young under-footman were to contradict the butler. Sergeant-Major Flannery's eyes bulged, and he drank coffee in a marked manner.

"Don't you talk nonsense, my girl," he said shortly.

"A girl can speak, can't she? A girl can make a remark, can't she?"

"Certainly she can speak," replied Mr. Flannery. "Undoubtedly she can make a remark. But," he added with quiet severity, "let it be sense. That young lady was the most beautiful young lady I've ever seen. She had eyes"—he paused for a telling simile—"eyes," he resumed devoutly, "like twin stars." He turned to Mrs. Evans, "When you've got that case's breakfast ready, ma'am, perhaps you would instruct someone to bring it out to me in the garden and I'll take it up to him. I shall be smoking my pipe in the shrubbery."

"You're not going already, Mr. Flannery?"

"Yes, ma'am."

"But you haven't finished your breakfast."

"I have quite finished my breakfast, ma'am," said Sergeant-Major Flannery. "I would not wish to eat any more."

He withdrew. To the pleading in the eyes of Rosa he pointedly paid no attention. He was not unaware of the destructive effect which the moustache nestling between his thumb and forefinger had wrought on the girl's heart, but he considered rightly that if you didn't keep women in their place occasionally, where were you? Rosa was a nice little thing, but nice little things must not be allowed to speak lightly of goddesses.

In the kitchen which he had left conversation had now resolved itself into a monologue by Mrs. Evans, on the Modern Girl. It need not be reported in detail, for Mrs. Evans on the Modern Girl was very like all the other members of the older generation who from time to time have given their views on the subject in the pulpit and the press. Briefly, Mrs. Evans did not know what girls were coming to nowadays. They spoke irreverently in the presence of their elders. They lacked respect. They thrust themselves forward. They annoyed good men to the extent of only half-finishing their breakfasts. What Mrs. Evans's mother would have said if Mrs. Evans in her girlhood had behaved as Rosa had just behaved was a problem which Mrs. Evans frankly admitted herself unable to solve.

And at the end of it all the only remark which Rosa vouchsafed was a repetition of the one which had caused Sergeant-Major Flannery to leave the table short one egg and a slice of bacon of his normal allowance.

"I didn't think she was so beautiful," said Rosa, tossing a bobbed auburn head.

Whether this deplorable attitude would have reduced Mrs. Evans to a despairing silence or caused her to repeat her ob-

servations with renewed energy will never be known, for at this
moment one of the bells above the dresser jangled noisily.

"That's Him," said Mrs. Evans. "Go and see what He wants."
She usually referred to the proprietor of Healthward Ho by
means of a pronoun with a capital letter, disapproving, though
she recognized its aptness, of her assistant's preference for the
soubriquet of Old Monkey Brand. "If it's his breakfast, tell
him it'll be ready in a minute."

Rosa departed.

"It's not his breakfast," she announced, returning. "It's the
case upstairs's breakfast. Old Monkey Brand wants to have a
look at it before it's took him."

"Don't call him Old Monkey Brand."

"Well, it's what he looks like, isn't it?"

"Never mind," replied Mrs. Evans. and resumed her specula-
tions as to what her mother would have said.

"He's to have some bacon and eggs and toast and a potted
coffee," said Rosa, showing rather a lack of interest in Mrs.
Evans's mother. "And old Lord Twist wants to have a look at
it before it's took him. It all depends what you call beautiful,"
said Rosa. "If you're going to call anyone beautiful that's got
touched-up hair and eyes like one of those vamps in the pictures,
well, all I can say is. . . ."

"That's enough," said Mrs. Evans.

Silence reigned in the kitchen, broken only by the sizzling of
bacon and the sniffs of a modern girl who did not see eye to eye
with her elders on the subject of feminine beauty.

"Here you are," said Mrs. Evans at length. "Get me one of
them trays and the pepper and salt and mustard and be careful
you don't drop' it."

"Drop it? Why should I drop it?"

"Well, don't."

"There was a woman in *Hearts and Satins* that had eyes just
like hers," said Rosa, balancing the tray and speaking with the
cold scorn which good women feel for their erring sister. "And
what she didn't do! Apart from stealing all them important
papers relating to the invention. . . ."

"You're spilling that coffee."

"No, I'm not."

"Well, don't," said Mrs. Evans.

Out in the garden, hidden from the gaze of any who might

spy him and set him to work, Sergeant-Major Flannery lolled in the shrubbery, savouring that best smoke of the day, the after-breakfast pipe. He was still ruffled, for Dolly had made a deep impression on him and any statement to the effect that she was not a thing of loveliness ranked to his thinking under the head of blasphemy.

Of course, he mused, there was this to be said for the girl Rosa, this rather important point to be put forward in extenuation of her loose speech—she worshipped the ground he walked on and had obviously spoken as she did under the sudden smart of an uncontrollable jealousy. Contemplated in this light her remarks became almost excusable, and, growing benevolent under the influence of tobacco, Mr. Flannery began to feel his resentment changing gradually into something approaching tenderness.

Rosa, when you came to look at it squarely, was, he reflected, rather to be pitied than censured. Young girls, of course, needed suppressing at times and had to be ticked off for their own good when they got above themselves, but there was no doubt that the situation must have been trying to one in her frame of mind. To hear the man she worshipped speaking with unrestrained praise of the looks of another of her sex was enough to upset any girl. Properly looked at, in short, Rosa's outburst had been a compliment, and Sergeant-Major Flannery, now definitely mollified, decided to forgive her.

At this moment he heard footsteps on the gravel path that skirted the shrubbery, and became alert and vigilant. He was not supposed to smoke in the grounds of Healthward Ho because of the maddening effect the spectacle could not fail to have upon the patients if they saw him. He knocked out his pipe and peered cautiously through the branches. Then he perceived that he need have had no alarm. It was only Rosa. She was standing with her back to him, holding a laden tray. He remembered now that he had left instructions that the Case's breakfast should be brought out to him, preliminary to being carried up the ladder.

"Mr. Flanner-ee!" called Rosa, and scanned the horizon.

It was not often that Sergeant-Major Flannery permitted himself any action that might be called arch or roguish, but his meditations in the shrubbery, added to the mellowing influence of tobacco, had left him in an unusually light-hearted mood. The sun was shining, the little birds were singing, and Mr. Flannery felt young and gay. Putting his pipe in his pocket, accordingly, he crept through the shrubbery until he was immediately behind the girl and then in a tender whisper uttered the single word:

"Boo!"

All great men have their limitations. We recognize the inevitability of this and do not hold it against them. One states, therefore, not in any spirit of reproach but simply as a fact of historical interest, that tender whispering was one of the things that Sergeant-Major Flannery did not do well. Between intention and performance there was, when Mr. Flannery set out to whisper tenderly, a great gulf fixed. The actual sound he now uttered was not unlike that which might proceed from the foghorn of an Atlantic liner or a toast-master having a fit in a boiler shop, and, bursting forth as it did within a few inches of her ear without any warning whatsoever, it had on Rosa an effect identical with that produced on Colonel Wyvern at an earlier point in this chronicle by John Carroll's sudden bellow outside the shop of Chas. Bywater, Chemist. From trivial causes great events may spring. Rosa sprang about three feet. A sharp squeal escaped her and she dropped the tray. After which, she stood with a hand on her heart, panting.

Sergeant-Major Flannery recognized at once that he had done the wrong thing. His generous spirit had led him astray. If he had wished to inform Rosa that all was forgotten and forgiven he should have stepped out of the shrubbery and said so in a few simple words face to face. By acting, as it were, obliquely and allowing himself to be for the moment a disembodied voice, he had made a mess of things. Among the things he had made a mess of were a pot of coffee, a pitcher of milk, a bowl of sugar, a dish of butter, vessels containing salt, mustard and pepper, a rack of toast and a plateful of eggs and bacon. All these objects now littered the turf before him: and, emerging from the shrubbery, he surveyed them ruefully.

"Oo-er!" he said.

Oddly enough, relief rather than annoyance seemed to be the emotion dominating his companion. If ever there was an occasion when a girl might excusably have said some of the things girls are so good at saying nowadays, this was surely it. But Rosa merely panted at the Sergeant-Major thankfully.

"I thought you was the Case Upstairs!" she gasped. "When I heard that gashly sound right in my ear I thought it was him got out."

"You're all right, my girl," said Mr. Flannery. "I'm 'ere."

"Oh, Mr. Flannery!"

"There, there!" said the Sergeant-Major.

In spite of the feeling that he was behaving a little prematurely, he slipped a massive arm round the girl's waist. He also kissed her. He had not intended to commit himself quite so definitely as this, but it seemed now the only thing to do.

Rosa became calmer.

"I dropped the tray," she said.

"Yes," said Mr. Flannery, who was quick at noticing things.

"I'd better go and tell him."

"Tell Mr. Twist?"

"Well, I'd better, hadn't I?"

Mr. Flannery demurred. To tell Mr. Twist involved explanations, and explanations, if they were to be convincing, must necessarily reveal him, Mr. Flannery, in a light none too dignified. It might be that, having learned the facts, Mr. Twist would decide to dispense with the services of an assistant who, even from the best motives, hid in shrubberies and said 'Boo!' to maid-servants.

"You listen to me, my girl," he advised. "Mr. Twist is a busy gentleman that has many responsibilities and much to occupy him. He don't want to be bothered with no stories of dropped trays. All you just do is run back to the kitchen and tell Mrs. Evans to cook the Case some more breakfast. The coffee-pot's broke, but the cup ain't broke and the plate ain't broke and the mustardan-pepperan-salt thing ain't broke. I'll pick 'em up and you take 'em back on the tray and don't say nothing to nobody. While you're gone I'll be burying what's left of them eggs."

"But Mr. Twist put something special in the coffee."

"Eh? How do you mean?"

"When I took him in the tray just now, he said 'Is that the case-upstairs's breakfast?' and I said Yes, it was, and Old Monkey Brand put something that looked like a aspirin tablet or something in the coffee-pot. I thought it might be some medicine he had to have to make him quiet and keep him from breaking out and murdering all of us."

Mr. Flannery smiled indulgently.

"That case upstairs don't need nothing of that sort, not when I'm around," he said. "Doctor Twist's like all these civilians He gets unduly nervous. He don't understand that there's no need or necessity or occasion whatsoever for these what I may call sedatives when I'm on the premises to lend a 'and in case of any verlence. Besides, it don't do anybody no good always to be taking these drugs and what not. The case 'ad 'is sleeping-draught yesterday, and you never know it might not undermine his 'ealth to go taking another this morning. So if Mr. Twist asks you has the Case had his coffee, you just say 'Yes, sir,' in a smart and respectful manner, and I'll do the same. And then nobody needn't be any the wiser."

Mr. Flannery's opportunity of doing the same occurred not more than a quarter of an hour later. Returning from the task of climbing the ladder and handing in the revised breakfast at John's window, he encounted his employer in the hall.

"Oh, Flannery," said Mr. Twist.

"Sir?"

"The—er—the violent case. Has he had breakfast?"

"He was eatin' it quite hearty when I left him not five minutes ago, sir."

Chimp paused.

"Did he drink his coffee?" he asked carelessly.

"Yes, sir," replied Sergeant-Major Flannery in a smart and respectful manner.

"Oh! I see. Thank you."

"Thank *you*, sir," said Sergeant-Major Flannery.

II

In describing John as eating his breakfast quite hearty, Sergeant-Major Flannery, though not as a rule an artist in words, had for once undoubtedly achieved the *mot juste*. Hearty was the exact adjective to describe that ill-used young man's method of approach to the eggs and bacon and coffee which his gaoler had handed in between the bars of the window. Neither his now rooted dislike of Mr. Flannery nor any sense of the indignity of accepting food like some rare specimen in a Zoo could compete in John with an appetite which had been growing silently within him through the night watches. His headache had gone, leaving in its place a hunger which wolves might have envied. Placing himself outside an egg almost before Sergeant-Major had time to say "Oo-er!", he finished the other egg, the bacon, the toast, the butter, the milk and the coffee, and, having lifted the plate to see if any crumbs had got concealed beneath it and finding none, was compelled reluctantly to regard the meal as concluded.

He now felt considerably better. Food and drink had stayed in him that animal ravenousness which makes food and drink the only possible object of a man's thought's and he was able to turn his mind to other matters. Having found and swallowed a lump of sugar which had got itself overlooked under a fold of the napkin, he returned to the bed and lay down. A man who wishes to think can generally do so better in a horizontal position. So John lay on the bed and stared at the ceiling, pondering.

He certainly had sufficient material for thought to keep him occupied almost indefinitely. The more he meditated upon his present situation the less was he able to understand it. That the villain Twist, wishing to get away with the spoils of Rudge Hall, should have imprisoned him in this room in order to gain time for flight would have been intelligible. John would never have been able to bring himself to approve of such an action, but he had to admit its merits as a piece of strategy.

But Twist had not flown. According to Sergeant-Major Flannery, he was still on the premises, and so, apparently, was his accomplice, the black-hearted Molloy. But why? What did they think they were doing? How long did they suppose they would be able to keep a respectable citizen cooped up like this, even though his only medium of communication with the outer world were a more than usually fat-headed Sergeant-Major? The thing baffled John completely.

He next turned his mind to thoughts of Pat, and experienced a feverish concern. Here was something to get worried about. What, he asked himself, must Pat be thinking? He had promised to call for her in the Widgeon Seven at one o'clock yesterday. She would assume that he had forgotten. She would suppose . . .

He would have gone on torturing himself with these reflections for a considerable time, but at this moment he suddenly heard a sharp, clicking sound. It resembled the noise a key makes when turning in a lock, and was probably the only sound on earth which at that particular point in his meditations would have had the power to arrest his attention.

He lifted his head and looked round. Yes, the door was opening. And it was opening, what was more, in just the nasty, slow, furtive, sneaking way in which a door would open if somebody like the leper Twist had got hold of the handle.

In this matter of the hell-hound Twist's mental processes John was now thoroughly fogged. The man appeared to be something very closely resembling an imbecile. When flight was the one thing that could do him a bit of good, he did not fly: and now, having with drugs and imprisonment and the small-talk of Sergeant-Majors reduced a muscular young man to a condition of homicidal enthusiasm, he was apparently paying that young man a social call.

However, the mental condition of this monkey-faced, waxed-moustached bounder and criminal was beside the point. What was important was to turn his weak-mindedness to profit. The moment was obviously one for cunning and craftiness, and John accordingly dropped his head on the pillow, cunningly closed his eyes, and craftily began to breathe like one deep in sleep.

The ruse proved effective. After a moment of complete silence, a board creaked. Then another board creaked. And then he heard the door close gently. Finally, from the neighbourhood of the door, there came to him a sound of whispering. And across the years there floated into John's mind a dim memory. This whispering . . . it reminded him of something.

Then he got it. Ages ago . . . when he was a child . . . Christmas Eve . . . His father and mother lurking in the doorway to make sure that he was asleep before creeping to the bed and putting the presents in his stocking.

The recollection encouraged John. There is nothing like having done a thing before and knowing the technique. He never had been asleep on those bygone Christmas Eves, but the gift-bearers had never suspected it, and he resolved that, if any of the old skill and artistry still lingered with him, the Messrs. Twist and Molloy should not suspect it now. He deepened the note of his breathing, introducing into it a motif almost asthmatic.

"It's all right," said the voice of Mr. Twist.

"Okay?" said the voice of Mr. Molloy.

"Okay," said the voice of Mr. Twist.

Whereupon, walking confidently and without any further effort at stealth, the two approached the bed.

"I guess he drank the whole pot-full," said Mr. Twist.

Once more John found himself puzzling over the way this man's mind worked. By pot he presumably meant the coffee-pot standing on the tray and why the contents of this should appear to him in the light of a soporific was more than John could understand.

"Say, listen," said Mr. Twist. "You go and hang around outside the door, Soapy."

"Why?" inquired Mr. Molloy, and it seemed to John that he spoke coldly.

"So's to see nobody comes along, of course."

"Yeah?" said Mr. Molloy, and his voice was now unmistakably dry. "And you'll come out in a minute and tell me you're all broke up about it but he hadn't got the ticket on him after all."

"You don't think . . . ?"

"Yes, I do think."

"If you can't trust me that far . . ."

"Chimpie," said Mr. Molloy, "I wouldn't trust you as far as a snail could make in three jumps. I wouldn't believe you not even if I knew you were speaking the truth."

"Oh, well, if that's how you feel . . ." said Mr. Twist, injured. Mr. Molloy, still speaking in that unfriendly voice, replied that that was precisely how he did feel. And there was silence for a space.

"Oh, very well," said Mr. Twist at length.

John's perplexity increased. He could make nothing of that "ticket". The only ticket he had in his possession was the one Bolt, the chauffeur, had given him to give to his uncle for some bag or other which he had left in the cloak-room at Shrub Hill station. Why should these men . . .

He became aware of fingers groping towards the inner pocket of his coat. And as they touched him he decided that the moment had come to act. Bracing the muscles of his back he sprang from the bed, and with an acrobatic leap hurled himself towards the door and stood leaning against it.

III

In the pause which followed this brisk move it soon became evident to John, rubbing his shoulders against the oak panels and glowering upon the two treasure-seekers, that if the scene was to be brightened by anything in the nature of a dialogue the ball of conversation would have to be set rolling by himself. Not for some little time, it was clear, would his companions be in a condition for speech. Chimp Twist was looking like a monkey that has bitten into a bad nut, and Soapy Molloy like an American Senator who has received an anonymous telegram saying "All is discovered. Fly at once." This sudden activity on the part of one whom they had regarded as under the influence of some of the best knock-out drops that ever came out of Chicago had had upon them an effect similar to that which would be experienced by a group of surgeons in an operating-theatre if the gentleman on the slab were to rise abruptly and begin to dance the Charleston.

So it was John who was the first to speak.

"Now, then!" said John. "How about it?"

The question was a purely rhetorical one, and received no reply. Mr. Molloy uttered an odd, strangled sound like a faraway cat with a fishbone in its throat, and Chimp's waxed moustache seemed to droop at the ends. It occurred to both of them that they had never realized before what a remarkably muscular, well-developed young man John was. It was also borne in upon them that there are exceptions to the rule which states that big men are always good-humoured. John, they could not help noticing, looked like a murderer who had been doing physical jerks for years.

"I've a good mind to break both your necks," said John.

At these unpleasant words, Mr. Molloy came to life sufficiently to be able to draw back a step, thus leaving his partner nearer than himself to the danger-zone. It was a move strictly in accordance with business ethics. For if, Mr. Molloy was arguing, Chimp claimed seventy per cent. of the profits of their little venture, it was only fair that he should assume an equivalent proportion of its liabilities. At the moment, the thing looked like turning out all liabilities, and these Mr. Molloy was only too glad to split on a seventy—thirty basis. So he moved behind Chimp, and round the bulwark of his body, which he could have wished had been more substantial, peered anxiously at John.

John, having sketched out his ideal policy, was now forced to descend to the practical. Agreeable as it would have been to take these two men and bump their heads together, he realized that such a course would be a deviation from the main issue. The important thing was to ascertain what they had done with the loot, and to this inquiry he now directed his remarks.

"Where's that stuff?" he asked.

"Stuff?" said Chimp.

"You know what I mean. Those things you stole from the Hall."

Chimp, who had just discovered that he was standing between Mr. Molloy and John, swiftly skipped back a pace. This caused Mr. Molloy to skip back, too. John regarded this liveliness with a smouldering disfavour.

"Stand still!" he said.

Chimp stood still. Mr. Molloy, who had succeeded in getting behind him again, stood stiller.

"Well?" said John. "Where are the things?"

Even after the most complete rout on a stricken battlefield a beaten general probably hesitates for an instant before surrendering his sword. And so now, obvious though it was that there was no other course before them but confession, Chimp and Soapy remained silent for a space. Then Chimp, who was the first to catch John's eye, spoke hastily.

"They're in Worcester."

"Whereabouts in Worcester?"

"At the depôt."

"What depôt?"

"There's only one, isn't there?"

"Do you mean the station?"

"Sure. The station."

"They're in the Left Luggage place at the station in Worcester," said Mr. Molloy. He spoke almost cheerfully, for it had suddenly come to him that matters were not so bad as he had supposed them to be, and that there was still an avenue unclosed which might lead to a peaceful settlement. "And you've got the ticket in your pocket."

John stared.

"That ticket is for a bag my uncle sent the chauffeur to leave at Shrub Hill."

"Sure. And the stuff's inside it."

"What do you mean?"

"I'll tell you what I mean," said Mr. Molloy.

" 'Atta-boy!" said Chimp faintly. He, too, had now become aware of the silver lining. He sank upon the bed, and so profound was his relief that the ends of his moustache seemed to spring to life again and cease their drooping.

"Yes, sir," said Mr. Molloy, "I'll tell you what I mean. It's about time you got hep to the fact that that old uncle of yours is one of the smoothest birds this side of God's surging Atlantic Ocean. He was sitting in with us all along, that's what he was doing. He said those heirlooms had never done him any good and it was about time they brought him some money. It was all fixed that Chimpie here should swipe them and then I was to give the old man a cheque and he was to clean up on the insurance, besides. That was when he thought I was a millionaire that ran a museum over in America and was in the market for antiques. But he got on to me, and then he started in to double-cross us. He took the stuff out of where we'd put it and slipped it over to the depôt at Worcester, meaning to collect it when he got good and ready. But the chauffeur gave the ticket to you, and you came over here, and Chimpie doped you and locked you up."

"And you can't do a thing," said Chimp.

"No, sir," agreed Mr. Molloy, "not a thing, not unless you want to bring that uncle of yours into it and have him cracking rocks in the same prison where they put us."

"I'd like to see that old bird cracking rocks, at that," said Chimp pensively.

"So would I like to see him cracking rocks," assented Mr. Molloy cordially. "I can't think of anything I'd like better than to see him cracking rocks. But not at the expense of me cracking rocks, too."

"Or me," said Chimp.

"Or you," said Mr. Molloy, after a slight pause. "So there's the position, Mr. Carroll. You can go ahead and have us pinched, if you like, but just bear in mind that if you do there's going to be one of those scandals in high life you read about. Yes, sir, real front-page stuff."

"You bet there is," said Chimp.

"Yes, sir, you bet there is," said Mr. Molloy.

"You're dern tooting there is," said Chimp.

"Yes, sir, you're dern tooting there is," said Mr. Molloy.

And on this note of perfect harmony the partners rested their case and paused, looking at John expectantly.

John's reation to the disclosure was not agreeable. It is never pleasant for a spirited young man to find himself baffled, nor is it cheering for a member of an ancient family to discover that the head of that family has been working in association with criminals and behaving in a manner calculated to lead to rock-cracking.

Not for an instant did it occur to him to doubt the story. Although the Messrs. Twist and Molloy were men whose statements the prudent would be inclined to accept as a rule with reserve, on this occasion it was evident that they were speaking nothing but the truth.

"Say, listen," cried Chimp, alarmed. He had been watching John's face and did not like the look of it. "No rough stuff!"

John had been contemplating none. Chimp and his companion had ceased to matter, and the fury which was making his face rather an unpleasant spectacle for two peace-loving men shut up in a small room with him was directed exclusively against his Uncle Lester. Rudge Hall and its treasures were sacred to John; and the thought that Mr. Carmody, whose trust they were, had framed this scheme for the house's despoilment was almost more than he could bear.

"It isn't us you ought to be sore at," urged Mr. Molloy. "It's that old uncle of yours."

"Sure it is," said Chimp.

"Sure it is," echoed Mr. Molloy. Not for a long time had he and his old friend found themselves so completely in agreement. "He's the guy you want to soak it to."

"I'll say he is," said Chimp.

"I'll say he is," said Mr. Molloy. "Say listen, let me tell you something. Something that'll make you feel good. I happen to know that old man Carmody is throwing the wool over those insurance people's eyes by offering a reward for the recovery of that stuff. A thousand pounds. He told me so himself. If you want to get him good and sore, all you've got to do is claim it. He won't dare hold out on you."

"Certainly he won't," said Chimp.

"Certainly he won't," said Mr. Molloy. "And will that make him good and sore!"

"Will it!" said Chimp.

"Will it!" said Mr. Molloy.

"Wake me up in the night and ask me," said Chimp.

"Me, too," said Mr. Molloy.

Their generous enthusiasm seemed to have had its effect. The ferocity faded from John's demeanour. Something resembling a smile flitted across his face, as if some pleasing thought were entertaining him. Mr. Molloy relaxed his tension and breathed again. Chimp, in his relief, found himself raising a hand to his moustache.

"I see," said John slowly.

He passed his fingers thoughtfully over his unshaven chin.

"Is there a car in your garage?" he asked.

"Sure there's a car in my garage," said Chimp. "Your car."

"What!"

"Certainly."

"But that girl went off in it."

"She sent it back."

So overwhelming was the joy of these tidings that John found himself regarding Chimp almost · with liking. His car was safe after all. His Arab Steed! His Widgeon Seven!

Any further conversation after this stupendous announcement would, he felt, be an anti-climax. Without a word he darted to the door and passed through leaving the two partners staring after him blankly.

"Well, what do you know about that?" said Chimp.

Mr. Molloy's comment on the situation remained unspoken, for even as his lips parted for the utterance of what would no doubt have been a telling and significant speech, there came from the corridor outside a single, thunderous "Oo-er!" followed immediately by a sharp, smacking sound, and then a noise that resembled the delivery of a ton of coals.

Mr. Molloy stared at Chimp. Chimp stared at Mr. Molloy.

"Gosh!" said Chimp, awed.

"Gosh!" said Mr. Molloy.

"That was Flannery!" said Chimp, unnecessarily.

" 'Was,' " said Mr. Molloy, "is right."

It was not immediately that either found himself disposed

to leave the room and institute inquiries—or more probably, judging from that titanic crash, a post-mortem. When eventually they brought themselves to the deed and crept palely to the head of the stairs they were enabled to see, resting on the floor below, something which from its groans appeared at any rate for the moment to be alive. Then this object unscrambled itself and, rising, revealed the features of Sergeant-Major Flannery.

Mr. Flannery seemed upset about something.

"Was it you, sir," he inquired in tones of deep reproach. "Was it you, Mr. Twist, that unlocked that Case's door?"

"I wanted to have a talk with him," said Chimp, descending the stairs and gazing remorsefully at his assistant.

"I have the honour to inform you," said Mr. Flannery formally, "that the Case has legged it."

"Are you hurt?"

"In reply to your question, sir," said Mr. Flannery in the same formal voice, "I *am* hurt."

It would have been plain to the most casual observer that the man was speaking no more than the truth. How in the short time at his disposal John had managed to do it was a mystery which baffled both Chimp and his partner. An egg-shaped bump stood out on the Sergeant-Major's forehead like a rocky promontory, and already he was exhibiting one of the world's most impressive black eyes. The thought that there but for the grace of God went Alexander Twist filled the proprietor of Healthward Ho with so deep a feeling of thankfulness that he had to clutch at the banister to support himself.

A similar emotion was plainly animating Mr. Molloy. To have been shut up in a room with a man capable of execution like that—a man, moreover, nurturing a solid and justifiable grudge against him, and to have escaped uninjured was something that seemed to him to call for celebration. He edged off in the direction of the study. He wanted a drink, and he wanted it quick.

Mr. Flannery, pressing a hand to his wounded eye, continued with the other to hold Chimp rooted to the spot. It was an eye that had much of the quality of the Ancient Mariner's, and Chimp did not attempt to move.

"If you had listened to my advice, sir," said Mr. Flannery coldly, "this would never have happened. Did I or did I not say to you, Mr. Twist, did I or did I not repeatedly say that it was imperative and essential that that Case be kept securely under lock and key? And then you go asking for it, sir, begging for it, pleading for it, by opening the door and giving him the opportunity to roam the 'ouse at his sweet will and leg it when so disposed. I 'ad just reached the 'ead of the stairs when I see him. I said Oo-er! I said, and advanced smartly at the double to do my duty, that being what I am paid for an' what I draw my salary for doing, and the next thing I know I'd copped it square in the eye and him and me was rolling down the stairs together. I bumped my 'ead against the woodwork at the bottom or it may have been that chest there, and for a moment all went black and I knew no more." Mr. Flannery paused. "All went black and I knew no more," he repeated, liking the phrase. "And when I come to, as the expression is, the Case had gone. Where he is now, Mr. Twist, 'oo can say? Murdering the patients as like as not or . . ."

He broke off. Outside on the drive, diminishing in the distance, sounded the engine of a car.

"That's him," said Mr. Flannery. "He's gorn!"

He brooded for a moment.

"Gorn!" he resumed. "Gorn to range the countryside and maybe 'ave 'alf a dozen assassinations on his conscience before the day's out. And you'll be responsible, Mr. Twist. On that Last Awful Day, Mr. Twist, when you and I and all of us come up before the Judgment Seat, do you know what'll 'appen? I'll tell you what'll 'appen. The Lord God Almighty will say, angry-like, ' 'Oo's responsible for all these corpses I see laying around 'ere?' and 'E'll look at you sort of sharp, and you'll have to rise up and say 'It was me, Lord! I'm responsible for them corpses. If I'd of done as Sergeant-Major Flannery repeatedly told me and kep' that Case under lock and key, as the saying is, there wouldn't have been none of these poor murdered blokes.' That's what you'll 'ave to rise and say, Mr. Twist. I will now leave you, sir, as I wish to go into the kitchen and get that young Rosa to put something on this nasty bruise and eye of mine If you have any further instructions for me, Mr. Twist, I'll be glad to attend to them. If not, I'll go up to my room and have a bit of a lay down Good morning, sir."

The Sergeant-Major had said his say. He withdrew in good

order along previously prepared lines of retreat. And Chimp, suddenly seized with the same idea which had taken Soapy to the study, moved slowly off down the passage.

In the study he found Mr. Molloy, somewhat refreshed, seated at the telephone.

"What are you doing?" he asked.

"Playing the flute," replied Mr. Molloy shortly.

"Who are you 'phoning to?"

"Dolly, if you want to know. I've got to tell her about all this business going bloo-ey, haven't I? I've got to break it to her that after all her trouble and pains she isn't going to get a cent out of the thing, haven't I?"

Chimp regarded his partner with disfavour. He wished he had never seen Mr. Molloy. He wished he might never see him again. He wished he were not seeing him now.

"Why don't you go up to London and tell her?" he demanded sourly. "There's a train in twenty minutes."

"I'd rather do it on the 'phone," said Mr. Molloy.

⋆ 14 ⋆

News for John

I

THE sun whose rays had roused Sergeant-Major Flannery
from his slumbers at Healthward Ho that morning had
not found it necessary to perform the same office for Lester
Carmody at Rudge Hall. In spite of the fact that he had not
succeeded in getting to sleep till well on in the small hours,
Mr. Carmody woke early. There is no alarm clock so effective
as a disturbed mind.

And Mr. Carmody's mind was notably disturbed. On the
previous night he had received shock after shock, each more
staggering than the last. First, Bolt, the chauffeur, had revealed
the fact that he had given the fateful ticket to John. Then Sturgis,
after letting fall in the course of his babblings the information
that Mr. Molloy knew that John had the ticket, had said
that that young man, when last seen, had been going off
in the company of Dolly Molloy. And finally, John had
not only failed to appear at dinner but was not to be
discovered anywhere on the premises at as late an hour as
midnight.

Having breakfasted, contrary to the habit of years, quickly
and sketchily, Mr. Carmody, who had haunted the stable-
yard till midnight, went there again in the faint hope of finding
that his nephew had returned. But except for Emily, who barked
at him, John's room was empty. Mr. Carmody wandered out
into the grounds, and for some half-hour paced the gravel
paths in growing desolation of soul. Then, his tortured nerves
becoming more and more afflicted by the behaviour of one of
the under-gardeners who, full of the feudal spirit, insisted on
touching his hat like a clockwork toy every time his employer
passed, he sought refuge in his study.

It was there, about an hour later, that John found him.

Mr. Carmody's first emotion on beholding his long-lost nephew was one of ecstatic relief.

"John!" he cried, bounding from his chair.

Then, chilling his enthusiasm, came the thought that there might be no occasion for joy in this return. Probably, he reflected, John, after being drugged and robbed of the ticket, had simply come home in the ordinary course of events. After all, there would have been no reason for those scoundrels to detain him. Once they had got the ticket, John would have ceased to count.

"Where have you been?" he asked in a flatter voice.

A rather peculiar smile came and went on John's face.

"I spent the night at Healthward Ho," he said. "Were you worried about me?"

"Extremely worried."

"I'm sorry. Doctor Twist is a hospitable chap. He wouldn't let me go."

Mr. Carmody, on the point of speaking, checked himself. His position, he suddenly saw, was a delicate one. Unless he were prepared to lay claim to the possession of special knowledge, which he certainly was not, anything in the nature of agitation on his part must inevitably seem peculiar. To those without special knowledge Mr. Twist, Mr. Molloy and Dolly were ordinary respectable persons and there was no reason for him to exhibit concern at the news that John had spent the night at Healthward Ho.

"Indeed?" he said carefully.

"Yes," said John. "Most hospitable he was. I can't say I liked him, though."

"No?"

"No. Perhaps what prejudiced me against him was the fact of his having burgled the Hall the night before last."

More and more Mr. Carmody was feeling, as Ronnie Fish had no doubt felt at the concert, that he had been forced into playing a part to which he was not equal. It was obviously in the rôle that at this point he should register astonishment, and he did his best to do so. But the gasp he gave sounded so unconvincing to him that he hastened to supplement his words.

"What! What are you saying? Doctor Twist?"

"Doctor Twist."

"But . . . But . . .!"

"It's come as quite a surprise to you, hasn't it?" said John. And for the first time since this interview had begun Mr. Carmody became alive to the fact that in his nephew's manner there was a subtle something which he did not like, something decidedly odd. This might, of course, simply be due to the circumstance that the other's chin was bristling with an unsightly growth and that his eyes were red about the rims. Perhaps it was merely his outward appearance that gave the suggestion of the sinister. But Mr. Carmody did not think so. He noted now that John's eyes, besides being red, were strangely keen. Their expression seemed, to his sensitive conscience, accusing. The young man was looking at him—yes, undoubtedly the young man was looking at him most unpleasantly.

"By the way," said John, "Bolt gave me this ticket yesterday to give to you. I forgot about it till it was too late."

The relatively unimportant question of whether or not there was a peculiar look in his nephew's eyes immediately ceased to vex Mr. Carmody. All he felt at this instant was an almost suffocating elation. He stretched out an unsteady hand.

"Oh, yes," he heard himself saying. "That ticket. Quite so, of course. Bolt left a bag for me at Shrub Hill station."

"He did."

"Give me the ticket."

"Later," said John, and put it back in his pocket.

Mr. Carmody's elation died away. There was no question now about the peculiar look in his companion's eye. It was a grim look. A hard, accusing look. Not at all the sort of look a man with a tender conscience likes to have boring into him.

"What—what do you mean?"

John continued to regard him with that unpleasantly fixed stare.

"I hear you have offered a reward of a thousand pounds for the recovery of those things that were stolen, Uncle Lester."

"Er—yes. Yes."

"I'll claim it."

"What!"

"Uncle Lester," said John, and his voice made a perfect match for his eye, "before I left Healthward Ho I had a little talk with Mr. Twist and his friend Mr. Molloy. They told me a lot of interesting things. Do you get my meaning, or shall I make it plainer?"

Mr. Carmody, who had bristled for a moment with the fury of a parsimonious man who sees danger threatening his cheque-book, sank slowly back into his chair like a balloon coming to rest.

"Good!" said John. "Write out a cheque and make it payable to Colonel Wyvern."

"Colonel Wyvern?"

"I am passing the reward on to him. I have a particular reason for wanting to end all that silly trouble between you two, and I think this should do it. I know he is simply waiting for you to make some sort of advance. So you're going to make an advance—of a thousand pounds."

Mr. Carmody gulped.

"Wouldn't five hundred be enough?"

"A thousand."

"It's such a lot of money."

"A nice round sum," said John.

Mr. Carmody did not share his nephew's views as to what constituted niceness and roundness in a sum of money, but he did not say so. He sighed deeply and drew his cheque-book from its drawer.

It was as if some malignant fate had brooded over him, he felt, ever since this business had started. From the very first, life had been one long series of disbursements. All the expense of entertaining the Molloy family, not to mention the unspeakable Ronnie Fish. . . . The car going to and fro between Healthward Ho and Rudge at six shillings per trip . . . . The five hundred pounds he had had to pay to get Hugo out of the house. . . . And now this appalling, devastating sum. Money going out all the time! Money . . . money . . . money. . . . And all for nothing!

He blotted the cheque and held it out.

"Don't give it to me," said John. "You're coming with me now to Colonel Wyvern's house, to hand it to him in person with a neat little speech."

"I shan't know what to say."

"I'll tell you. And after that," said John, "you and he are going to be like two love-birds." He thumped the desk. "Do you understand? Love-birds."

"Very well."

There was something in the unhappy man's tone as he spoke, something so crushed and forlorn, that John could not but melt a little. He paused at the door. It crossed his mind that he might possibly be able to cheer him up.

"Uncle Lester," he said, "how did you get on with Sergeant-Major Flannery at Healthward Ho?"

Mr. Carmody winced. Unpleasant memories seemed to be troubling him.

"Just before I left," said John, "I blacked his eye and we fell downstairs together."

"Downstairs?"

"Right down the entire flight. He thumped his head against an oak chest."

On Mr. Carmody's drawn face there hovered for an instant a faint flickering smile.

"I thought you'd be pleased," said John.

II

Colonel Wyvern hitched the celebrated eyebrows into a solid mass across the top of his nose, and from beneath them stared hideously at Jane, his parlourmaid. Jane had just come into the morning-room, where he was having a rather heated conversation with his daughter, Patricia, and had made the astounding statement that Mr. Lester Carmody was waiting in his front hall.

"Who?" said Colonel Wyvern, rumbling like a thunder-cloud.

"Sir, please, sir, Mr. Carmody."

"Mr. Carmody?"

"And Mr. Carroll, sir."

Pat, who had been standing by the French windows, caught in her breath with a little click of her firm white teeth.

"Show them in, Jane," she said.

"Yes, Miss."

"I will not see that old thug," said Colonel Wyvern.

"Show them in, Jane," repeated Pat, firmly. "You must, father," she said as the door closed. "He may have come to apologize about that dynamite thing."

"Much more likely he's come about that business of yours. Well, I've told you already and I say it again that nothing will induce me . . ."

"All right, father. We can talk about that later. I'll be out in the garden if you want me."

She went out through the French windows, and almost simultaneously the door opened and John and his uncle came in.

John paused in the doorway, gazing eagerly towards the garden.

"Was that Pat?" he asked.

"I beg your pardon," said Colonel Wyvern.

"Was that Pat I thought I caught a glimpse of, going into the garden?"

"My daughter has just gone into the garden," said Colonel Wyvern with cold formality.

"Oh?" said John. He seemed about to follow her but a sudden bark from the owner of the house brought him to a halt.

"Well?" said Colonel Wyvern, and the monosyllable was a verbal pistol-shot. It brought John back instantly from dreamland, and, almost more than the spectacle of his host's eyebrows, told him that life was stern and life was earnest.

"Oh, yes," he said.

"What do you mean, Oh yes?"

John advanced to the table, meeting the Colonel's gaze with a steady eye. There is this to be said for being dosed with knock-out drops and shut up in locked rooms and having to take your meals through bars from the hands of a Sergeant-Major whom only a mother could love—it fits a normally rather shy and diffident young man for the battles of life as few other experiences would be able to fit him. The last time he and this bushy-eye-browed man had met John had quailed. But now mere eye-brows meant nothing to him. He felt hardened, like one who has been through the furnace.

"I suppose you are surprised to see us here?"

"More surprised than pleased "

"My uncle was anxious to have a few words with you."

"I have not the slightest desire . . ."

"If you will just let me explain . . ."

"I repeat, I have not the slightest desire . . ."

"SIT DOWN!" said John.

Colonel Wyvern sat down, rather as if he had been hamstrung. The action had been purely automatic, the outcome of that involuntary spasm of acquiescence which comes upon most people when someone speaks very loudly and peremptorily in their presence. His obsequiousness was only momentary and he was about to inquire of John what the devil he meant by speaking to him like that, when the other went on.

"My uncle has been very much concerned," said John, "about that unfortunate thing that happened in the park some weeks ago. It has been on his mind."

The desire to say something almost inhumanly sarcastic and the difficulty of finding just the right words caused the Colonel to miss his chance of interrupting at this point. What should have been a searing retort became a mere splutter.

"He feels he behaved badly to you. He admits freely that in grabbing you round the waist and putting you in between him and that dynamite he acted on the spur of an impulse to which he should never have yielded. He has been wondering ever since how best he might heal the breach. Haven't you, Uncle Lester?"

Mr. Carmody swallowed painfully.

"Yes."

"He says 'Yes'," said John, relaying the information to its receiving station. "You have always been his closest friend, and the thought that there was this estrangement has been preying on my uncle's mind. This morning, unable to endure it any longer, he came to me and asked my advice. I was very glad to give it him. And I am still more glad that he took it. My uncle will now say a few words . . . Uncle Lester!"

Mr. Carmody rose haltingly from his seat. He was a man who stood on the verge of parting with one thousand pounds in cool cash, and he looked it. His face was haggard, and his voice, when he contrived to speak, thin and trembling.

"Wyvern, I . . ."

". . . thought . . ." prompted John.

"I thought," said Mr. Carmody, "that in the circumstances. . . ."

"It would be best . . ."

"It would be best if . . ."

Words—and there should have been sixty-three more or

them—failed Mr. Carmody. He pushed a slip of paper across the table and resumed his seat, a suffering man.

"I fail to . . ." began Colonel Wyvern. And then his eye fell on the slip of paper, and pomposity slipped from him like breath off a razor-blade. "What—what— ?" he said.

"Moral and intellectual damages," said John. "My uncle feels he owes it to you."

Silence fell upon the room. The Colonel had picked up the cheque and was scrutinizing it as if he had been a naturalist and it some rare specimen encountered in the course of his walks abroad. His eyebrows, disentangling themselves and moving apart, rose in an astonishment he made no attempt to conceal. He looked from the cheque to Mr. Carmody and back again.

"Good God!" said Colonel Wyvern.

With a sudden movement he tore the paper in two, burst into a crackling laugh and held his hand out.

"Good God!" he cried jovially. "Do you think I want money? All I ever wanted was for you to admit you were an old scoundrel and murderer, and you've done it. And if you knew how lonely it's been in this infernal place with no one to speak to or smoke a cigar with . . ."

Mr. Carmody had risen, in his eyes the look of one who sees visions and beholds miracles. He gazed at his old friend in awe. Long as he had known him, it was only now that he realized his true nobility of soul.

"Wyvern!"

"Carmody," said Colonel Wyvern, "how are the pike. ?"

"The pike ?" Mr. Carmody blinked, still dazed. "Pike ?"

"In the moat. Have you caught the big one yet ?"

"Not yet."

"I'll come up and try for him this afternoon, shall I ?"

"Yes."

"He says 'Yes'," said John, interpreting.

"And only just now," said Colonel Wyvern, "I was savaging my daughter because she wanted to marry into your family!"

"What's that ?" cried Mr. Carmody, and John clutched the edge of the table. His heart had given a sudden ecstatic leap, and for an instant the room had seemed to rock about him.

"Yes," said Colonel Wyvern. He broke into another of his

laughs, and John could not help wondering where Pat had got that heavenly tinkle of silver bells which served her on occasions when she was amused. Not from her father's side of the family.

"Bless my soul!" said Mr. Carmody.

"Yes," said Colonel Wyvern. "She came to me just before you arrived and told me that she wanted to marry your nephew Hugo."

★ 15 ★

Plain Speech from an Ancestor

I

SOME years before, in pursuance of his duties as a member of the English Rugby Football fifteen, it had become necessary for John one rainy afternoon in Dublin to fall on the ball at a moment when five or six muscular Irish forwards full of Celtic enthusiasm were endeavouring to kick it. Until this moment he had always ranked that as the most unpleasant and disintegrating experience of his life.

His fingers tightened their clutch on the table. He found its support grateful. He blinked, once very quickly as if he had just received a blow in the face, and then a second time more slowly.

"Hugo?" he said.

He felt numbed, just as he had felt numbed in Dublin when what had appeared to be a flock of centipedes with cleated boots had made him the object of their attentions. All the breath had gone out of him, and though what he was suffering was at the present more a dull shock than actual pain, he realized dimly that there would be pain coming shortly in full measure.

"Hugo?" he said.

Faintly blurred by the drumming of the blood in his ears, there came to him the sound of his uncle's voice. Mr. Carmody was saying that he was delighted. And the utter impossibility of remaining in the same room with a man who could be delighted at the news that Pat was engaged to Hugo swept over John like a wave. Releasing his grip on the table, he laid a course for the French windows and, reaching them, tottered out into the garden.

Pat was walking on the little lawn, and at the sight of her his numbness left John. He seemed to wake with a start, and waking, found himself in the grip of a great many emotions

229

which, after seething and bubbling for awhile, crystallized suddenly into a white-hot fury.

He was hurt all over and through and through, but he was so angry that only subconsciously was he aware of this. Pat was looking so cool and trim and alluring, so altogether as if it caused her no concern whatever that she had made a fool of a good man, raising his hopes only to let them fall and encouraging him to dream dreams only to shatter them, that he felt he hated her.

She turned as he stepped on to the grass, and they looked at one another in silence for a moment. Then John, in a voice which was strangely unlike his own, said "Good morning."

"Good morning," said Pat, and there was silence again.

She did not attempt to avoid his eye—the least, John felt, that she could have done in the circumstances. She was looking straight at him, and there was something of defiance in her gaze. Her chin was tilted. To her, judging from her manner, he was not the man whose hopes she had frivolously raised by kissing him that night on the Skirme, but merely an unwelcome intruder interrupting a pleasant reverie.

"So you're back?" she said.

John swallowed what appeared to be some sort of obstruction half-way down his chest. He was anxious to speak, but afraid that, if he spoke, he would stammer. And a man on an occasion like this does not wish to give away by stammering the fact that he is not perfectly happy and debonair and altogether without a care in the world.

"I hear you're engaged to Hugo," he said, speaking carefully and spacing the syllables so that they did not run into each other as they showed an inclination to do.

"Yes."

"I congratulate you."

"You ought to congratulate him, oughtn't you, and just say to me that you hope I'll be happy?"

"I hope you will be happy," said John, accepting this maxim from the Book of Etiquette.

"Thanks."

"Very happy."

"Thanks."

There was a pause.

"It's—a little sudden, isn't it?"

"Is it?"

"When did Hugo get back?"

"This morning. His letter arrived by the first post, and he came in right on top of it."

"His letter?"

"Yes. He wrote asking me to marry him."

"Oh?"

Pat traced an arabesque on the grass with the toe of her shoe.

"It was a beautiful letter."

"Was it?"

"Very. I didn't think Hugo was capable of it."

John remained for a moment without speaking. He searched his mind for care-free, debonair remarks, and found it singularly short of them.

"Hugo's a splendid chap."

"Yes."

"Yes—so bright!"

"Yes."

"Nice-looking fellow."

"Yes."

"A thoroughly good chap."

"Yes."

John found that he had exhausted the subject of Hugo's qualities. He relapsed into a grey silence and half thought of treading on an offensively cheerful worm which had just appeared beside his shoe and seemed to be asking for it.

Pat stifled a little yawn.

"Did you have a nice time yesterday?" she asked carelessly.

"Not so very nice," said John. "I daresay you heard that we had a burglary up at the Hall? I went off to catch the criminals and they caught me."

"What!"

"I was fool enough to let myself be drugged, and when I woke up I was locked in a room with bars on the windows. I only got out an hour or so ago."

"Johnnie!"

"However, it all ended happily. I've got back the stuff that was stolen."

"But, Johnnie! I thought you had gone off picnicking with that Molloy girl."

"It may have been her idea of picnicking. She was one of the gang. Quite the leading spirit, I gather."

He had lowered his eyes, wondering once more whether it would not be judicious to put it across that worm after all, when an odd choking sound caused him to look up. Pat's mouth had opened, and she was staring at him wide-eyed. And if she had ever looked more utterly beautiful and marvellous, John could not remember the occasion. Something seemed to clutch at his throat, and the garden, seen indistinctly through a mist, danced a few steps in a tentative sort of way, as if it were trying out something new that had just come over from America.

And then, as the mist cleared, John found that he and Pat were not, as he had supposed, alone. Standing beside him was a rugged and slightly unkempt person clad in a bearskin which had obviously not been made to measure, in whom he recognized at once that Stone Age Ancestor of his who had given him a few words of advice the other night on the path leading to the boat-house.

The Ancestor was looking at him reproachfully. In appearance he was rather like Sergeant-Major Flannery, and when he spoke it was with that well-remembered voice.

"Oo-er," said the Ancestor, peevishly twiddling a flint axe in his powerful fingers. "Now you see, young fellow, what's happened or occurred or come about, if I may use the expression, through your not doing what I told you. Did I or did I not repeatedly urge and advise you to be'ave towards this girl in the manner which 'as been tested and proved the correct one by me and all the rest of your ancestors in the days when men were men and knew how to go about these matters? Now you've lost her, whereas if you'd done as I said . . ."

"Stay!" said a quiet, saintly voice, and John perceived that another form had ranged itself beside him.

"Still, maybe it's not too late even now . . ."

"No, no," said the newcomer, and John was now able to see that this was his Better Self, "I really must protest. Let us, please, be restrained and self-effacing. I deprecate these counsels of violence."

"Tested and proved correct . . ." inserted the Ancestor. "I'm giving him good advice, that's what I'm doing. I'm pointing out to 'im, as you may say, the proper method."

"I consider your advice subversive to a degree," said Better

Self coldly, "and I disapprove of your methods. The obviously
correct thing for this young man to do in the circumstances
in which he finds himself is to accept the situation like a gentleman. This girl is engaged to another man, a good-looking,
bright young man, the heir to a great estate and an excellent
match . . ."

"Mashed potatoes!" said the Stone Age Ancestor coarsely.
"The 'ole thing 'ere, young fellow, is you just take this girl
and grab her and 'old 'er in your arms, as the saying is, and
never mind how many bright, good-looking young men she's
engaged to. 'Strewth! When I was in me prime you wouldn't
have found me 'esitating. You do as I say, me lad, and you
won't regret it. Just you spring smartly to attention and grab
'er with both 'ands in a soldierly manner."

"Oh, Johnnie, Johnnie, Johnnie!" said Pat, and her voice
was a wail. Her eyes were bright with dismay, and her hands
fluttered in a helpless manner which alone would have been
enough to decide a man already swaying towards the methods
of the good old days when cave-men were cave-men.

John hesitated no longer. Hugo be blowed! His Better Self
be blowed! Everything and everybody be blowed except this
really excellent old gentleman who, though he might have
been better tailored, was so obviously a mine of information
on what a young man should know. Drawing a deep breath
and springing smartly to attention, he held out his arms in
a soldierly manner, and Pat came into them like a little boat
sailing into harbour after a storm. A faint receding sigh told
him that his Better Self had withdrawn discomfited, but the
sigh was drowned by the triumphant approval of the Ancestor.

"Oo-er," boomed the Ancestor thunderously

"So this is how it feels!" said John to himself.

"Oh, Johnnie!" said Pat.

The garden had learned that dance now. It was simple once
you got the hang of it. All you had to do, if you were a tree,
was to jump up and down, while, if you were a lawn, you just
went round and round. So the trees jumped up and down and
the lawn went round and round, and John stood still in the
middle of it all, admiring it.

"Oh, Johnnie," said Pat. "What on earth shall I do?"

"Go on just like you are now."

"But about Hugo, I mean."

Hugo? Hugo? John concentrated his mind. Yes, he recalled now, there had been some little difficulty about Hugo. Wha was it? Ah, yes.

"Pat," he said, "I love you. Do you love me?"

"Yes."

"Then what on earth," demanded John, "did you go and do a silly thing like getting engaged to Hugo for?"

He spoke a little severely, for in some mysterious fashion all the awe with which this girl had inspired him for so many years had left him. His inferiority complex had gone completely. And it was due, he gathered, purely and solely to the fact that he was holding her in his arms and kissing her. At any moment during the last half-dozen years this childishly simple remedy had been at his disposal and he had not availed himself of it. He was astonished at his remissness, and his feeling of gratitude towards that Ancestor of his in the baggy bearskin who had pointed out the way became warmer than ever.

"But I thought you didn't care a bit for me," wailed Pat.

John stared.

"Who, me?"

"Yes."

"Didn't care for you?"

"Yes."

"You thought I didn't care for you?"

"Well, you had promised to take me to Wenlock Edge and you never turned up and I found you had gone out in your car with that Molloy girl. Naturally I thought . . ."

"You shouldn't have."

"Well, I did. And so when Hugo's letter came it seemed such a wonderful chance of showing you that I didn't care. And now what am I to do? What can I say to Hugo?"

It was a nuisance for John to have to detach his mind from what really mattered in life to trivialities like this absurd business of Hugo, but he supposed the thing, if only to ease Pat's mind, would have to be given a little attention.

"Hugo thinks he's engaged to you?"

"Yes."

"Well, he isn't."

"No."

"Then that," said John, seeing the thing absolutely clearly, "is all we've got to tell him."

"You talk as if it were so simple!"

"So it is. What's hard about it?"

"I wish you had it to do instead of me!"

"But of course I'll do it," said John. It astonished him that he should have contemplated any other course. Naturally, when the great strong man becomes engaged to the timid, fluttering little girl, he takes over all her worries and handles in his efficient, masculine way any problem that may be vexing her.

"Would you really, Johnnie?"

"Certainly."

"I don't feel I can look him in the face."

"You won't miss much. Where is he?"

"He went off in the direction of the village."

"Carmody Arms," diagnosed John. "I'll go and tell him at once." And he strode down the garden with strong masterful steps.

II

Hugo was not in the Carmody Arms. He was standing on the bridge over the Skirme, his elbows resting on the parapet, his eyes fixed on the flowing water. For a suitor recently accepted by—presumably—the girl of his heart, he looked oddly downcast. His eye, when he turned at the sound of his name, was the eye of a fish that has had trouble.

"Hullo, John, old man," he said in a toneless voice.

John began to feel his way into the subject he had come to discuss.

"Nice day," he said.

"What is?" said Hugo.

"This."

"I'm glad you think so. John," said Hugo, attaching himself sombrely to his cousin's coat sleeve, "I want your advice. In many ways you're a stodgy sort of a Gawd-help-us, but you're a level-headed kind of old bird, at that, and I want your advice. The fact is, John, believe me or believe me not, I've made an ass of myself."

"How's that?"

"I've gone and got engaged to Pat."

Having exploded this bomb-shell, Hugo leaned against th
parapet and gazed at his cousin with a certain moody satisfac
tion.

"Yes ?" said John.

"You don't seem much surprised," said Hugo, disappointed

"Oh, I'm astonished," said John. "How did it happen ?"

Hugo, who had released his companion's coat sleeve, nov
reached out for it again. The feel of it seemed to inspire him

"It was that bloke Bessemer's wedding that started the whol
trouble," he said. "You remember I told you about Ronnie'
man, Bessemer ?"

"I remember you said he had remarkable ears."

"Like aeroplane wings. Nevertheless, in spite of that he go
married yesterday. The wedding took place from Ronnie'
flat."

"Yes ?"

Hugo sighed.

"Well, you know how it is, John, old man. There's somethin
about a wedding, even the wedding of a gargoyle like Bessemer
that seems to breed sentimentality. It may have been the claret
cup. I warned Ronnie from the first against the claret-cup
A noxious drink. But he said—with a good deal of truth, n
doubt—that if I thought he was going to waste champagne
on a blighter who was leaving him in the lurch without a tea
I was jolly well mistaken. So we more or less bathed in claret-
cup at the subsequent festivities, and it wasn't more than an
hour afterwards when something seemed to come over me all
in a rush."

"What ?"

"Well, a sort of aching, poignant feeling. All the sorrows
of the world seemed to be laid out in front of me in a solid
mass."

"That sounds more like lobster."

"It may have been the lobster," concluded Hugo. "But
I maintain that the claret-cup helped. Well, I just sat there,
bursting with pity for the whole human race, and then suddenly
it all seemed in a flash, as it were, to become concentrated on
Pat."

"You burst with pity for Pat ?"

"Yes. You see, an idea suddenly came to me. I thought about
you and Pat and how Pat, in spite of all my arguments, wouldn't

ook at you, and all at once there flashed across me what I took
o be the explanation. Something seemed to whisper to me
hat the reason Pat couldn't see you with a spy-glass was that
ill these years she had been secretly pining for me."

"What on earth made you think that?"

"Looking back on it now, in a clear and judicial frame of mind,
I can see that it was the claret-cup. That and the general ghastly,
oppy atmosphere of a wedding. I sat straight down, John,
old man, and I wrote a letter to Pat, asking her to marry me.
I was filled with a sort of divine pity for the poor girl."

"Why do you call her the poor girl? She wasn't married to
you."

"And then I had a moment of sense, so I thought that before
I posted the letter I'd go for a stroll and think it over. I left
the letter on Ronnie's desk, and got my hat and took a turn
round the Serpentine. And, what with the fresh air and everything, pretty soon I found reason returning to her throne. I
had been on the very brink, I realized, of making a most con-
summate chump of myself. Here I was, I reflected, on the
threshold of a career, when it was vitally necessary that I should
avoid all entanglements and concentrate myself wholly on my
life-work, deliberately going out of my way to get myself hitched
up. I'm not saying anything against Pat. Don't think that.
We've always been the best of pals, and if I were backed into a
corner and made to marry someone I'd just as soon it was her.
It was the principle of the thing that was all wrong, if you see
what I mean. Entanglements. I had to keep myself clear of
them."

Hugo paused and glanced down at the water of the Skirme,
as if debating the advisability of throwing himself into it. After a
while he resumed.

"I was bunging a bit of wedding cake to the Serpentine ducks
when I got this flash of clear vision, and I turned straight round and
legged it back to the flat to destroy that letter. And when I got
there the letter had gone. And the bride's mother, a stout old
lady with a cast in the left eye, who was still hanging about
the kitchen, finishing up the remains of the wedding feast,
told me without a tremor in her voice, with her mouth full of
lobster mayonnaise, that she had given it to Bessemer to post
on his way to the station."

"So there you were," said John.

"So there," agreed Hugo, "I was. The happy pair, I knew were to spend the honeymoon at Bexhill, so I rushed out an grabbed a taxi and offered the man double fare if he woul get me to Victoria station in five minutes. He did it with second to spare, but it was too late. The first thing I saw on reachin the platform was the Bexhill train pulling out. Bessemer's fac was visible in one of the front coaches. He was leaning out c the window, trying to detach a white satin shoe which som kind friend had tied to the door handle. And I slumped bac against a passing porter, knowing that this was the end."

"What did you do then?"

"I went back to Ronnie's flat to look up the trains to Rudge Are you aware, John, that this place has the rottenest trai service in England? After the five-sixteen, which I'd missec there isn't anything till nine-twenty. And, what with havin all this on my mind and getting a bit of dinner and not keepin a proper eye on the clock, I missed that, too. In the end, had to take the three a.m. milk train. I won't attempt to describ to you what a hell of a journey it was, but I got to Rudge a last, and, racing like a hare, rushed to Pat's house. I had sort of idea I might intercept the postman and get him to giv me my letter back."

"He wouldn't have done that."

"He didn't have to, as things turned out. Just as I got t the house, he was coming out after delivering the letters. think I must have gone to sleep then, standing up. At any rate I came to with a deuce of a start, and I was leaning agains Pat's front gate, and there was Pat, looking at me, and I sai 'Hullo!' and she said 'Hullo!' and then she said in rather a rumm sort of voice that she'd got my letter and read it and would b delighted to marry me."

"And then?"

"Oh, I said 'Thanks awfully' or words to that effect, anc tooled off to the Carmody Arms to get a bite of breakfast. Whicl I sorely needed, old boy. And then I think I fell asleep again because the next thing I knew was old Judwin, the coffee room waiter, trying to haul my head out of the marmalade After that I came here and stood on this bridge, thinking thing over. And what I want to know from you, John, is what is to be done."

John reflected.

"It's an awkward business."

"Dashed awkward. It's imperative that I oil out, and yet don't want to break the poor girl's heart."

"This will require extraordinarily careful handling."

"Yes."

John reflected again.

"Let me see," he said suddenly, "when did you say Pat got ngaged to you?"

"It must have been around nine, I suppose."

"You're sure?"

"Well, that would be the time the first post would be delivered, ouldn't it?"

"Yes, but you said you went to sleep after seeing the post-an,"

"That's true. But what does it matter, anyway?"

"It's most important. Well, look here, it was more than ten inutes ago, wasn't it?"

"Of course it was."

John's face cleared.

"Then that's all right," he said. "Because ten minutes ago at got engaged to me."

III

A light breeze was blowing through the garden as John eturned. It played with sunshine in Pat's hair as she stood y the lavender hedge.

"Well?" she said eagerly.

"It's all right," said John.

"You told him?"

"Yes."

There was a pause. The bees buzzed among the lavender.

"Was he—?"

"Hard hit?"

"Yes."

"Yes," said John in a low voice. "But he took it like a sports-nan. I left him almost cheerful."

He would have said more, but at this moment his attention vas diverted by a tickling sensation in his right leg. A suspicion hat one of the bees, wearying of lavender, was exploring the

surface of his calf, came to John. But, even as he raised a han
to swat the intruder, Pat spoke again.

"Johnnie."

"Hullo?"

"Oh, nothing. I was just thinking."

John's suspicion grew. It felt like a bee. He believed it was
bee.

"Thinking? What about?"

"You."

"Me?"

"Yes."

"What were you thinking about me?"

"Only that you were the most wonderful thing in the world.

"Pat!"

"You are, you know," said Pat, examining him gravely
"I don't know what it is about you, and I can't imagine wh
I have been all these years finding it out, but you're the dearest
sweetest, most angelic . . ."

"Tell me more," said John.

He took her in his arms, and time stood still.

"Pat!" whispered John.

He was now positive that it was a bee, and almost as positiv
that it was merely choosing a suitable spot before stinging him
But he made no move. The moment was too sacred.

After all, bee-stings were good for rheumatism.